Mosaic $15 Nov 2007

THE SPACE BETWEEN

THE SPACE BETWEEN

DON AKER

Harper*Trophy*Canada™
An imprint of HarperCollins*PublishersLtd*

First edition

Published by Harper*Trophy*Canada™, an imprint of HarperCollins Publishers Ltd.

Harper*Trophy*Canada™ is a trademark of HarperCollins Publishers.

HarperCollins books may be purchased for educational, business, or sales promotional use through our Special Markets Department.

HarperCollins Publishers Ltd
2 Bloor Street East, 20th Floor
Toronto, Ontario, Canada
M4W 1A8

www.harpercollins.ca

Library and Archives Canada Cataloguing in Publication

Aker, Don, 1955–
The space between / Don Aker.—
1st ed.

ISBN-13: 978-0-00-200850-1
ISBN-10: 0-00-200850-5

I. Title.

PS8551.K46S62 2007   jC813'.54
C2007-902219-7

HC 9 8 7 6 5 4 3 2 1

Printed and bound in the United States
Designed by Sharon Kish

For Frank Pecora:
teacher, writer, visionary, friend.
1942-2005
You and Dylan Thomas were right.

I'm going to Mexico to get laid.

I scan those seven words a couple times before drawing a line through them twice and then looping over the letters with my pen again and again, making them impossible to read. I doubt that Ms. Bradford would take the time to decipher the original writing—she *says* she considers cross-outs "the equivalent of erasures"—but it doesn't pay to take chances. Sometimes what a teacher says and does are two different things.

But I am. Going to Mexico to get laid, I mean. I'm practically eighteen. My birthday is only two days away and I've never slept with a girl, something I'm determined to change the first chance I get.

Of course, the fact that I'm flying there with my mother, my aunt and my younger brother might suggest the likelihood of that happening is slim. But I'm a person with a purpose, so that has to count for something. Even Ms. Bradford understands the importance of purpose. Every day when we walk into her Grade 12 English class, she's got the lesson objective already on the board, and the first thing we have to do is copy it at the top of a new page in our binders. It's supposed to help us focus on the purpose of the lesson, something she learned in an educational psychology course to encourage "scaffolding," teacher-talk for making connections between this lesson and the ones before it. Personally, I think it's just a way to shut us up in the first few moments of the period, but maybe it does both. I'll give her the benefit of the doubt. After all, I owe her for letting me miss a week of her classes.

I think for a bit about how Ms. Bradford might write this objective:

Find a like-minded, compatible partner and proceed to lose one's virginity.

I've surprised myself by actually recording this in my notebook, and I begin doing the line and loop thing all over again.

"You won't get much value if you don't leave some of it on the page, Jace." This from my mother, who obviously hasn't been reading the *Maclean's* magazine she brought with her on the plane. It's open on her lap, but she hasn't turned a page in over ten minutes. I thought she was watching Lucas, but I guess I was wrong.

I continue lining and looping, wondering if she read what I wrote from across the aisle. I don't think so. My mother isn't the kind of person to invade someone else's privacy. But, again, you never really know people. My older brother, Stefan, proved that.

I clear my throat. "It's exploratory writing," I tell her. "The teacher *expects* us to cross things out. It's all about finding our voice."

She sighs, and I know her practical nature would like to comment on "voice," question the value of looking for something you can't lose in the first place, but she says nothing. I watch as she adjusts herself minutely in her seat, something she's done repeatedly during the four and a half hours we've been in the air.

It's automatic, something I doubt she's even aware she's doing. It's because of long days in the restaurant, cooking over the two stoves in the kitchen or, if things get really busy, waiting on tables out front. Her back is a wreck, although you'd never know it to look at her. Tall and slim with long black hair, she carries herself like one of those people paid to teach poise to clumsy kids. Even when things fall apart in the kitchen and orders are backed up ten tables deep, she never rushes, never loses that quiet calm and grace. She's so *not* like my father.

On the other side of her, next to the window, sits Lucas, his eyes focused on some point in front of his face. To see him like that, you'd think he was mesmerized by the movie that's playing on the monitor in front of him, but I know he isn't seeing it, isn't hearing the dialogue on the earbuds plugged into his seat. He's gone again, disappeared inside his nine-year-old head, listening to sounds or non-sounds only he can hear. Physically, he's a smaller version of our father, dark and sturdy, but that's where the similarity ends. Lucas can sit for hours without making a sound, while Pop never stops talking.

I look at my watch, still set on Atlantic Standard Time—11:19—and think of Pop at the restaurant. He'll already be gearing up for the Saturday lunch crowd, neatly printing the specials on the chalkboard while calling greetings to early customers and barking at the waitresses, Monica and Estelle, to refill the sugar bowls and the salt and pepper shakers. Always talking, talking, the air around him a tidal wave of words.

His business card reads "Evander Antonakos," but he's "Van" to my mother and their friends—not to mention the people who return to the Parthenon Grill time after time. "Repeaters are the key to success," Pop often expounds, along with a dozen other sayings he's picked up over the years, some from a restaurateurs' conference he attended a while back but most of them from my Uncle Stavros, who has two restaurants in Halifax, a third in Sydney and plans for a fourth in the Annapolis Valley. He's one very successful businessman, my Uncle Stavros. He owns a huge house in Halifax's South End, a summer home in Chester, four vehicles (one of them a vintage Porsche Spyder 550 I'd give my left arm to drive for a day), a 36-foot sailboat that he keeps moored at the Armdale Yacht Club (and takes out maybe once every summer) and enough disposable cash on hand to pay for anything else he wants. Like this vacation the four of us are taking to the Mayan Riviera.

I turn to my left and look across the other aisle at my Aunt Mara nursing yet another vodka martini. She's my mother's sister, only a year younger, although you'd never know it to look at her. A fair amount of Stavros's disposable cash has paid for some fancy nip-and-tucking that, besides taking ten years off her, has made her one of those people that men turn and stare at when they pass her on the street. Not that she wasn't good-looking to start with—pre-Stavros family photos clearly show that—but her nose is a work of art, and there's not even the hint of a wrinkle around those dark Mediterranean eyes. A sleeker, more brittle version of my mother, Mara looks as though she should be clinging to the arm of some jet-setting rock star, instead of the stem of a nearly empty martini glass. Scratch that. It's a *newly* empty martini glass, and I can already see her reaching for the button that will bring a flight attendant carrying another full one. She's given them strict instructions to keep them coming, and they do. That's what flying First Class gets you.

A burst of raucous laughter erupts behind us, and I know its source without having to look. But I look anyway. Laying my notebook on the empty seat to my left—Stavros paid for all six seats in our row so Mara would have no one on either side of her—I turn to peer through an opening in the curtain that separates First Class from Economy. Sure enough, the hockey players are at it again, giving one of the female flight attendants a hard time. Her face is pink and I can tell her smile is pasted on as she says something I can't hear to the jerks crammed into the Airbus's four-seat centre row and spilling over into a fifth seat across the aisle. A male flight attendant stands behind her, and his deeper voice sends snippets of his comments through the curtain: " . . . kind of behaviour is unacceptable . . ." and " . . . not be tolerated . . ." The kinds of things you'd expect to hear from a high-school principal, instead of a harried Air Canada employee in the final hour of a flight from Halifax to Cancun. But this group of five has been the centre of considerable attention all morning, even before they finished checking in at the airport.

My father dropped Mom, Lucas, Mara and me at Halifax International at five o'clock this morning, almost two hours before our flight was scheduled to leave, but there were already long lines of travellers snaking around those chrome posts in the terminal. Definitely not the best time to be taking a vacation, since it's the week in February when the universities and colleges shut down for their midwinter break—which explains why the average age of the people lined up around us was about twenty. Very few of them looked to be teenagers like me, and almost none were as young as my brother, the obvious reason being that people our age are still in school in February. But Mara told Stavros she needed to get away, and Mara gets pretty much whatever she wants, whenever she wants it. Stavros asked my father if he could spare Mom and me from the restaurant because he couldn't go himself, and he insisted on paying the whole shot, just to have someone to keep Mara company. My father couldn't really say no, not after everything my uncle has done for him. And certainly not after what my mother has been through this past year. I guess you could say we've all been through it, but it hit my mother the hardest. That's what everyone says, anyway.

We had just joined the much shorter line for Executive and First Class passengers when five guys wearing Dalhousie

University jackets came through the terminal's revolving entry-way. *Burst* through is more like it, since every person in the place immediately swivelled to stare at them. Judging from the noise they were making, I expected to see twenty people storm in, but there were only the five, whooping and yukking it up like they'd just won the Super 7 Lottery. All five wore the Dalhousie Torrents' hockey insignia, and I immediately recognized the tallest member of the group: Connor MacPherson, the Torrents' right wing. MacPherson's picture had already been in the *Chronicle-Herald*'s sports section at least a dozen times that year, the last one for tying the league record for goals in a single season. With several weeks of play still left, he'd beat it easily. A world-class athlete, they said.

And, apparently, a world-class asshole.

Even after my family and I got our boarding passes, checked our bags and began making our way toward the security scanners, we could still hear all five laughing and horsing around in the Economy Class lineup. One of those airport rent-a-cops had already asked them to settle down, but I got the impression he was a huge Torrents fan because he didn't sound too threatening. I half expected him to ask MacPherson for his autograph.

Airlines must make a killing this time of year—there were restless mobs milling around each of the departure gates we passed on the way to our own. Luckily, there were a few seats still available at Gate 23, and the four of us sat down to wait the hour and a half until we boarded. Despite how early it was, a man across from me was immersed in work, his fingers flying over a Toshiba notebook open on his lap. It had one of those polished chrome casings, and the raised cover mirrored both Lucas and me perfectly. As usually happens when I see a reflection of the two of us together, I couldn't get over how different we looked. Both of us have dark complexions and wavy black hair, but Lucas is solid and compact—"built low to the ground, like me," my father used to joke—while I take after my mother's side of the family, taller and longer-limbed. Mr. Winaut, my junior high basketball coach, was disappointed when I told him I was giving up the game at the end of our Grade 9 season to work in my father's restaurant after school. "You'd have no trouble making the senior team next year," he told me, but it didn't matter. My father needed me. He needs me now even more, which is why I gave up volleyball last year, too. But I still play soccer, both school league and summer play. People will expect you to give up everything if you let them.

We'd only been sitting there a few minutes when a girl about my age sat down beside Toshiba-guy. "I got you this," she said, handing him a Tim Horton's coffee in a lidded cup. You could tell she'd only been out of bed a short time, like the rest of us— her blond hair was pulled back in a casual ponytail—but she definitely looked better than anyone else around, with the possible exception of Mara. Despite her fair hair, her skin was darker than mine—darker, in fact, than anyone else's in the departure lounge. She'd obviously been preparing for the southern sun on a tanning bed. She reminded me a little of my girlfriend, Cynthia—*ex*-girlfriend, as of last week—which made me dislike her on the spot. Ponytail carried herself in that easy, confident way that pretty girls have when they know they're being watched. And there were definitely a lot of people watching, including two older married men sitting nearby, their eyes darting in her direction when their wives weren't looking—and when they weren't gazing at Mara, of course. Aging predators on the prowl. Guys like that make my skin crawl.

But even they don't irk me as much as guys like the five Torrents, who barrelled down the aisle of the departure lounge a half-hour later and, to the obvious dismay of several of the people on our flight, stopped at our gate. Of course, by this time all the seats near the gate were occupied, but that didn't stop them from dropping their carry-ons near the wall of windows overlooking the tarmac and sprawling across them. All five were roaring at some comment one of them had just made, while behind them under glaring floodlights, our Air Canada Airbus 340 waited by the passenger ramp, fresh snow collecting on its wings. I'd really been looking forward to leaving winter and the restaurant behind for a week, but the prospect of five hours on a plane with that group of knuckleheads suddenly took the edge off my excitement.

Okay, I admit it. I'm not a hockey fan. Which, I know, earns me membership in a very small group of Canadians. But the whole rink scene never appealed to me: all those people screaming from the stands, goading players to drop their gloves and fight. Parents are often the worst, shrieking at their kids to beat the shit out of each other. Of course, some of my feeling about hockey probably has to do with Stefan, but mostly it's the mentality of the blood-thirsty fans. Mostly.

When the Air Canada employee at the departure gate finally announced that the passengers could begin boarding, MacPherson and his troop clambered to their feet, high-fiving each other and cheering like idiots. Several people in nearby seats rolled their eyes, and I heard Ponytail mutter, "Why don't you guys give it a rest?" Which immediately made me rethink my previous bias—Cynthia definitely would not have made a remark like that; she might have *thought* it, but she wouldn't have said it out loud. Toshiba-guy, who I assumed was Ponytail's father, immediately shushed her, but not before MacPherson replied, "Why don't you come over here and let me rest it *on you*, baby?" Followed, of course, by more whoops from the other four.

"Now see here—" Toshiba-guy began, but two uniformed men standing near the gate intervened, moving quickly to the five and speaking to them in low tones. Whatever they said had the desired effect because the group didn't say anything more.

That didn't stop MacPherson, though, from pursing his lips at Ponytail in an exaggerated air-kiss. I could hear her murmur what sounded like "Prick!" under her breath, and then the First Class passengers were called to board.

The warning the hockey players received at the departure gate worked for most of the flight, but during the last hour they've gotten considerably louder again. Some of it probably has to do with the drinks they've been knocking back ever since the flight attendants began selling them, but, whatever the reason, I'm definitely glad to be sitting in First Class. Even through the narrow opening in the curtain, I can see misery lining the faces of the passengers cramped together with them in Economy.

I look over at my mother again, but she's still staring unseeingly at the magazine on her lap. I wonder if the hockey players have made her think of Stefan, wonder what images are passing before her eyes. And then, of course, they're passing before my own.

The pilot comes over the PA announcing that we've begun our descent into Cancun, and behind me in Economy I hear some-one sitting near the curtain mutter, "Thank Christ!"

The water below us becomes land and the plane dips one wing, turning toward the sun. As we begin our approach to the airport, I force myself to think of palm trees and hot sand. Lithe, tanned girls in string bikinis. And my objective, buried twice beneath heavy loops and lines in my notebook.

Anything but the images forming and reforming in my head.

| 2 |

I thought entering a foreign country would be a bigger deal than this. Officials barely glance at our passports before stamping them. I guess two women, an almost-eighteen-year-old male and a nine-year-old boy don't quite fit the profile of a terrorist cell.

Once we get our bags off the rotating carousel, we move directly to another counter for luggage inspection, something I've been dreading since we landed. Each of us is told to press a button at the end of the counter—my mother, of course, presses for Lucas, who continues to stare behind him at the carousel revolving along its oval track—and a green light comes on above another official, who just waves us through. I guess if we'd gotten a red light they'd have searched every bag, and I'm nearly weak with relief because I've tucked several packages of condoms inside some of my socks. Trojans, in various colours. Ribbed and lubricated. Definitely not something I'd want to try explaining to my mother during our first minutes in Mexico. In front of family and immigration officials.

Outside the terminal, dozens of buses idle noisily in neat rows, while taxis and other vehicles weave through crowds of tourists scanning the parking lot for their package-tour personnel. Representatives from a dozen different travel companies wave brightly coloured signs, but I'm barely aware of them as moist heat hits us like a hammer. The temperature in the Yucatan Peninsula in mid-February is usually around twenty-five degrees Celsius, but I read on the Internet it's been three to four degrees higher this year, and I'm sure today's morning temperature beats even that. Environmentalists blame the increase on global warming, and I know I should be bothered by this unhappy fact—I've seen enough disaster films to recognize the impact it can have—but anything that might bring an end to snow in Nova Scotia can't be all bad.

While I stand, dazzled by the sun and the heat, Mara curtly refuses the services of at least four Mexicans who demand to carry our luggage, their hands already outstretched for payment. Instead, she peers through the throng and beckons to a short man with shiny black hair combed straight back who is holding up a sign that says "Kouklakis." It's even spelled right, which I know would have pleased Uncle Stavros if he'd been here. Stavros says he's given up counting the ways people have misspelled his surname, but the most memorable is "Kookylakes." In Canada, he usually shortens it to "Klakis" to make it easier for non-Greeks, but he has to use the passport spelling for international travel.

The man with the sign rushes over, grabs our suitcases and points behind him to a long white limousine with tinted windows, its trunk lid open to reveal a cavern-like carpeted space within. While he collects our things and places them with exaggerated care in the trunk, we slide inside the leather interior of the air-conditioned vehicle, where two bench seats face each other over a well stocked mini-bar. Stavros has ensured that, even on the ground, Mara travels First Class.

The cool of the limo's seats feels great against my skin, and I'm suddenly conscious of the sweat that, in the few moments we were outside, has pooled at the small of my back and under my arms. I can't wait to get out of my clothes and into my trunks and T-shirt, which several people on the plane had the foresight to do before we landed. Even the hockey players—swaying somewhat from their booze-buzz—were wearing shorts and tanks as they stood waiting for their bags to appear on the carousel. I wish I'd thought to bring light clothes in my carry-on, but I plan to unpack at the resort in seconds—after making sure my socks are stowed someplace safe.

I look at Lucas, who is sitting across from me and gazing intently at the dome light above his head. "Hey, buddy," I murmur, "you ready for the beach?"

His eyes make a circle of the car's interior before finally resting on me. "Um," he says, and he smiles. "Beach."

———

Thirty-five minutes later, we arrive at our resort, and I lower my tinted window for a better look. Having seen the pictures in the brochure that Stavros gave my mother with our tickets, I knew it would be nice—a hotel doesn't get five stars for nothing—but up close the Mayan Empress Resort Hotel is a universe beyond nice. When the wrought-iron gate, guarded by two armed men in grey uniforms, opens to allow our limousine to enter, I feel like I'm on one of those TV programs that show how the super-rich live. Exactly as described in the brochure, towering royal palms and shorter silver thatch palms line a long brick driveway that curves past ornate fountains, flower beds and shrubs sculpted into the shapes of animals: one a rearing horse, another a huge bird in flight, still another that looks like an Egyptian sphinx. Men in coveralls move through the greenery clipping, raking, spraying everything and carrying away fallen palm leaves as huge as hammocks. The air is heavy with smells of exotic flowers, their blooms like splashes of colour against the green landscape, and I smile as I hear Lucas draw great breaths, his face aglow with these new sensations. I can see that Mom, too, is impressed by our surroundings, her face mirroring some of my brother's awe. Only Mara seems unaffected by this beauty.

Mara said little during the drive from the airport. After all those martinis, I expected her to fall asleep, but she knows how to hold her liquor, which probably has something to do with all that ouzo she grew up around. But my mother grew up around it too, and she can't put the booze away like Mara. Not that she tries—a glass of wine with dinner is usually the most she ever drinks. My mother's a lot more conservative than her sister. It's even something of a joke on their side of the family: *If Sophia won't do it, you can be sure that Mara has—at least twice.* Sometimes it surprises me that the two of them are so close. They're more like best friends than sisters, which explains why Mom's the one Mara invited to come to Mexico with her.

While Mom pointed out interesting sites to Lucas during the drive, I jotted down some details in my other notebook, the one that I'm keeping for Mr. Sanderson, my Global Geography teacher. Like Ms. Bradford, he's asked me to keep a record of my trip to the Yucatan as an alternative to the work I'll miss at school, but while Bradford wants "emotional responses to my experiences," as she called them, Sanderson wants information about landforms, culture, industry, stuff like that. Fortunately, Ms. Surrette, who teaches Advanced Math, gave me some work ahead of time, and I finished that a couple days ago.

My buddy Rod Burgess kidded me about having to do school-work while I was away. "Jace," he crowed, "nothin' turns the chicks off faster than a dude doin' homework on the beach." Rod's the only person I've told about my breakup with Cynthia. And, of course, my primary objective.

I wasn't thrilled about Bradford's assignment—no one in the Antonakos family is big on sharing feelings—but I kind of liked what I had to do for Sanderson. It beat lugging that godawful

Global textbook to Mexico and answering questions at the end of each chapter.

So, while I jotted down observations and Mom tried to engage Lucas in the landscape, Mara sat back, drank two more vodka martinis and stared at the limo's ceiling. I couldn't help wondering what was going on in her head. She was the one who'd wanted to take this vacation in the first place, but from the blank expression on her face, you'd think we were still in sub-zero Halifax on our way to Home Depot.

Now that we're at the resort, though, I forget about Mara's strange silence and enjoy the sights around us. The limo eases to a stop in front of the hotel entrance, and a man in a crisp white uniform opens the car door. I'm out of there in no time.

"Welcome to the Mayan Empress," the man says in perfect English. He's shorter than I am, as are most of the men I've seen since we landed, the only exceptions being the two armed guards at the entrance. At six feet tall, I seem to dwarf both our driver and the man who has greeted us, as well as many of the male staff who bustle around the lobby we now enter.

At least, I *think* it's the lobby. Three storeys high, with twin marble staircases curving away in opposite directions, the space could easily hold our house on Connaught Avenue four times over. Between the marble staircases, an enormous fountain fills an area that's open to the sky directly above it, and I can't help but wonder what happens when it rains. Maybe it doesn't. It probably wouldn't dare.

I realize I'm gawking, and I close my mouth just as another man in a white uniform crosses the lobby toward us, his shoes making important staccato sounds on the polished white marble floor. "Mrs. Kouklakis," he says, extending his hand to Mara, and I wonder how he knows who she is. But then I realize people working at places like this probably make it their business to identify vacationers by name, this personal touch just one of many intended to ensure their return. I hear my father's *Repeaters-are-the-key-to-success* mantra in my head, and I can't help but grin.

"I am Raoul Estavez, the hotel manager," the man continues, flashing a brilliant smile as he takes Mara's hand. "Welcome to the Mayan Empress. I trust your flight was a pleasant one?"

"Not really," Mara replies, and I know she's thinking about the hockey players in Economy.

Without missing a beat, Raoul folds his other hand over hers and says, "Let me assure you the same will not be true of your stay here. My staff and I are entirely at your disposal. Whatever you and your family require to make your vacation as enjoyable as possible, please do not hesitate to ask." He releases her hand and snaps his fingers, and three porters appear seemingly from nowhere. Pointing to the luggage our driver has deposited silently behind us, Raoul tells them, "You'll be taking these to Ocean 1."

He turns to me. "I understand, Mr. Antonakos, that you are celebrating a birthday during your stay with us. You will turn eighteen on Monday?"

I nod, my mouth falling open once again.

He smiles and turns to my mother. "With your permission, Mrs. Antonakos, Mr. Kouklakis has arranged for your older son to have a room of his own in honour of his birthday. Your younger son," and here he smiles at Lucas, who stands, staring at the fountain, "will, of course, be staying with you as originally planned. I hope this is satisfactory."

A room of my *own*? I can barely hear my mother's reply over the pounding of my heart.

"Is it in the same building?" she asks.

"Most certainly. In fact, it's a suite adjoining yours, with connecting doors that can be unlocked, if you prefer."

A *suite* of my own? I look at my mother and focus every fibre of my being on telepathically compelling her to say yes.

She turns to Mara. "Did you know about this?"

For the first time today, Mara actually smiles. "It was my idea," she says. "Jace should be able to come and go as he wants. It's his vacation, too."

I want to hug her. No, what I really want to do is pick her up and whirl her dizzily around the lobby, but I settle for saying, "Thanks, Mara." Anything more and I'm afraid my voice will crack.

"Happy birthday, Jace," she says.

My mother looks at me. "I guess I can't really say no to a present, now can I?" Something in her voice suggests she'd *like* to, but she doesn't. "Happy birthday," she says.

My grin threatens to split my face in half. I think about my objective in my notebook, my socks in my suitcase, and my very own suite. It's a good thing there's no roof over the fountain in the lobby because I feel a whoop coming on that could blow it clear off. That is, if I released it, which I don't. If Antonakos men know anything, it's how to keep things inside.

| 3 |

I spend most of the walk to Ocean 1 trying to keep my eyes in their sockets. Following the porters, who push our luggage on polished brass trolleys, we move along a path of interlocking red bricks interspersed here and there with intricate Mexican designs, two of them Mayan symbols for earth and sun that I recognize from research I did on the Internet for Mr. Sanderson last week. The path winds by flowered entrances to recreation facilities, bars and dining areas, all open to the air under enormous thatched roofs. Although it's two hours earlier here than in Nova Scotia, guests talk and laugh everywhere as they drink all-inclusive alcohol and eat their way through all-inclusive twenty-four-hour buffets. Each of them wears a white bracelet identical to the one now on my wrist, signifying to staff that we've paid for the right to indulge in this round-the-clock excess. According to a sign we passed at the entrance, people wearing differently coloured bracelets—or none at all—will be escorted off the property immediately. This white bracelet is my ticket to anything I want to order while I'm here, with one exception: the orange dot on mine and Lucas's tells bartenders we're underage and can't be served alcohol. That is, not until my birthday. Eighteen is the legal drinking age in Mexico, and on Monday I get to trade in my bracelet for one that's all white. Of course, I haven't mentioned this to my mother—after all, the legal drinking age in Nova Scotia is still nineteen—but, hey, when in Rome, right?

Continuing behind our porters, we pass three enormous, free-form, connecting pools, lined with white marble and inlaid with vivid blue tiles forming the words "Mayan Empress" in cursive script across the bottom. Three marble islands dot the pools, supporting more palm trees and vegetation, and a larger island, connected to the pool's outer edge by a footbridge, rises from the centre and forms a swim-up bar, already well attended by swimmers seated on underwater marble stools. And all around the pool, guests are draped in various positions over comfortable mesh loungers bearing the same Empress insignia, their oiled bodies glistening in the sunshine.

Most of these glistening bodies belong to women in their twenties or thirties. And five of them are topless.

Walking beside me, Mara pokes me in the ribs. "Jace," she says, smiling again, "it's rude to stare."

I cough in embarrassment, dragging my eyes from the pool area and forcing them to focus on my aunt. "Just enjoying the view," I tell her. I know my face is on fire, but there's little I can do about it. I'm just glad I'm not wearing loose trunks after all.

I don't know what I expected Ocean 1 to be, but I could never have imagined the building the porters lead us to. A three-storey structure facing the beach and surrounded by palm trees, Ocean 1 is all glass and white stucco, almost brilliant beneath the Mexican sun, and inside it is even more impressive. All our rooms are on the top floor. We leave Mara and one of the porters at her door and continue to mine.

I was hoping for a double bed, a decent bathroom and maybe a balcony. What I've got is a suite as big as a volleyball court that includes, to the left and right of the door, a private sauna and a bathroom with a Jacuzzi that could easily hold six people. The beach-facing part of the suite, whose floor is gleaming-white marble tile, contains a king-sized bed with at least ten pillows and a comforter the colour of clouds. Sitting in its centre is a white towel that someone has artfully folded into the shape of a swan. Amazing.

Opposite the bed is an enormous, intricately carved mahogany cabinet with enough drawers in it to make finding even fifty socks a challenge. To its left is a smaller cabinet that my porter opens to reveal a narrow refrigerator filled with Coronas, and to the right of the fridge, shelves lined with every type of booze I've ever heard of. Even the full bar at the Parthenon Grill doesn't have a selection like this.

Beyond the bed are three steps that lead down to a sitting area, where a leather sofa and loveseat are arranged in an L around a massive coffee table that's made of the same mahogany as the cabinets. Hanging on the wall opposite the long side of the L is an enormous flat-panel TV, and below that sits what I'm guessing is a state-of-the-art surround-sound audio system.

Beyond the living area are sliding glass doors that open to a balcony overlooking white sand and water that defies description. I want to call it turquoise, but even that doesn't sound right. It's the colour you'd get if you put blue and green together and then shone a light through it. Luminous.

"Beautiful, isn't it?"

I turn to my mother and Lucas standing behind me and simply nod my head. Words seem inadequate.

"Stefan would have loved this," she adds softly.

My sudden anger surprises even me, bubbling up from nowhere. "Stefan isn't here because he chose not to be," I tell her, not even trying to hide the resentment in my voice.

I see her wince and immediately regret my words. I quickly turn to Lucas, whose eyes are following the fan that rotates lazily above the bed, and I muss his hair. "How d'you like my room, buddy?" He continues to follow the fan, but he smiles, and that's enough for now. His smile is contagious.

"I'll take him down to the beach as soon as I get changed, okay?" I want to tell my mother I'm sorry, but this is almost the same thing.

"We'll get changed now, too," she says, nodding toward the wall that separates the suite she and Lucas will share from mine. "We can unpack later. I'm looking forward to getting in the water. I can't believe how hot and sticky it is. It's not even noon here yet."

We're talking about normal things again, the moment now behind us. She takes Lucas's hand and leads him toward the hallway, where their porter is still waiting, then turns.

"Jace?"

"Yeah?"

I expect her to say something about Stefan, and for a moment it seems as though she will, but then, "I don't want to unlock this, if that's okay with you." She gestures toward the adjoining door to the right of the larger cabinet. "It'll be easier to keep track of Lucas if there's only one exit from my room."

"You're sure?" I ask, with exaggerated nonchalance. I cannot *believe* my luck.

"It's not like you're going to be having wild orgies in here, right?"

I know she intends this as a joke, and I force a laugh. I just hope the sudden heat on my face isn't as obvious as it feels.

"After all," she continues as she steps into the hallway, "what would Cynthia say?"

This time I don't laugh. I just shut the door behind her and lean against it, my face pressed to the wood long after the latch has clicked into place.

What would Cynthia say? I think about those words as I change into the Hilfiger trunks I bought last week at the Campus Store on Quinpool Road. My one extravagance.

And then I think of some more words: *Who the hell* cares *what goddamn Cynthia Gregson would say?*

If I could, I'd give her front-row tickets to my first orgy.

I'm trying not to be bitter, but there's a limit. After all, *I* wasn't the one who went away last weekend to Moncton with her church group. *I* wasn't the one who seemed to forget all about the person she said she loved. *I* wasn't the one who hooked up with Corey Salter, the choir director's son, the second the chaperones were out of sight.

Okay, so it was more than a second. The second *day*, to be exact. But that doesn't change the fact that we've gone together since the end of grade ten and she dumps me for a guy whose finest hour was playing Bob Sheldon in our school's musical production of *The Outsiders*. Bob's the guy who gets stabbed in the park at the end of the first act while singing "Bad and Loving It." Corey got to wear a dye pack, but Keiran McKelvie, who was playing Johnny, stabbed him at least four times and the thing still wouldn't go off. By that time, some joker in the audience began calling out offers to lend a hand, so Corey finally reached up inside his own shirt and burst the pack himself. But instead of staining his shirt, the dye shot up through his collar squirting him full in the face. He looked like an exploded ketchup bottle.

This is the guy Cynthia cheated on me with last week.

I can only assume he was luckier with his dick than his dye pack.

Besides the betrayal, the thing that really pisses me off is that Cynthia seldom let me get past first base with her the whole time we were together. "Jace," she'd say, taking my hand off her breast and sliding it to safer territory, "you know we can't." And I *knew* we couldn't. I certainly wasn't going to force the girl I loved into doing something she wasn't ready for. I respected her too much to do that. *Despite* the fact that most of the guys I know scored home runs long ago, a lot of them in junior high. I'd accepted that this was a huge step and Cynthia just wasn't ready to take it. Just as I'd accepted the fact that I returned home from most of our dates to a cold shower or a Kleenex.

What I *couldn't* accept was her sleeping with Corey Do-or-Dye Salter.

I knew something was wrong the minute I saw her when she got back from Moncton—she kept laughing at everything I said. I'm not that funny. I try to be, and I have my moments, but more often than not Cynthia just rolls her eyes.

Rolled her eyes. Sometimes I forget that we're past tense now.

But forgetting the other thing? Not a chance.

When it finally came out, she tried to explain what had happened, but I wasn't in much of a mood to listen. I didn't react well, which is another way of saying I went ape-shit. When she tried to make me understand that she and Corey connected on, as she put it, "an entirely different level," I pretty much lost it, yelling about how I'd been trying to make *that* kind of connection with her for a hell of a lot longer than Corey had. Which sort of explains where my head was at the time. It was easier to be a prick about the sex part than to show her how much she'd hurt me.

I'm not proud of how I acted. Afterwards, I wished I hadn't lashed out at her the way I did, but what guy responds rationally to finding out he's been cheated on? She must have expected my meltdown. What *I* didn't expect was what she told me next, when I finally calmed down enough to listen to what she had to say—that she'd been ready to break it off with me last year. And she *would* have, she said, if it hadn't been for Stefan.

A knock on the door jolts me from my thoughts.

"Jace?"

My mother. I sigh. I still haven't told her or Pop about Cynthia. How can I? Like they need more proof I'm not my brother, who'd already dumped a busload of girlfriends by the time he was my age. Always the dump*er,* never the dump*ee.* Like me.

"Yeah?" I call, but my voice is thick, my reply little more than a gargle. I clear my throat and try again. "Yeah, Mom?"

"Are you ready yet?" she asks through the door.

"As I'll ever be," I say, then realize that's Stefan's line. I resist the urge to kick something, anything. Instead, I grab the swan towel from the bed and head for the door. Just before I open it, I arrange my face into something like a smile.

| 4 |

The beach is unbelievable.

From my balcony, it looked like a Hollywood special effect, absolutely too amazing to be true. From the water's edge, it's dazzling, like standing on the surface of the sun. That is, if the sun were made of the finest, softest substance imaginable. The white sand sears the soles of my feet, but I let it, thinking of all that snow we've left behind. I can't imagine a beach better than this. Which immediately makes me feel like a traitor because we've got some terrific beaches back home. When tourists think of Nova Scotia's shores, most of them probably picture the house-sized boulders of Peggy's Cove or the rugged coastline of the Eastern Shore, no doubt imagining the province to be one endless chunk of rock carved by pounding surf, the Nova Scotia they see on calendars and coffee mugs. Sure, there are lots of places like that, but there are some great beaches, too. Like Rissers, Hubbards, Crystal Crescent, the kilometres of sand stretching along the Northumberland Strait. But they're different from what I'm standing on now. This is the prototype of the *perfect* beach.

Then I notice the artfully placed retaining walls that, from a distance, look like rock but are actually moulded concrete, and

I'm suddenly aware that what I'm looking at isn't completely natural. The sand is real, of course, but the beach is wider here than what I see extending beyond the limits of the resort in either direction. And I remember something I read on the Internet last week: much of the Empress's oceanfront is man-made, reconstructed after two hurricanes hammered the Yucatan a couple of years ago. In a way, I guess it's a designer beach. I look down at the logo on my Hilfiger trunks and wonder if there's some logo buried beneath this sand. But only for a moment. Who cares if it isn't real? For the next seven days, I'll have zero trouble pretending it is. Especially if the topless sunbathers on the loungers behind me are going to be here all week. A few of them aren't much older than I am.

A hand tugs at mine and I look down at Lucas. He's smiling, but there are sudden tears on his cheeks, his eyes watering from the sun's brilliance, and for a moment something in my chest catches, makes me think of the smiles that have hidden so many tears in our family this past year. But I shrug it off, refusing to give in to such thoughts. Stefan isn't going to ruin this, too. Not if I can goddamn help it.

"So, you ready for a swim?" I point to the waves that curl toward us, the heads of several swimmers rising and falling as the surf sweeps beachward.

Lucas says nothing. Still grinning, he charges at the water and I race behind him, my shouts filling for a while the hollow part inside me.

====

"So, how's the water?" Mara asks. She and my mother are sipping drinks in the shade of a palm tree. My mother's, I'm sure, is a Diet Pepsi, but Mara's is one of those bright-pink tropical concoctions complete with fruit and tiny umbrella. After my birthday on Monday, I plan to try one. Maybe five.

"Water's great. Why haven't you gone in yet?" I ask. My mother has been in and out two or three times, but Mara hasn't stirred from her lounger.

Mara raises her glass to me. "First things first," she says.

My mother frowns, but she says nothing. Mara's husband is, after all, paying for everything, including the Diet Pepsi in her own hand.

I sip my piña colada—minus the alcohol, of course—and the three of us watch Lucas playing in the waves. We'll be lucky to get him out of there before dark. Lucas loves water. And I don't mean that in the way some people say they love french fries or foreign films. Lucas *really* loves water. Which has to do with his autism.

He was diagnosed shortly after he turned four. He seemed perfectly fine in his first three years, which is the tipoff that his real condition is childhood disintegrative disorder, but since he exhibits all the symptoms of autism and both conditions fall under the same umbrella of pervasive developmental disorders, it's easier to respond with just one word than three when people ask. And they do. All the time.

My parents first noticed something was wrong when Lucas began wetting and soiling himself after he'd been toilet-trained for more than a year. At first, they thought these were just relapses or the results of laziness or waiting too long—kids get playing and don't want to stop to use the bathroom, and then everything comes too fast for them to make it there when they finally do. By itself, that wasn't a huge deal, but then there were other things, signs that something more was going on.

Because most of my parents' friends and family have older kids like Stefan and me, my mother enrolled Lucas in a nursery school program so he'd have children his own age to play with a few times each week. Once he got over the fear of being left for awhile, he loved it. I remember going sometimes with my mother to pick him up, and when we got there he'd usually be in the centre of a group stacking blocks or rolling balls or crawling through big cloth tubes, always squealing and giggling. But then we began arriving to find him off by himself more, just sitting there gazing at something nobody else was interested in. I was thirteen at the time, but even I could tell something wasn't right. He began to speak less and less to us, and it seemed to get harder for him to do things he'd done easily only months before, like putting the wooden pieces of his Ernie and Big Bird puzzles in the right slots. It was like somebody had replaced my bright, talented little brother with a completely different person. Someone who now sat silent for long periods of time, who stared off into space and shit his pants, who didn't seem to know or even care who we were half the time.

My parents took him to be tested, and I remember the weeks of waiting for a final diagnosis, watching my parents cling to false hope that this was just a phase that would pass. But it didn't.

Lucas basically won the anti-lottery, because fewer than five kids in ten thousand get childhood disintegrative disorder. In fact, according to a weird statistics website that Rod found, you're seventeen times more likely to board a plane with a drunk pilot than to be diagnosed with CDD. Which, if you think about it, really isn't all that comforting.

No one actually knows what causes CDD, but most scientists feel it's linked to problems with the central nervous system. Whatever its cause, the really tough part is finding out that there's no cure. Once you've got it, it's got you.

There are treatments, though, the same ones they give kids with autism. After the diagnosis, my parents took Lucas to a team of specialists who, in addition to recommending regular speech and language therapies, suggested others with fancy names like "auditory integration training" and "applied behavioural analysis." All of them are intensive, hard work. And expensive, because our health care doesn't pay for all of it. Which explains why my parents could never have afforded a vacation like this themselves. And why both of them work such long hours at the restaurant.

It's probably no surprise that having a younger brother with CDD means you don't get the lion's share of attention in the household. Combine that with having an older brother able to do everything better than anyone else and you don't even get the *lamb's* share. In fact, I'm pretty much the *shaved* lamb between thumb-thick slices of *psomi horiatiko,* the Greek bread my mother still makes from scratch sometimes.

Stefan's the kind of guy only a masochist would want for an older brother: outstanding student with one of the highest grade-point averages in the history of the district, triple-A hockey player who won division MVP three years running, student council president elected by a landslide, valedictorian at his graduation, where he received more scholarship offers than anyone from our school in the last ten years. Handsome guy, too, with no short-age of girls ringing the phone off the hook and leaving message after message.

Then, of course, there was me. "So, you're Stefan's brother," a new round of teachers would say to me each September, and I'd see in their eyes this expectation of greatness that always fizzled by the middle of the month. Not that I'm a total loser. I get respectable Cs and the occasional B in most of my courses—the exception being History, which is often an A—and I've pulled quite a few soccer games out of the toilet with some fancy foot-work and what the coach calls "sheer guts." But no way am I in Stefan's league. Never was. Never will be.

Rod claims I have "middle-child syndrome," although I don't think it's an actual condition, certainly nothing like "childhood disintegrative disorder" or "firstborn son"—which, let's face it, is cause for celebration in lots of Greek families. Rod showed me a ton of Internet sites where middle-child-syndrome sufferers whine online about getting lost in the shuffle. There are even blogs where grown men and women write long entries about how they were ignored as children, how they were always trying to prove themselves to their parents but no one noticed. I think if you're in your thirties or forties and still moaning about Mommy and Daddy not giving you enough attention when you were younger, then you've got bigger problems than being a middle child. I saw this cartoon in a magazine once that showed a mouse looking at a hunk of cheddar and telling a bigger mouse, "Cheese is just a substitute for the love you never gave me," and I pictured all those bloggers curled up on psychologists' couches saying different versions of the same thing. Reading their entries, I felt like signing on and telling them to grow some balls. Try having a younger brother with CDD and an older brother voted Most Likely To Do Whatever He Goddamn Wants and *then* you'll know what it's like to get lost in the shuffle.

Take meals, for example. I've seen enough movies to know that most people imagine Greek mealtimes to be this big free-for-all where everyone around the table babbles at full volume about every moment of their day. Maybe that's true for some Greeks, but when Stefan lived at home, mealtime for me was mainly about disappearing. Pop or Mom asking Stefan about his classes, hockey schedule, student council, latest girlfriend. Mom or Pop reminding Lucas to focus on his food or to drink his milk. Me passing the salt and pepper. Or the butter. There was a time I used to try sharing stuff about my own day, telling them about a class or about soccer or about plans Rod and I had made, but often I'd be in the middle of saying something when Pop would ask Stefan about his next game or Mom would tell Lucas to try eating more than one pea at a time. *The Invisible Teenage Virgin*, starring Jace Antonakos. A few years ago, a wireless phone company developed an ad campaign around the slogan "Can you hear me now?" and I briefly considered getting those five words tattooed on my forehead. I doubt, though, that anyone named Antonakos would have noticed.

Thinking about all this now, I could get really bummed out. That is, if I let myself. But I don't. What's the point? It's not like it would make a difference. Too much has happened for me to expect anything to change. Besides, I'm on the Mayan Riviera—or, as the Mexicans call it, the *Riviera Maya*. Whatever its name, it's as far from our house on Connaught Avenue as I'm ever likely to get, and I've got other thoughts to occupy my mind. The Mayan Riviera is the place where Jace Antonakos will finally become a man.

=====

As I predicted, it's a major battle getting Lucas out of the water, but we can't let him stay in any longer. It's already been well over an hour. The 45 SPF sunblock my mother put on him is supposed to be waterproof, but not even paint could stay on a kid who rolls and tumbles endlessly in those swells. Lucas loves to bodysurf, and he's been riding wave after wave right to the water's edge, stopping only when a breaker deposits him on the sand, at which point he leaps up and charges back in.

"Luke, buddy," I say to him as I catch his arm during another approach to the beach. I still can't get over how warm the water is as I stand knee-deep, attempting to nab a nine-year-old. "Time to get something to eat, okay?" I tug his arm, but he flails away from me.

"*Nuh*-uh," he says, already pivoting to head back out.

"C'mon, Lucas." I hate being the bad guy, but he's getting too strong for my mother. I reach out, grab the waist of his trunks and try to pull him to me.

Big mistake. He wriggles out of them and churns away from

me, his ass cheeks like two white moons flashing in the waves.

"Lucas!" Mortified, I plunge after him, holding his trunks in my hand. He's fast, but my years of lessons at the Dalplex pool pay off and in a moment I overtake him. The only thing to do is to get in front of him. He doesn't like obstacles.

"No!" he hollers as I wrap an arm around him. "*NO!*"

"Lucas!" I speak as firmly as I can without shouting and, treading water with one arm, I hold him close with the other as he continues to struggle. A wave washes over us both but I don't let go. I cough and snort the water out of my nostrils and hold him even tighter. "No, Lucas. Stop. Lunch now, beach later."

Another wave swamps us, and this time he's the one with water down his throat and up his nose. Sputtering, he clings to me, his arms a sudden vise around my neck, and I feel him stop struggling. I turn us toward the beach and scissor-kick repeatedly until there's sand beneath my feet again, then stand and pull him to his feet beside me.

"You need these?"

I turn to see a hand holding Lucas's trunks, which I apparently lost during my pursuit. The hand is attached to the arm of a girl, and it takes me a whole split second to recognize Ponytail from the Halifax departure lounge. Except her hair is no longer pulled back; it falls instead in wet waves around her face. She's wearing a white bikini that, also wet, leaves little to the imagination. But my imagination roars into overdrive anyway. I stand there staring at her and suddenly feel like I'm the one with CDD, like I've somehow lost the power of speech. I take the trunks.

"You're welcome," she says after a moment.

Common courtesy finally kicks in. "Uh, sorry," I say. "Thanks." I gesture with the swimsuit. And then realize that Lucas is still naked beside me. I whirl around and cover his groin with the trunks, forcing him lower in the water. "Put these on, buddy," I hiss. I'm trying to get his feet through the legs of the wet material, but it's a lot harder getting the trunks on than off. It's like they're suddenly six sizes too small for him, and I can only get one foot into one leg. The wrong leg, as it turns out.

"Here, Jace. Give him to me." My mother wades in beside me with a towel, wrapping it around Lucas's waist and pulling him to his feet. He no longer struggles, seemingly resigned to leaving the water now, and she guides him effortlessly toward the sand.

I turn back to Ponytail, but she's no longer there. I scan the swimmers in the waves but she isn't among them. I continue to stand there for a moment, hoping to catch a glimpse of her, but I see nothing. It's like she was never even there.

I shake my head.

You'd think I'd be used to people leaving by now. But I'm not.

| 5 |

I just stand there, my knife suspended in mid-air. I can't bring myself to cut it.

"Jace," says my mother, "people are waiting."

I turn and see she's right. People who earlier today wore only swimsuits—or less—are now lined up behind me in evening wear, women in fancy dresses and men in slacks, shirts and ties. A few of them are even wearing dinner jackets. For me, the strangest part is seeing shoes instead of sandals or bare feet. Even though we've only been at the resort a few hours, my toes now feel oddly trapped inside the patent-leather shoes that I bought in December to wear to our school's Snowflake Ball. With Cynthia.

"May I help you, sir?" This from a Mexican server in a chef's hat standing behind "The Carvery."

Lunch was at the Beachside Café, offering twenty-four hour casual dining, just steps from the sand. I was having so much fun in the surf with Lucas that I only stopped long enough to wolf down a slice of pizza and some Coke. Because of the time difference, evening meals are served two hours later here than in Halifax, and by the time we were getting dressed for dinner I was starving. I'd devoured the complimentary fruit basket in my room and was considering a return visit to the Beachside Café, but my mother stopped me. She promised we'd be first in line for dinner, instead.

Now I wish we weren't.

It feels somehow wrong to touch the food on display. The buffet looks more like an exhibit of fine art than stuff we're meant to eat. All around us, melons, pineapples and other tropical fruits have been carved into the shapes of exotic birds and fish, with tiny tomatoes pierced with toothpicks for their bright, round eyes. Large blocks of ice have been meticulously chiselled into flamenco dancers. Beads of water form on the edges of their upswirled ice dresses, and draped around the dancers' shoulders are gorgeous flowers that Mara has told me are actually edible. I've never seen anything so unusual or so beautiful.

"Sir?" the server prompts again.

"Uh, no," I mumble. "I can do it." And I do, using a razor-sharp blade to slice off a strip of sirloin that folds itself neatly onto my plate. I slice again and another strip joins the first. I have to swallow twice to keep from drooling.

Besides the Beachside Café, there are four à la carte restaurants at the Empress, but guests need to make reservations to have dinner there. That's why we've decided to eat at the Empire Room, the large dining room located off the hotel lobby that, according to the resort brochure, serves "spectacular buffets" every evening. The moment we entered, I knew "spectacular" was an understatement.

Like everything else at the resort, the Empire Room is fancier than any dining room I've ever seen before. And enormous. At least a hundred tables made of rich, dark wood are covered with white linen cloths, and fresh flowers stand in crystal vases at the centre of each one. Along one side of the dining room are various "stations," each one serving a different kind of food. The Carvery, of course, serves several kinds of meat, while a seafood station serves nine kinds of fish, including squid, scallops and escargot. A pasta station offers more than a dozen different dishes, and a vegetable station serves potatoes, carrots, corn, peas, beans and a variety of Mexican foods, each prepared several different ways—potatoes alone, for example, come baked, boiled, roasted, fried, whipped and in two other forms I don't even recognize. And, of course, there's a salad station, where Mara is now dishing up. She's rail-thin, but I overheard her earlier telling my mother how she needs to lose at least five pounds. Amid all this gourmet food, there's even a fast-food station that serves hot dogs, hamburgers and several kinds of pizza, obviously intended for younger guests whose tastes are quite a bit simpler. Like Lucas. I know he doesn't understand that we can have whatever we want in any amount and as often as we please; he stood frozen in front of the fast-food station staring at the choices until I asked the server to put a hot dog and a slice of pepperoni pizza on his plate. My brother could *live* on hot dogs and pepperoni pizza.

The part of the buffet that seizes *my* attention is the dessert station, and I gaze longingly at it as I make my way to our table. I can't help it, I'm a sugar freak. As far as I'm concerned, the main course is only a formality people endure to get to the star attraction, and I see there are dozens of star attractions that I'll be sampling in the days ahead. Cheesecakes, Black Forest cakes, pies, tortes, tarts, cookies, puddings, custards, flans, fruit dishes—if anything's missing, I can't imagine what it might be. I nearly trip over my feet scanning everything on my way past.

When we first arrived at the Empire Room, the maitre d' took our names and led us to a table that he said would be ours every evening. This way, he explained, we'll always have the same waiter, who will make it his business to learn our particular food and drink preferences. Another advantage is that we'll know where to meet if we arrive separately. Of course, we're free to choose another table if we'd like, but none of us wants to. On the eastern side of the dining room our table stands near a floor-to-ceiling opening that overlooks the grounds and the ocean beyond. I suspect we won't be making too many reservations at the à la carte restaurants. I can't imagine any of them being better than this.

Once we're all seated, our waiter appears, a short, dark man with a thousand-kilowatt smile. Dressed in a white shirt, black slacks and a short black jacket with satin trim and a white rose in the lapel, he looks more likely to break into song than take our drink orders. In hesitant but capable English, he tells us his name is Nabor, and he pours us bottled spring water—guests are advised never to drink tap water, which is often contaminated in Mexico—then asks each of us if there's anything else he can bring. Mara orders white wine, Mom orders red, and I order milk for myself and Lucas. What I'd really like is a beer, which I see several people drinking at nearby tables, but I know better than to suggest it. I'm biding my time until Monday.

The meal tastes as incredible as it looks. Several times I leave our table to get food at different stations, returning to find that Nabor has whisked away my dirty dishes and discreetly swept up my crumbs. Even Mara attempts a non-salad dish—pasta with fennel—and, although she takes only two bites of it, it's obvious she enjoys it.

Lucas is uncharacteristically animated. Often, he spends meal-times focused on his silverware, drawn to the light reflected from it. And there's certainly plenty of light reflected here. Massive crystal chandeliers hang from the frescoed ceiling several metres above us, sending light cascading in all directions. Surprisingly, though, Lucas seems to follow our conversation around the table this evening, his eyes moving from one person to another, and I catch my mother smiling as she watches his face. I can't recall the last time she's smiled like this, unforced and unrehearsed. She even looks rested.

At home, she often returns from the restaurant exhausted, yet she works tirelessly each afternoon with Lucas from the moment he gets out of school. He's on an individualized program plan at his elementary school, and he spends each day in a regular Grade 4 classroom with an educational assistant trained in the various therapies the team of specialists devised for him. But both my parents know that Lucas will have a better chance if they work with him, too, and he's progressed more in the last five years than even his doctors could have hoped. He still lives in a world entirely his own, still has bad weeks—even bad months—when he seems to regress more than he improves, but he's a remarkable kid. Sure, there are times when I resent the extra care he requires, the extra work he creates for all of us, but Lucas never fails to remind me how special things are, even the most ordinary and mundane. Like the way light reflects off silverware. Who else could make me appreciate something like that?

I reach over and muss his hair and he turns to me. "You enjoyin' yourself, buddy?" I ask.

A smile creases his face, and then, of course, all of us are smiling. Even me.

=====

"I think I'm gonna puke," I moan as we leave the dining room. I'm surprised at how quickly the night comes in Mexico. If it weren't for the lights along the path, I don't think we would be able to find our way. The sky is studded with stars, but there's no moon yet. A breeze has sprung up, gently moving the branches of the palm trees overhead, and the slightly cooler air feels terrific against my skin. Despite my sunblock, I got burned today. Not a lot, but enough to teach me to reapply faster tomorrow or spend more time in the shade.

"You think that third piece of cheesecake was maybe a bit much?" Mara asks. I can tell she's teasing, but that doesn't change the fact that my stomach feels like it'll split any second. I'm in agony.

My mother yawns. "I know it's only eight o'clock here, but my body's still two hours ahead. Lucas and I are going to turn in."

My brother walks silently beside her, his upturned face staring into each light we pass. It's like he's reading a story whose words only he can see. He yawns too, and I know he'll be asleep in no time. *Out like a light,* I muse, then grin at the unintentional pun. Cynthia would have groaned if I'd said that out loud.

Then, of course, I'm thinking of Cynthia again, and it really pisses me off that she's followed me to Mexico like this. I remind myself of Rod's comment about the first four letters of her name and how therapeutic it can be to change one vowel.

"Turn in?" Mara is incredulous. "We came all this way and you want to spend your first night in Mexico in *bed?*" She shakes her head and then looks at me. "What about you, Jace? How about the two of us go watch the show?"

I'd forgotten about the show. According to the resort brochure, there's live entertainment every evening at the outdoor theatre beyond the pool. Singers and dancers perform a different production each night of the week. The pictures in the brochure reminded me of those glitzy ads you sometimes see for Las Vegas. As impressive as this place is, though, I figure the singers and dancers who work at a resort are the kind of people who can't get jobs anywhere else, so I don't expect much. But anything beats returning to my room and pretending to watch my flat-panel, all the while imagining what Cynthia's doing with Corey. And vice versa.

"Sure," I say. "Why not?" We've come to a place where the path divides, and signs chiselled into large flat stones tell us that the left fork leads toward Ocean 1 while the other leads to the theatre.

My mother leans toward me and, for one Twilight Zone Second, I think she's going to kiss me, something she hasn't done for a very long time. But she just puts her hand on my arm. "Don't stay out too late, okay?" she warns.

Mara snorts. "Sophia, the guy's on vacation. Give him a break."

I see my mother about to say something, but she only shrugs. Taking Lucas's hand in hers, she moves off toward Ocean 1 while Mara and I turn right.

I look back to see my mother put her arm around my brother's shoulders, and I marvel that she can do this, can still pull someone close to her when she's spent so much of the last year pushing others away.

===

"Amazing, aren't they?" Mara asks, applauding the singers on stage, who have just completed another set of their *Around the World* show featuring imitations—both physical and musical—of several international pop stars. I have to admit I was wrong about resort performers. Some of these people are actually better than the stars they're imitating, and the audience has applauded wildly after every number. Like everything else at the Empress, the show is spectacular.

I grin at Mara over my drink, which I'm hoping people around us will think is a rum and Coke, despite the orange dot on my bracelet. "They're fantastic," I say.

It feels weird not having to pay extra to see the show, just one of several all-inclusive entertainment options the resort offers its guests. Lucas would have loved it, and I think I'll encourage my mother to bring him tomorrow night. According to the resort's brochure, tomorrow's *Salute to the 80s* promises "an homage to *Dirty Dancing.*" Dirty dancing aside, Lucas will love all that movement and colour.

I, on the other hand, plan to enjoy more of the *non*-show movement and colour I've been appreciating during the last half-hour. Three tables away and facing the stage, Ponytail is oblivious to the fact that I've been staring at her since she sat down with her father. She's wearing a short green dress that clings to every curve, and each time she moves in her chair, the material shimmers and slides over her skin. Ten seconds after this performance began, I had to lay a napkin on my lap to keep Mara from seeing exactly how much I enjoyed it.

The girl's blond hair is up again but not in a ponytail this time. It's pinned so curls fall around her face and down her neck, making her appear older than she is. Of course, I don't really know *what* her age is, and I'll feel pretty stupid if it turns out that's her *husband* she's with. I don't think so, though—the guy looks a lot older. More to the point, he's barely touched her. If she were with me, I wouldn't be able to keep my hands off her.

As it is, I can't keep my eyes off her. Throughout the last set, Ponytail turned to Toshiba-guy and made frequent comments, smiling and gesturing toward the performers. I've imagined what she's been saying to him, imagined what her voice sounds like when she isn't criticizing loud-mouthed Torrents or returning swimming trunks to naked nine year olds. I've imagined, too, what she smells like, what her skin might feel like beneath my fingertips. Now I'm imagining what she would taste like, her lips full and red against mine.

And then I surprise myself by realizing that I haven't thought of Cynthia once in the last thirty minutes. I suspect she and Corey are probably somewhere doing a little dirty dancing of their own, but for the very first time, I really don't care. Much.

Okay, so maybe that's not entirely true. But for the first time in almost a week, I feel something other than self-pity at the centre of my thoughts.

A crash to my left makes everyone in our section jump.

"Ooops! My bad!" Then guffaws.

Mara and I turn toward the disturbance and see a waiter bending over a tray of drinks now lying shattered on the floor.

He's quickly picking up shards of glass while another waiter approaches with napkins to wipe up the liquid. Behind them stand the five Dalhousie Torrents, newly arrived and obviously drunk, Connor MacPherson raising a beer and grinning foolishly at everyone now staring at them.

Something else that I thought was gone for good.

In the face of *this* spectacle, the prospect of a week at the Mayan Empress Resort Hotel suddenly loses some of its appeal.

| 6 |

Yawning, I drop my notebook and stretch lazily on the lounger I claimed earlier this morning. Last night at dinner, I overheard someone say that you have to get up early if you want one right on the beach, so I set my alarm for seven o'clock, and this morning I took four towels from my room and laid them on loungers before heading to breakfast. Even at that hour, several workers were already raking the sand and carrying out the white resin loungers, placing them in perfectly parallel rows on the sand.

I wish the parallel lines in my notebook had filled as quickly as those loungers did. For someone who got up early, I haven't got much besides a seat on the beach to show for it. The notebook on the sand beside me reveals everything I've written since I arrived.

I wonder

I look at those two words and think of various ways I could finish that thought. It's one of the writing prompts Ms. Bradford gave us. She took a creative writing course last summer and now she's big on prompts. They're supposed to "prime the pump," as she puts it. I've got a handout with more than a hundred of them taped inside the cover of my notebook:

If I had
If I weren't
The heaviness of

And on and on and on. What crap teachers come up with sometimes.

Gazing around me, I let my mind finish some of those thoughts.

If I had an ice cube, I'd drop it on the back of the babe lying face down a few loungers to my right. She arrived after I did, and she's untied her bikini strings so she'll get a no-line tan. My mind conjures that after-ice-cube moment over and over again.

If I weren't so horny, I'd go for a swim, but there's no way I could hide the tent in my trunks if I stood up right now.

The heaviness of my—

Okay. Enough's enough. Forcing my mind back to the task at hand, I pick up the notebook, determined to get at least a little work done. My mother and Lucas are eating a late breakfast in the Beachside Café, Mara is still in bed—which is no surprise after all the booze she knocked back yesterday and last night—and I really need to take advantage of this time to myself. Bradford's assignment is to write at least three hundred words each day, and I only have these two. I tore out the page I wrote my objective on yesterday—better safe than sorry.

I wonder

I look out at the water, wondering, then press the pen against the paper.

I wonder how the barrel

"Is this taken?"

I look up to find Ponytail standing over me in her white bikini, and I immediately drop my notebook over my crotch. "Huh?"

"This," she says, pointing to the lounger on my left that has my towel draped across it. "Is somebody using this?"

"No," I lie, reaching over to retrieve my towel. Four minus one. Mara will have to fend for herself.

"Thanks," she says. She sits down, then reaches into a straw beach bag and pulls out a bottle of suntan lotion. Squirting some into both palms, she begins applying it to her face, then to her shoulders, arms and stomach, and finally to her legs and feet. After returning the bottle to the bag, she pulls out an iPod, inserts a pair of earbuds, then puts on sunglasses and lies back, her hair a yellow fan beneath her head. All of this I'm watching out of the corner of my eye, longing for a bigger notebook.

I force myself to look at the scene before me. When I first arrived, the ocean was like glass, but a breeze has come up and there's quite a swell now. Several windsurfers zip back and forth over the waves, and two four-person catamarans, bearing the Empress's insignia on their bright sails, skate across the rolling blue-green seascape. A speedboat with the same insignia is anchored just metres off the beach, and several people in scuba gear are clambering aboard, obviously heading out for the reef dive I saw posted on the activities board by the pool. It's as though we're a race of water-breathers, living on and under the sea.

I turn slightly, thinking I hear familiar music coming from Ponytail's earbuds. Of course, all music sounds familiar when heard from the wrong end of an earbud, thin and tinny. But as I listen, it tugs at my memory, and I struggle to place it. No luck.

I'm dying to say something to her. I rack my brain for some remark, but everything sounds so lame in my head. *Come here often?* Yeah, right. The kind of thing some slob would say in a seedy bar. *Great weather, huh?* Like I'm eighteen going on eighty.

And after all, this *is* the Mayan Riviera. People don't pay big bucks to lie out in *lousy* weather.

From this angle, I can't even tell if her eyes are open behind those dark lenses. She could already be asleep, like so many of the earbud-wearing sunbathers lying in parallel rows on either side of us.

I sigh and turn back to the ocean. The speedboat is powering up now, and it churns the surf behind as it roars off, its bow almost completely clear of the waves. It skips across the water and then disappears around the point.

"Hard to believe we're here, isn't it?"

It takes me a moment to realize the comment is directed at me, and I turn to see Ponytail sitting up, taking the earbuds from her ears and pressing the controls on her iPod. The music stops.

"Mmm," I say. I'm trying for nonchalance, but I could not be less cool.

"I'm Kate," she says. "Kate Townsend. I'm the one who—"

"—rescued my brother's trunks," I finish for her, my embarrassment at that moment returning. "Look, about that, I should've thanked—"

"Forget it," she says. "You had your hands full."

I don't know how to respond to this, don't know whether her words are a statement of fact or a joke about Lucas's bare ass. "I'm Jace," I tell her simply.

She nods. "We came on the same flight yesterday," she says. "You sat across from my dad and me at the airport."

So Toshiba-guy *is* her dad. I'm as pleased by this as I am surprised by her revelation. I've had so much practice being invisible in my family that I always think nobody notices me. "I saw you there, too. And last night at the show." I suddenly wish I hadn't said that last part, which makes me sound like a stalker.

She doesn't seem to notice. "Weren't they amazing?"

"Yeah," I agree, but I want to say *Not nearly as amazing as you.*

Up close like this, she's even prettier. I fumble with my notebook, making sure it's still covering my crotch.

She nods at the notebook. "You a writer?"

I almost laugh out loud. "Just doing homework."

Her eyebrows arch. "Aren't you off this week?" she asks.

Then I realize her mistake. She thinks I'm a university student. Like *she* must be. I hear Rod's voice in my head—*Nothin' turns the chicks off faster than a dude doin' homework on the beach*—and then stare at the five words I've written in my notebook. I imagine five others in their place: *Man, you're such a loser.* At least I don't have to worry about the tent in my trunks any more. I feel like I've just had a cold shower.

"No," I mutter, my face burning, "I took the week off school. I'm in Grade 12."

"Me, too," she offers, and I almost don't hear what she says next because the sudden smile on her face makes my pulse pound in my ears. "The company my dad works for brought us down here. It's supposed to be like a bonus, but he has meetings all day." She shrugs. "I brought along schoolwork too, but it's definitely not getting done this morning." She gestures toward the water and takes a deep breath. "Life doesn't get any better than this, does it?"

I shake my head in agreement. It absolutely does not.

But life can always get worse, another voice in my head reminds me.

And, as if to prove the point, life offers up five Dalhousie Torrents in beachwear. Coronas in hand, they swagger out through the palm trees behind us and onto the sand, laughing and slapping each other on the back. A regular jock-fest, and me without my autograph book. I swallow the urge to swear.

Kate does not. "Jesus," she murmurs. "*Way* too early for these assholes." Quickly gathering up her things, she stands and says, "Nice meeting you, Jake."

Jace, I want to tell her, but she's already moving off down the beach. I see she's just as attractive from behind.

Apparently, one of the Torrents thinks so, too. "Hey! Blondie!" one guy calls after her. "Don't let *us* chase you away."

But Kate ignores him, just keeps walking, and I see him mouth the word *bitch* to his buddies.

I watch until she turns and disappears along a path that leads up toward the pool, and I regret not having said something more to her. Even *goodbye* would have been nice. As it is, she doesn't even know my name.

"Your friend comin' back?"

I turn and look up at Connor MacPherson. From this angle, he appears seven feet tall, and he's got the kind of abs you see on the covers of fitness magazines. I'm in pretty good shape, but this guy's got a six-pack you could scrub clothes on. He must do a thousand crunches a day.

"Well, *is* she?" he prompts, impatience in his voice.

I look at the lounger beside me and I suppress a groan. No towel. "I doubt it," I tell him. Grudgingly.

"Great," he says, and he sets a Dalhousie athletic bag on the sand beside it. He unzips it, pulls out a football and tosses it to one of the other Torrents.

"You playin', Connor?" the Torrent asks.

MacPherson shakes his head. "You guys go ahead, Barn. I wanna soak up some sun."

Barn, whose name is more than appropriate given that he's almost as big as one, nods and salutes MacPherson with his Corona. Taking long swallows, he and the others drain their bottles and let them fall to the sand—only a few steps from a basket obviously provided for empty drink containers—then move down toward the water and begin tossing the football back and forth.

MacPherson sprawls out on the lounger beside me, and I can almost hear the resin groan under his considerable bulk. He looks up at the cloudless Caribbean sky for a moment, then sighs noisily and calls to his buddies, "Life doesn't get any better than this, does it?"

I literally have to bite back the words. I'd like to tell life to fuck off.

| 7 |

Mom and Lucas didn't make it down to the beach after all. Turns out Mom took Lucas back to their suite after breakfast so they could put on their swimsuits, and she made the mistake of leaving the TV remote where he could get it. When she came out of the bathroom dressed for the beach, she found my brother curled up on the leather sofa immersed in a Discovery Channel program on boats.

Lucas is obsessed with boats. Which has a lot to do with his obsession with water. He has over a hundred miniature boats at home, some that people have bought for him, but lots he's made himself out of everything imaginable. Wood, of course, but also stuff you'd throw away—everything from tinfoil to candy wrappers. But they're not crude like you'd think. All of them *look* like boats, right down to little masts that support tiny flags meticulously drawn on scraps of paper. And they all float, too. Using a huge sheet of plastic and a wooden frame, Pop built him a large, shallow tub in the basement where Lucas stages these incredible regattas, like the ones we've seen at Stavros's yacht club, and he'll stay down there for hours at a time if we let him. His favourite TV program is a children's series about a talking tugboat, and he owns every episode ever released on DVD, which he'll watch over and over again like it's the very first time.

The moment Lucas spied that Discovery Channel program, there was nothing my mother could do to get him away from the flat-panel. All of us learned a long time ago that it's not as simple as shutting off the TV or trying to distract him. Once he fixates on something, nothing else exists for him, and trying to remove it or shut if off can really upset him. Which wasn't such a problem when he was five or six, but now that he's nine, he can be a real handful. Sometimes the only thing you can do is wait it out.

Which I find my mother doing when I return to their suite. I wasn't surprised when Mara was a no-show, but I got a little worried when Mom and Lucas didn't appear. And I got tired of watching the Torrents prove to everyone on the beach just how amazing they are. It seemed like every few seconds one of them interrupted their football game to bet on something: who could run the fastest, throw the farthest, jump the highest, tackle the hardest—important stuff like that. Whoever lost the bet had to chug a beer, which then turned into a bet about who could chug the most, and I figured that was leading to a pissing contest, when four bikini-clad girls joined the group. One of the Torrents thought it would be fun if the girls rode on their shoulders—which didn't do much for their game, since three of them were half tanked by that time, but having those long legs draped around their necks seemed to make scoring a lot less important. On the beach, anyway. I was pretty sure double digits were a given when those Torrents finally returned to their rooms.

MacPherson didn't even have to get off his lounger. Two female fans who'd obviously recognized the hockey star ran up and introduced themselves to him, hovering over the guy and hanging on his every word: *Oooo, Connor* this and *Oooo, Connor* that. It was embarrassing. For me, anyway, sitting centimetres away. I finally got up to leave, and my ass wasn't off my lounger more than two seconds before both girls parked themselves on it. I just left the remaining towels behind on the other two loungers. It would have been too humiliating to collect them after all that time.

"Hey, bud," I say now as I sit down beside Lucas. "How about we get you outside?"

But, of course, I don't exist for him right now. He continues to stare at the flat-panel while a commentator describes the construction of a cruise ship that will eventually carry passengers throughout the Caribbean, south to Brazil and north along the eastern seaboard of the United States. I don't know how much of this Lucas actually understands, but it's like he can't tear his eyes away. It's almost like porn for him.

Which is something I happen to know quite a bit about.

Rod sometimes works evenings and weekends at a twenty-four-hour video rental store downtown, and he sneaks out DVDs from the "Adults Only" room when the manager isn't there. At first, I couldn't believe they actually make stuff like that—or, more to the point, that you can get it in Nova Scotia. Some of the guys I know brag about watching it on cable whenever they want, but I'd never seen anything like it before. Pop claims that minimum-tier programming has everything we need. It doesn't.

The first time I watched one of those DVDs at Rod's place, I was speechless. I must have looked just like Lucas: eyes glued to the screen, mouth open. After the third or fourth porno, though, you realize they're not big on plot. Guy wakes up and gets laid. Guy goes shopping and gets laid. Guy goes to the dentist and gets laid. (I clearly do *not* live in this guy's neighbourhood.) Sometimes when I'm bored in English class, I picture Bradford trying to discuss character arcs in films like *Hotter Than Hell* or *Wicked Wives Will*. It would probably take her all of four seconds, but at least she'd have the full attention of every guy in the room.

Lucas continues to stare at the television, and I turn to my mother, who shrugs. "It's on all day," she says. "Back-to-back shows on boat construction. Can you believe it?"

I think of the irony. We're looking at gorgeous shots of the Caribbean on this huge plasma flat-panel, yet we can't get my brother outside to put his feet in it. I just shake my head. "Is Mara up yet?" I ask.

"She called a few minutes ago. She says she's ready to get something to eat."

Which, I bet, means she's ready to get something to drink, but I don't say this. "Why don't you two go to lunch? I'll stay here with Lucas."

I can see the relief on my mother's face. "Are you sure?" she asks.

"Yeah. I've got schoolwork anyway. This'll give me a reason to do some of it." I put my hand on Lucas's shoulder, but he slides out from under it, his eyes never leaving the TV.

"We won't be gone too long. Call for room service if you get hungry, okay?" She's out the door in seconds, as if she's afraid I'll suddenly change my mind.

I make sure the door is locked behind her so Lucas can't wander off, then leave him in front of the TV and step out on the balcony, sitting in one of the cushioned wicker chairs and putting my feet up on the railing. Like all the balconies in Ocean 1, this one has a white, wrought-iron top railing with Plexiglas below it so none of the view is obstructed. Beyond the palm trees to my right, I can see the football game has broken up, four of the Torrents and their Torrent-riders now romping in the waves. I don't see MacPherson anywhere and I assume he's in one of the bars entertaining his adoring female fans with endless tales of athletic prowess. More likely, though, he's entertaining them in his room. Guy goes to the beach and gets laid.

I riffle the blank pages of my notebook, thinking of that

minimum word count again. Three hundred per day. Daunting.
I turn to the first page and read the five I wrote earlier:

I wonder how the barrel

They surprise me. I'd forgotten what I'd written. What I'd
actually allowed myself to write.

I pick up my pen, hold it above the paper for a long moment,
then place it deliberately on the line, finishing what I've started.

I wonder how the barrel of the gun felt in your mouth.

I put my pen down and look through the Plexiglas at the
waves rolling toward the beach below, one after the other in
endless succession. The fact that life keeps unfolding despite the
tragedies it brings us somehow surprises me at that moment, on
that balcony, above that beach. Behind me in surround-sound,
a man talks about turbine rotation and propeller size and water
displacement ratios, making everything sound explicable and
exact. As if anything could be.

———

Sometimes it's like a light shutting off, and that's what happens
this time. One minute Lucas is totally fixated on the screen and
the next he's on the balcony looking at me with this *What-are-
you-waiting-for?* expression on his face. Like *I'm* the one who's
been holding *him* up all this time. He points toward the water.
"Beach," he says.

"You bet, buddy," I say, ruffling his hair. After the last few minutes, I'd like to put my arms around him and pull him close, but
I don't. Lucas doesn't much like being hugged, sometimes not
even by our mother. No one in the Antonakos family has ever
been big on physical displays of affection, anyway.

I stand up and my notebook falls to my feet. I take a step forward to pick it up but my toe kicks it, sending it flying through the narrow space between the Plexiglas and the balcony floor. I watch in disbelief as it sails through the air and arcs downward, its flight ending abruptly in the branches of a silver thatch palm.

"Unbelievable," I mutter. "Shit!"

"Shit!" Lucas parrots back to me, and I whirl to face him. Of all the times for him to actually be listening.

"No," I tell him. "No shit." And then I grin. *No shit.* Right. "C'mon, Lukey. I've got some climbing to do."

Outside on the path, I count over four balconies from the end of Ocean 1, trying to determine which tree the notebook is in, and I narrow it down to two possibilities. The silver thatch palms are shorter than the royals so their branches are only a couple metres over my head, but this doesn't help much. Except for small horizontal ridges their trunks are bare, and I wonder how I can possibly climb them. I remember the film Mr. Sanderson showed us last week about the Caribbean economy, the shots of Dominican workers in bare feet scaling tall coconut palms in seconds. I am definitely no coconut climber.

I glance around to see if there are workers who might be able to help me, but all I see are a man and a woman in servers' uniforms carrying trays of drinks and food. I try pushing against the trunk of the first tree to see if I can dislodge the notebook if it's up there, but I may as well be pushing against a concrete wall. And, my luck running true to form, the breeze blowing earlier this morning has subsided and the branches hang motionless above us. I feel another *Shit!* coming on, but I don't give in to it. Lucas is staring at me closely, probably wondering why I've suddenly developed such an interest in tropical trees.

Then I get an idea. "Lucas," I say, pointing to the branches above us. "Remember the book I was writing in?" He continues to stare at me, and I have no idea if he understands what I'm talking about, but I press on. "I think it's up there. Can you stand on my shoulders and get it for me, buddy?"

He turns toward the water and says, "Beach."

"Yeah, yeah, we'll go down to the beach in a minute, okay? Right now, I need you to do this for me." I lock my fingers into a cup and bend down. "Put your foot in here, okay?"

He looks at me and smiles. I don't know if he finds what I'm doing funny or if he's thinking about something else entirely. Like turbine rotation or water displacement ratios. Hilarious stuff like that.

I find myself growing impatient, which is a complete waste of time. I may as well lose my patience with this palm tree.

Then Lucas surprises me by putting his hands on my shoulders and his sandaled foot in my hands. I hoist him up—no small feat when you consider how solid he is—and he grabs hold of the trunk of the silver thatch palm, steadies himself, then hauls himself up and puts his feet on my shoulders.

"Great, buddy," I tell him. "Now jiggle the branches, okay?"

But Lucas is looking out at the water again. "Beach," he says, clearly impressed by this new vantage point.

"Later," I hiss as the edges of his sandals dig into my shoulders. Why didn't I put on a T-shirt? "Reach up and grab the branches, Lucas. Shake 'em."

He shifts his weight and his sandal scrapes skin off my right shoulder. I grit my teeth, biting back quite a bit more than *Shit!*

"You takin' this act on the road?"

I turn my head to see Connor MacPherson standing in the path, grinning. I stifle a groan as I imagine how we must look: Lucas hugging a palm tree while teetering on my shoulders, me telling him to grab branches. Silver thatch molesters.

I bend my knees and lower Lucas to the ground. "Lost something," I mumble.

"Up there?" MacPherson asks, his grin even broader.

At least he's alone, but I doubt I'd be any more embarrassed if all five Torrents were there sharing shit-eating smiles at my expense.

"A book," I tell him, then realize just how ridiculous *that* sounds. Like I was reading while parasailing through palm trees. Jesus. "Forget it. I've got another one anyway." I put my hand on Lucas's shoulder. "C'mon, bud. Let's get you in the water," I say, nudging him toward the beach.

"Sure you don't want some help?"

I don't even turn around. The smirk I imagine on that jerk's face probably pales beside the real thing. I just shrug and keep walking. *Asshole!*

———

Mom and Mara eventually find us on the beach, me nursing a sandal burn while Lucas bodysurfs. The high salt content in the water stung my shoulder so I didn't stay in long. I doubt that Lucas is even aware I'm not in there with him. I'm watching him closely, though, making sure he stays within the area marked off with a buoy-lined rope. Signs in several languages warn guests that farther down the beach the bottom drops off quickly, and it's safer to swim within the roped section.

Mom and Mara have brought along chicken wraps and tall glasses of a fruit drink the colour of grenadine, the stuff they put in Tequila Sunrises. Mara, of course, is drinking the real thing. At least a double. Maybe even a triple.

I get up and give my mother one of the two loungers I'd left towels on earlier, and I sit on the sand. Mara raises the back of the other one and then lies down without spilling a drop.

I'd forgotten I was so hungry. The chicken wrap is delicious, spicier than I'm used to, which makes my nose run, but definitely the best chicken wrap I've ever tasted. Because Lucas is still in the water, I eat his, too. I'll get him another one later.

"You're frowning, Sophia," Mara says to my mother, who is watching Lucas ride the waves. "You're not worrying about the restaurant, are you?"

My mother grimaces, and I see the guilt on her face. "I know I shouldn't. I'm sure Van's doing fine without me."

"Of course he is," says Mara. She takes another sip of her Sunrise. "I wonder what he'd think of this place."

"He'd focus on the food," says my mother, "so he'd approve." She looks at me. "What do you think Cynthia would say about it, Jace?"

Cynthia again. *Jesus!* I don't care what that bitch would say, so I just mumble syllables around a chunk of spicy chicken. Thankfully, no one asks me to repeat myself. Still chewing, I look at Lucas, and soon all three of us are watching him in the waves.

"Sophia," Mara says after a moment.

"Mmm?" my mother asks absently.

There's a pause. I turn to Mara, who's looking at my mother but nodding her head at me. "Sophia," she says again, and this time there's a tone in her voice, an undercurrent of meaning.

My mother looks at her questioningly, then something seems to pass between them and Mom nods. She turns to me, her eyes narrowing, and I suddenly think I know what this is about.

They found the condoms.

My heart does a quick two-step and I can barely hear the surf above the bloodrush in my ears.

"What were you planning to do, Jace?" Mom asks.

"Do?" I ask around another mouthful of chicken. I try to swallow but a wad of wrap lodges in my throat and I nearly choke. Sputtering, I reach for a bottle of spring water and drain at least half of it, slowly, buying time while I consider what to say.

"You must have some idea," says Mara, and I hear that tone again. Teasing? Accusing?

"About what?" I ask, taking another drink while I try to think of reasons that might actually justify all those rubbers in my sock drawer: I've developed an unusual fondness for latex, I'm overly concerned about penis sunburn, I use them as flotation devices . . .

"About what you'd like to do while we're here," my mother says.

I set the bottle down, relief flooding through me—this isn't about the rubbers after all.

"I thought we were doing it," I tell them, glancing at the dozens of other Empress guests on the beach who are doing it too. Eating, relaxing, soaking up that incredible Caribbean sun. I resist the urge to say that life doesn't get any better than this.

"There's plenty to do *off* the resort, if you want," Mara tells me.

"I don't feel much like shopping."

Mara scowls. "I don't mean that," she says, then looks at Mom. "Although I *do* plan to take your mother into Playa del Carmen sometime this week to look around." Playa del Carmen is a seaside town a few minutes' drive from here that has some upscale stores, along with the usual shops where local people sell their goods. Something else I learned in the Empire Room last night. People will tell you anything when you're waiting to be served at a buffet.

"What, then?" I ask.

My mother reaches into her beach bag and pulls out some glossy brochures. "I got these in the lobby. Lots of tour groups offer half-day and full-day trips to attractions in the area, and the Empress staff recommend quite a few."

I flip through them. Scuba diving, snorkelling on reefs, visits to cigar factories, excursions into the interior on monster trucks— you name it, they've got it. Then something catches my eye. "This looks interesting," I say, holding up a brochure.

My mother looks at Mara. "What'd I tell you?" she says.

Smiling, Mara takes the brochure from me and flips through it. "Right. A tour of the Mayan ruins in Tulum."

All my family and friends know how much I like that stuff. Rod kids me about it when I go over to his place and immediately turn on the History Channel, which we don't get at home. I could watch those specials on ancient civilizations for hours, how they'll excavate a site millimetres at a time, uncovering evidence of lives we can only guess about. I like how sometimes the most amazing discoveries lie just beneath the surface. Rod, of course, will grab the remote and flip to something like female mud wrestling or infomercials where really hot women demonstrate exercise equipment. We joke about people from the future unearthing a mud wrestling video or a rusted Thigh Master and trying to envision our twenty-first-century lives based on that stuff. Scary when you think about it.

"Do they have those tours every day?" I ask Mara.

"The bus leaves here each morning around 7:30 and gets back shortly after noon," she says. She turns the brochure over, showing me the back. "Since you're off the resort anyway, it only makes sense to try the whole-day package." She points at the word "Xel-ha" at the top of the paper. "This place is a water park. The full-day tour takes you to Tulum in the morning and then the water park in the afternoon."

I shake my head. "The tour of the ruins sounds great, but I'm not a water park kinda guy."

"It's not what you think," Mara tells me. "When I first heard about it, I pictured something like Blizzard Beach at Disney World. But the tour organizer in the lobby says it's an *eco*-park, a huge natural lagoon off the ocean where people swim with sea life, snorkel through caves, raft down rivers, things like that. She says everyone who goes there loves it."

Of course, a tour organizer is *paid* to say stuff like that, but I study the pictures more closely and it really doesn't look like one of those hokey theme parks after all, the ones with flumes and fancy inner-tubes and hour-long lineups. I nod. "Looks like fun," I say.

Mara smiles. "Good. You're booked to go tomorrow."

"You're kidding."

She shakes her head.

"Great," I say. "So we leave at 7:30?"

"Not *we*," says my mother. "*You*." When she sees the surprise on my face, she explains that it's too long a day for Lucas so the three of them will stay at the resort. "We'd only slow you down," she says. "This way you can enjoy yourself without having to worry about us. After all, tomorrow's *your* day, Jace."

It's then that I remember: I turn eighteen tomorrow.

"It's your birthday present," continues my mother. "From your father and me."

"A day all to yourself," Mara says.

A day all to myself. Like the spray of a rock smashing water, those five words wash over me, flooding me with sudden memories of the last day I spent alone—at home. Nearly a year ago. In March. I have to push back the images crowding my brain, focus instead on the brochure in my hand.

"Thanks, Mom," I say.

"Should be lots of people your own age there," offers Mara.

I study the glossy photos of young men and women smiling by ancient stone structures, young men and women smiling by turquoise lagoons, and I imagine myself there with them. Smiling. All the women in the pictures wear skimpy shorts and tank-tops or even skimpier swimsuits, and suddenly I'm thinking of Kate Townsend, wondering if she's a ruins-and-water-park kind of person. Without even trying, my brain suddenly conjures other memories, recent ones this time, images of her on this beach, in the water, in her bikini, and in seconds I'm smiling for real. Kate Townsend, I'm convinced, is *definitely* that person. Kate Townsend will *absolutely* be on that tour tomorrow. With me. All to myself.

Wishful thinking, maybe, but one hell of a birthday present.

8

It's quite a group that assembles in the lobby around 7:20 the next morning. I really didn't know what to expect, but it certainly wasn't this. Except for a couple who look to be in their late twenties and, judging by the way they hold hands and gaze constantly into each other's eyes, probably on their honeymoon, most of the forty-some people here are middle-aged or older. After seeing those pictures on the brochure, I figured that a tour including a visit to a water park would attract a lot more people my age, but I was obviously wrong. Like I was obviously wrong about Kate Townsend being a ruins-and-water-park kind of person. I've scanned the lobby a dozen times and she's not here. She's probably not even out of bed yet.

And, of course, that's all it takes. Immediately, an image fills my mind: Kate lying on a Mayan Empress bed, her blond hair spilling over her pillow, her tanned skin vivid against the white sheet draped across her body. I feel my own body responding to the picture in my head, and I force my brain to visualize other things. Ruins. Water parks. Middle-aged people with cameras around their necks. Middle-aged people who will later be wearing swimsuits at Xel-ha. And *that* does it. I'm good to go.

And, apparently, so is the group. A man wearing a nametag

and a cap with "Tulum Tours" written on it walks to the fountain in the centre of the lobby and greets us. "Good morning," he says, musically rolling the *r* in the second word. "My name is Roberto, and I'll be accompanying you to Tulum and Xel-ha today." I'm surprised by the way he says the second name, pronouncing the first syllable *shell*. I would have said *zel*. And I would have been wrong.

Roberto holds up a clipboard. "I have the names here of everyone who has paid for the full-day tour. When I read yours, please take a seat on the bus outside. Give your receipt to the driver as you get on."

My name, of course, is first. After thirteen years in school, I'm used to "Antonakos" being at or near the top of every alphabetical list. I leave the lobby and board the huge motorcoach idling outside, passing my receipt to the man behind the wheel and moving to the back of the bus.

One by one, other members of the tour group get on, most of them in pairs but a few in larger groups. I watch the seats fill up and begin to suspect I'm the only one here by myself today. I shrug. Isn't that what this is all about, anyway? A day all to myself? But, looking at seat partners chatting to seat partners, I suddenly feel out of place. A fifth wheel.

Clipboard still in hand, Roberto gets on the bus after everyone has boarded. Glancing at his watch, he says, "There are still three other people to come. It's not quite 7:30, so please feel free to ask me questions while we wait."

Hands immediately go up, but I don't listen to the questions or to Roberto's responses. Instead, I'm thinking about who those three other people might be, fervently hoping that one of them is Kate. I've even crossed my fingers.

Through the window, I see a man and a woman old enough to be my grandparents emerge from the lobby entrance and head toward the bus, and I frown. Still one more to go, though.

After they get on and settle themselves into seats, Roberto looks at his watch. "One more minute, people," he tells us.

But it's not a minute. No sooner are these words out of his mouth than the last passenger appears. I can't believe it.

I watch this person board the bus, give a receipt to the driver, then move down the aisle. My row is one of only three with a seat still empty, and I refuse to believe my luck as the latecomer moves past the other two and plunks down into the one by me.

"Morning," Connor MacPherson says.

I grunt something like a greeting and turn to the window again, grimacing as the bus releases its air brakes and eases forward. *Happy fucking birthday, Jace.*

———

I don't hear much of the tour-talk that Roberto begins as the driver guides the bus out through the Empress gates and onto the road. All I can think about as we pick up speed is the jerk sitting beside me. Of all the people to get stuck with on this bus, why does it have to be *this* asshole? I'd even have preferred the old guy sitting two seats ahead on the other side of the aisle. He looks to be at least eighty, with two canes, a scrawny neck and a bald head that bobs up and down as the bus rocks along, reminding me of those dumb plastic dogs that people used to put in the back windows of cars. Depressing, yeah, but even he'd be better than Connor MacPherson. I keep thinking of that moment on the path yesterday, of MacPherson's comment about Lucas and me taking our act on the road. And now here we are together on the road to Tulum. I remember last week when Ms. Bradford droned on and on about irony while most of the class zoned out, unable or unwilling to offer examples of irony in real life. *Well, Bradford,* I muse, *I've got one for you now.* If I had my English notebook, I'd even write it down. But I only have the one I'm using for Mr. Sanderson's Global Geography. And I doubt Sanderson's big on irony.

The tires whine beneath us and, soon after we make a right turn, the sound is interrupted frequently by thuds and whumps as we roll over cracks and dips in the pavement that make the whole bus shudder. The road we're now on clearly doesn't receive the same maintenance as the groomed boulevard that runs past the Riviera resorts, and, as if to prove the point, our right tires hit a hole that would rival a coffee table in surface area, jolting us like berries in a blender set on "pulse." My ass actually leaves the seat momentarily and a collective cry of surprise fills the bus. Roberto grins at us apologetically.

"Rough road," MacPherson says.

The hockey player's keen powers of observation underwhelm me. "Mmm," I reply. I look at my watch and, seeing we're still only minutes into the hour-long drive to Tulum, I groan.

"Even the roads back home aren't this bad," the mountain beside me continues. Out of boredom, no doubt, so I don't bother responding. It's not my job to entertain hockey heroes. It is, after all, my birthday, right?

The bus hits another bump and everyone rocks from side to side, including the honeymooners, who still haven't taken their eyes off each other. I look again at the guy with the canes and wonder how many birthdays *he's* seen come and go. And then, noticing how he faces forward rather than talking to the person beside him, I realize that he's all by himself on this bus too. Old and alone. And suddenly I get this feeling that I'm looking at myself in one of those weird flash-forward moments, somehow seeing myself in the future. As if being young and alone isn't depressing enough already.

And then, of course, I'm thinking of Cynthia. As much as I try not to, I see her face before me, the way the corners of her eyes crinkle when she laughs, the way she bites her lower lip when she's concentrating on something, the way she—

I turn to the window and try to focus on the terrain that

slides by. Try to convince myself the sudden ache in my chest is indigestion, hunger pangs, anything but the emptiness I refuse to acknowledge. I remind myself I'm in *Mexico,* for Christ's sake. It's my birthday, and I have the entire day to myself to do whatever I want. Whatever *I* want.

I hear Roberto tell us that the highway we're travelling on runs parallel to the ocean for a while, but we can't see it beyond the glass. Farther inland, where we are now, the landscape is mostly trees and scrub broken here and there by a few small houses and a store or two. But within moments I count what look to be four major construction sites. Construction appears to be big in the Yucatan, which probably has to do with tourism. I wonder what it's like for Mexicans who struggle along on a few pesos a day to help build huge resorts that are enjoyed mostly by affluent people from other countries. More irony. I think about that some more and then decide it's worth jotting down, so I reach into my backpack between my feet, push aside my water bottle, hat, swim trunks, change of clothes, digital camera, tube of sunblock—stuff the brochure told tour members to bring—and pull out my Global Geography notebook. I momentarily wonder if MacPherson will think I'm a total loser—probably, in fact, already does—but I don't give a shit. It's not like he's anyone I want to impress.

I open the notebook and slide out the pen I've stuck inside the coil, then attempt to jot down the date as the bus rolls along. The movement makes my handwriting wavy, but I don't care. Rather than a minimum word-count, Sanderson's assigned me to record ten observations a day, and I'd like to get some written ahead of time so I can concentrate on enjoying myself. More to the point, so I can concentrate on my prime objective. After all, this is Monday. I only have five more days to get laid. In Mexico, I mean.

"That a diary?"

My eyes freeze on the page. Leave it to Tony Testosterone to assume I keep a diary. When I'm not baking cookies and bottling jam. I feel my ears burn. "No," I mutter without looking up. "Homework." Hearing myself say it, though, I almost cringe. Suddenly I'm a fifth-grader on a field trip. The one who gets to carry the whistle and the attendance sheet.

"You still in high school?"

Still. The word rankles. "Grade 12." I try to get my pen moving again so he'll shut up.

"I remember my Grade 12," MacPherson says. Like it was, oh, thirty years ago.

I want to remind him he's only been out of high school two years himself, something I remember reading in one of those newspaper articles. But instead I just murmur, "Mmm."

He holds out his hand. "I'm Connor, by the way."

"Jace," I say. I shake his plate-sized palm, and for a second I'm afraid mine will break as his fingers grip, viselike, around it. I'm relieved when he lets go.

"Good to meet you, Jason."

First Kate calls me "Jake," and now this guy thinks I'm "Jason." What is it with names in Mexico? "It's *Jace*," I tell him, exaggerating the single syllable.

"Jace," he repeats. "Never heard that before."

I think of yesterday on the beach and feel like commenting that he probably meets more girls than guys, but I don't. "It's Greek."

He nods. "You *look* Greek."

Right. And you *look like a poster boy for steroid abuse.* I turn back to my notebook and begin writing the time under the date, but another huge pothole results in a diagonal scrawl across the paper. *Christ!* I tear out the page, ball it up and jam it into my backpack, then begin another.

"Does it mean something? Your name?"

"Mmm." I look out the window at the trees flashing by, thinking of a Family Studies assignment I had to do in Grade 7: draw our family tree and write a paragraph about the people on each branch. Besides their ages and where they were born, I didn't have much else to say about my parents and my brothers, so I looked for websites that gave origins of Greek names and pencilled in those details. Pop's and Lucas's names didn't really have meanings as much as backgrounds—"Evander" was a character in *The Aeneid*, a really long poem written by someone named Virgil, and "Lucas" was a form of "Luke," one of the authors of the New Testament. Stefan's name was something of a puzzle because different websites gave different meanings. One said it meant "constant," another defined it as "garland" or "wreath," while a third offered "crowned one." I went with the last definition. Even when I was in Grade 7, "crowned one" made a lot of sense—synonymous, really, with "firstborn son."

My mother's name and my own were much easier to nail down. "Sophia" meant "wisdom," which suits her—she's always been the one in our family that everyone depends on, the one with all the answers, the one who can look at problems as impossible as Lucas's CDD and find ways through them. *My* name, on the other hand, was a cosmic joke—I just didn't realize it in Grade 7.

"So," Himalaya prods again, "what's 'Jace' mean?"

"Healer," I grunt, turning away from the window. I rewrite today's date and the time on the paper, then draw a line under both just to give my pen something else to do.

"You born in Greece?"

Why won't he just *shut up*? "My parents were," I reply as I try to remember the thought I was about to write down. Something about construc—

"Interesting," he says, which is the universal code word for *You're boring the bejesus out of me.* I want to tell him he can shove his "interesting" up his ass, but I don't want to encourage him by talking.

"What's the course?"

I realize I'm clenching my jaws, and I force myself to ease up before I crack a molar. "Global Geography." I again struggle to grasp that vanishing tendril of thought. Mexican workers who—

"I took Global. It was okay."

I release a long sigh. Whatever my idea was, it's gone now. *Damn.*

"But my favourite was History," he adds.

I look at him, surprised. "You're kidding, right?" Of *course* he's kidding. Why'd I even ask?

He smiles, and I'm surprised he has teeth. Perfect teeth, in fact. Some of the goons that play for the provincial hockey team come into our restaurant sometimes, and a couple of them have huge gaps in their mouths, no doubt awaiting the services of a good prosthodontist. MacPherson's probably had most of his teeth capped or crowned already. Nothing about this guy is real. Like that remark about enjoying History.

"No, really," he says. "I loved History. Still do. It's my major at university. I go to Dal," he adds.

"I know." I point to his chest.

He looks down at the Dalhousie crest on his T-shirt, stretched tight across massive pecs, and he grins.

"You play for the Torrents," I tell him. Like he doesn't know.

He nods. "You flew on the same flight I did," he says, and for a second time I'm surprised someone noticed me. "You from Halifax too?" he asks.

I close my notebook—no point in trying to work now—and tell him where I live.

"Been there long?"

I suspect he's only talking to me because conversation is preferable to counting bumps in the road, but I have to admit I'm intrigued by the History thing. So I play along, tell him about both my parents immigrating with their families from small villages on the Aegean when they were kids, how they met at school in Halifax and married soon after graduation. He asks what they do and I tell him about the Parthenon.

"That's not far from the Dal campus," he says. "Been there a couple times. Really good food."

He's bullshitting me, I know, but I pretend not to notice. "You're *really* a History major?"

He nods. "Most of the guys I went to school with hated History. Thought it was boring. A waste of time learning about dead people."

"Yeah. My friends feel the same way," I tell him.

He nods again. "But it's not like that at all." He shrugs. "There are teachers out there who can *make* it painful, but I had one who showed me what it really is."

"What's that?"

"A movie."

Now I'm pissed all over again. Here I actually thought he might be serious, but he was bullshitting me all along, just passing the time on the way to Tulum. "Right," I say. I open up my notebook again and try to think of something to write. Anything, just so he'll take the hint and screw off.

He doesn't. Instead, he turns in his seat so he's facing me, no easy feat considering his bulk. "I mean it," he says. "Choose any period in history and you've got it all: setting, main character, conflict, everything. It's all one movie after another."

I look at him and wonder if he's for real, teeth notwithstanding. He *seems* like he's serious. Roberto is standing at the front of the bus, talking into a microphone about the site we're going to visit, and I think about why I chose to tour ruins rather than go scuba diving or monster-trucking. After all, MacPherson could be on the beach with multiple babes right now; instead, he's on a bus heading toward the crumbling remains of a Mayan civilization. I decide to give him the benefit of the doubt.

"So who was this teacher?"

"Ms. Tattersall. Grade 10 History. Whenever we started a new unit, she'd come to class dressed like a person who lived during the period we were going to study and she'd stand on her chair and recite some passage she'd found or maybe made up herself. She'd actually *be* that person. She'd stay in character the whole day, even when you saw her in the hall."

I shake my head.

"I know," he says, grinning, "sounds pretty lame. My buddies would roll their eyes, make fun of her when she wasn't looking." He settles back in his seat, and I get the weird impression he's seeing that Grade 10 classroom again. "I thought she was great," he sighs.

Oh, *now* I get it. Big deal. His interest had more to do with hormones than history.

But his next comment dispels that idea. "She was in her sixties and almost retired. In fact, I think she quit the year after I had her." He turns to me again. "That's what was so great about her. She could've spent her last year in the classroom coasting, but she didn't. She was always so fired up about how important history was, how we had so much to learn from it."

I nod at his last statement. "Yeah. That's the part most people don't see. Somebody said that the people who can't remember the past—"

"—are condemned to repeat it," he finishes for me. "George Santayana wrote that."

I couldn't be more stunned if he'd said he knits skate-warmers on road trips. "Santayana?"

"In his book *The Life of Reason*. He also wrote, 'Skepticism is the chastity of the intellect, and it is shameful to surrender it too soon or to the first comer.' Great line, huh?" he asks.

Connor MacPherson of the Dalhousie Torrents reciting quotations about history and philosophy. It's weird how people can totally surprise you. You'd think I'd be used to it after Cynthia—and after Stefan—but I'm not. I manage to nod.

"You like history?" he asks.

"Yeah," I say—with what I'm sure is entirely too much enthusiasm. Ordinarily, I'd worry about sounding like the world's biggest geek, but it's the first time I've talked to someone who seems to feel how I do. "I think of it as a mystery. You've got this outcome, this end result, and it's the backstory you're trying to figure out. It's as if you're a detective trying to piece together cause and effect."

"Like those *CSI* shows," he offers.

I find myself smiling. "Yeah. Especially when they deal with artifacts left behind by civilizations that died out, like we'll see today. Imagining what purpose something might have served, what need created it."

"So it's archaeology you like most," he observes. "You ever been to one of these sites before?"

I shake my head, thinking of the trip Stefan took last summer. With some help from our grandparents, Pop sent my brother to Greece right after graduation so he could see where our family came from. Stefan had accepted a full scholarship from Saint Mary's University so he really didn't need to work that summer, and Pop felt it was important for his oldest son to see the villages where he and my mother were born. "You can't really know who you are unless you understand where you came from," Pop said. So Stefan went, staying with aunts and uncles and cousins, touring Athens and then much of the country along the Aegean. He e-mailed us pictures of the sites he'd seen—the Parthenon, of course, and the Acropolis, the Theatre of Dionysus, the Library of Hadrian, but also more obscure places like the ruins of Tiryns and the Sanctuary of Asklepios in Epidaurus. I'd page through them on the screen again and again, imagining what it would be like to be there, to walk on the ground where civilization began.

The funny thing—no, the *ironic* thing—is that Stefan couldn't have cared less about those places, touring ruins and listening to guides tell their stories. None of that stuff ever interested him. He'd taken Ancient History in high school only because Mr. Conway, his guidance counsellor, had said it would round out his resumé. Knowing about our restaurant, one of our relatives took a photo of Stefan standing in front of the Parthenon and he e-mailed it to Pop. Studying that picture, though, I thought I could see boredom behind Stefan's pasted-on smile. He never once talked to me about the trip when he got back, and I was grateful for that.

"Ever think you'd like to be an archaeologist?"

I tell him I've thought about it a lot, something I'm more than a little surprised to find myself sharing. I've talked to this guy for ten minutes and he knows something I've never even told my best friend. But that's because I know what Rod's reaction would be—after he ruptured a lung laughing, of course: *Archaeologist? I thought you wanted to get* laid, *Jace, not embalmed.* And he'd have a point. Archaeology isn't exactly the ultimate babe-magnet.

It appears I'm not the only one thinking of friends. "My buddies," Connor says, "left on some monster-truck ride earlier this morning. It's a good thing they didn't come with us. It would've been painful."

"For them," I say.

He shakes his head. "For *us*. They're great guys, but they can get carried away sometimes."

So can you, I say to myself, remembering that scene in the airport with Kate. And the scene by the bar on our first night at the Empress.

"But then so can I," he says, surprising me all over again.

9

The bus rumbles to a dusty stop beside a long, low building that spills tiny outdoor souvenir shops into a parking area. We can't see the ruins, but Roberto warned us before we arrived that the actual entrance to the Tulum site is a kilometre down a dirt road. He said we could either walk or wait for a trolley to take us. I'd initially decided to walk—a kilometre seemed like no big deal—but when I step off the air-conditioned bus, the heat blankets me. It's like entering a sauna cranked up to "cook."

"You coming?" asks Connor, who has stepped off ahead of me.

"Think I'll wait for the trolley."

"You're kidding, right?" he says.

I shrug. Already I feel beads of sweat on my forehead.

"It's a kilometre, for Christ's sake." And then he adds, "Pussy."

Let's face it. When jocks play the "pussy" card, you're pretty much screwed.

"So what're you waiting for, asshole?" I mutter, shouldering my backpack and setting off across the parking lot. Connor falls into step beside me.

I have to admit part of me isn't as annoyed as I'm pretending to be. I can think of worse things than spending my birthday with someone who seems to like history as much as I do. Cynthia hated anything remotely resembling a museum. The whole time we were dating, her closest brush with the past was a visit to a used car lot when her brother was shopping for wheels.

I turn and see that Connor and I aren't the only ones who've decided to walk to the ruins. A handful of people from the bus—the few under fifty, including the honeymooners—are following us, the rest having chosen to wait on wooden benches for the trolley. I see that the old guy with the canes is among the people waiting. I don't blame him.

We don't get more than a hundred paces down the road before my shirt is soaked with sweat. Connor's is, too, and he drops his backpack, pulls off his Dalhousie T and jams it into a side pocket before continuing. I want to do the same, but I'm more than a little intimidated by the shape he's in.

"Jesus, how often do you work out?" I ask.

Walking sideways, he strikes one of those double-biceps body-builder poses, muscles flexing impressively, and then cracks up. His baritone laugh is even deeper than my father's. Pop still uses his on customers in the restaurant, but I haven't heard him laugh at home in a long time. Nearly a year.

"No, really. I wanna know. How often?"

"I'm usually at the gym four times a week using the weights, but I try to skip every day."

"Why would you want to skip if you get results like that?"

He looks at me quizzically, then laughs again. "Not *that* kind of skipping, schoolboy. *Rope* skipping."

It's my turn to laugh. "Somehow I can't picture a hockey player skipping rope."

He raises one eyebrow. "I bet there's lots a' things you can't picture a hockey player doing," he says. Then, "Skipping's a ter-rific aerobic workout, and great for coordination, too. Some of the world's best boxers are skippers." He bends down and picks up a rock, effortlessly sends it sailing high over the tangled mass of trees lining the road. "What about you?"

"What *about* me?"

"How often do *you* work out?"

"Not as often as I should." But I take off my T-shirt anyway. It's drenched.

"You're fine," he says, looking at me. "Good upper body. Strong legs. What's your sport?"

"Soccer."

"Thought so. You've got the legs for it. You must run in the off-season."

"Whenever I can, but working at the restaurant cuts into it."

"You ever play hockey?" he asks.

I shake my head. "My older brother did."

"Ever want to?"

"One hockey player in the family was enough."

We continue for a while in silence. I turn and see we've left the other walkers far behind. They're strung out in something like a single file, frequent spaces between them. Even from this distance, though, I can tell they're all as sweat-soaked as we are. None of them have removed clothing, though.

Then, "So what's your brother do now, Jace?"

It's been almost a year since someone's asked me this question and I'm surprised when it catches me, makes me draw a breath before answering. "Nothing. He's dead."

Connor stops. "Sorry, man."

I shrug, hoping he'll leave it alone. "It's okay. You didn't know."

But there's a sudden expression on his face, a flicker of eyes and the way he's looking now at some point on my forehead, that makes me wonder, oddly, if this is really true.

Seconds before we reach the entrance to the ruins, the trolley carrying the rest of the group passes us. The old guy with the canes waves as they rumble by, and I have to grin. Smart bugger.

Roberto, who also chose to ride the trolley, is the first off, and he advises us all to use the rest-stop before we continue because there are no facilities on the grounds of the ruins. "Also," he says in his precise English, "please drink as much water as you can. I do not want anyone getting dehydrated." I think about the construction sites we've driven by and wonder how Mexican labourers work outside in heat like this daily. And it isn't even summer here yet.

Pulling on our T-shirts, Connor and I make our way into a restroom and wait as several men ahead of us use the urinals. Two other tour groups arrived just before us, and I imagine every guide must offer the same advice about the facilities.

After we finish, we rejoin the others and listen as Roberto provides more background about the site. He tells us that Tulum is not as large as Chichen-Itza, the most-visited Mayan ruins in the Yucatan, but many feel that Tulum is more significant. "Considerable evidence," Roberto continues, "suggests that Tulum was one of the most important cities of the ancient Maya because both sea and land routes converged here. Artifacts from as far away as Central America have been discovered at this site."

When I think of how old the city is—Roberto told us that inscriptions date back as early as 564 AD—and how primitive travel was at that time, I realize just how incredible the discovery of those Central American artifacts must have been. I can tell by the look on Connor's face that he's equally amazed.

Not everyone in the group is as impressed as we are. A middle-aged couple wearing hats with "Idaho Rocks" on them and shirts that say "Idaho'ed it if I'd planted it" fan themselves vigorously with their brochures. "*Christ!*" the man murmurs. "It's a friggin' *furnace* out here." The woman tries to shush him, but her own skin glistens in agreement.

Roberto waves our group forward. As we walk, he tells us that the names of places in Mexico sometimes resulted from problems in communication between cultures. "When the Spanish conquistadors first arrived in this area, they asked the natives what they called their home, and the natives said, '*Yucatan,*' which was their word for 'I don't understand you.'" Several people in our group chuckle at this. "*Tulum* means 'wall' in the Mayan language," he continues, indicating the high stone structure to our right, "and the wall surrounding the remains of this ancient city offered protection from attack. The name *Tulum,* however, was given to it by the explorers who found it in the nineteenth century. Researchers now believe its actual name was *Zama,* which means 'dawn,' since the rising of the sun played a very important role in the lives and worship of its people."

Our group passes through a gap in the wall and an immense grassy area opens up before us, a variety of crude stone structures rising here and there toward the sun. Many of them are only a couple metres high, but off to our left are much taller structures perched on a cliff overlooking the bottle-green ocean. The stones, worn smooth from wind and rain, are various shades of grey, and everywhere we look iguanas, the same colour as the ruins, bask in the sun. Every few moments, a member of the tour group gives a startled gasp as an iguana, invisible until its movements betray it, flicks its tail and scurries off.

"Man," breathes Connor, "can you imagine what it must've been like to *find* this place?"

Looking at the wall, the ruins, the ocean moving toward the cliff face below, I imagine the movie unspooling in Connor's head. "It's really something," I say. And it is.

Idaho grunts behind me and I can tell he doesn't share the sentiment, but I don't give a shit. Walking through that opening is like stepping through a portal in time. If not for our clothing and digital cameras, you could almost imagine we were the explorers who rediscovered this site more than a hundred and fifty years ago. Or even the people who inhabited it ten times that many years earlier. It's as though time has frozen here, and I suddenly understand why buses have to park so far away. The absence of engines rumbling and tires turning helps create the illusion of other-worldliness. The only sounds we hear are waves breaking on the beach and the awed murmurs of visitors. Only Idaho is unfazed. Everyone else stares wide-eyed at the scene around us, snapping picture after picture that will no doubt be e-mailed to family and friends later in the day.

I think for a moment about e-mailing pictures of Tulum to Pop. I wonder what he'd think of these ruins, wonder if he'd see in them the beauty or the waste. But I decide against it, decide the ruin of our family is enough for my father. For any of us.

Roberto gathers us in the shade of one of the stone structures and asks us to peer into its dark interior toward a tiny rectangular opening on the ocean side of the building. "On the exact day of the spring equinox," he says, "the light of the rising sun passes directly through this window, signalling the beginning of planting." He opens a binder and holds it up to show us photos of the tiny window ablaze with light. Then he describes several other features of the stone structures related to the movement of the sun across the sky, all of them revealing the incredible understanding the ancient Mayans had of both calendars and celestial movement. Me, I'm lucky if I remember to set my alarm clock.

We move forward and stop in the shade of another building, where Roberto describes the people who would have used the various structures on the site, among them priests and members of the royal family. The doorways of the buildings are small, their lintels no higher than my shoulders, so obviously the Mayans weren't very big. Roberto shows us a book containing artistic interpretations of the Mayans that further support this impression, and I'm reminded of something Ms. Bradford told us during one of those self-esteem-building kicks that teachers get on sometimes: "You don't have to be big to have a huge impact on your world." Patronizing statements like that usually stimulate my gag reflex, but I suddenly find myself wishing I had my English notebook to record those words. They seem to have real importance here.

Roberto speaks some more about Mayan culture and customs reflected in Tulum's architecture, and then he invites us to explore the site on our own. I've been so caught up in what he's had to tell us that I'm surprised to see several people have already moved off, no doubt impatient for more photo ops. Connor, however, is right behind me, standing next to the old guy with the two canes.

"Need some help?" Connor asks. At first I think he means me, but then I realize he's talking to the old man, which surprises me yet again. I don't know what he expects to do—hoist the old guy up on his shoulders?—but the man shakes his head anyway.

"I am goot," he tells Connor, and I hear in his words an accent I don't recognize. Dutch? German? "You haff much to see. Go."

Connor nods, then looks at me. "You up for more walking, pussy?"

"After you, asshole," I grin.

═══

I doubt an eco-park can equal the spectacle of a lost civilization, but as noon approaches and the sun grows even hotter, I find myself looking forward to the lagoon at Xel-ha.

Leaving the ruins, all of us take the trolley back to the bus—even Connor, who repeatedly mops his face with the bottom of his T-shirt—and I can tell everyone's as glad as I am to hear the trip to Xel-ha won't be long.

It isn't. As our bus rolls into the park, Roberto offers some last-minute instructions and information, including the welcome news that our prepaid admission entitles us to eat as much as we want at any of the open-air restaurants around the lagoon. My stomach suddenly reminds me it's been hours since my breakfast at the resort, and I figure the lagoon can wait a little longer. I'm about to make this observation when Connor beats me to it.

"Let's get something to eat," he says as the bus shudders to a stop.

On Roberto's recommendation, we first head to the main building, where we pick up snorkelling equipment and towels, change into our trunks and leave our backpacks and clothing in secure lockers. Although we've only exchanged one burden for another, it feels good to leave something behind.

Lunch is a Chinese buffet in an enormous pavilion, and I heap as much food as I can on my plate. Connor does the same, and we find a table outdoors overlooking the water and sit down. The lagoon is maybe a kilometre or more across and stretches as far as we can see to our left and right, dotted here and there with groups of life-jacketed snorkellers whose flippered feet propel them along its surface. A warm breeze blows toward us carrying frequent squeals of "Did you see *that?*" and "What was *that* thing?" over the green, translucent water.

As we eat, Connor and I see the old man with the canes inching along the path, heading toward one of the many sets of wooden stairs that lead down into the lagoon. Except for the towel around his neck, he wears only trunks and sneakers now, his skin hanging in wrinkled pouches at his waist and above his bony knees. A bag containing his snorkel gear bumps against one cane each time he picks it up and puts it down.

"Gotta hand it to the old guy, huh?" Connor says around an eggroll.

I nod as we watch the man sit on a bench, laying both canes

to one side and taking off his sneakers. With what looks like tremendous effort, he slides on the flippers and tightens the straps at his heels, then stands up. That's when I notice he isn't wearing a life jacket.

The man puts a snorkel in his mouth, then pulls goggles over his eyes and inches slowly toward the staircase, lifting and lowering the flippers with exaggerated care. He eases his way down the steps and I can almost see his knuckles whiten as his hands grip both railings. When he reaches the water, he bends his knees slowly and lets himself fall gently forward. And then everything changes. The next moment, he's gliding smoothly across the surface of the lagoon, his legs moving in strong, rhythmic sweeps. It's as though we've witnessed a transformation, a rebirth of sorts. A few moments later, he's out of sight.

"Jesus," Connor says, shaking his head.

"Yeah," I reply. "Who'd 'a thought?"

He pushes his chair back and stands up. "You ready to get wet?"

"You bet," I say as I gather up my equipment.

A few moments later, we're sitting on the same bench the old guy used. Sliding on my flippers and life jacket, I look at the abandoned canes and sneakers and am amazed all over again by what we've seen the old guy do. I start to fasten the buckles on the life jacket, then slip it off and lay it on the bench.

"You're not wearing it?" Connor asks.

"*He* didn't," I reply, pointing at the canes.

"He probably signed a waiver." This from the guy who had to be silenced by airport security.

I grin. "*Now* who's being a pussy?"

I stand and frog-walk to the stairs, then I get a better idea. I move to the right and, holding my goggles and snorkel in one hand, I stand on the rocky ledge that borders this part of the lagoon. Below me, the water looks to be at least three metres deep, with brightly coloured fish flashing through it, and I can't wait to join them.

"Eat my splash," I say as I turn and dive into the—

"—hear me, Jace?"

I'm coughing—choking, more like it—and salt water scorches my throat and nose. There's a weight on my chest, pressing into me again and again. I suck in air and open my eyes. Connor and a woman kneel over me while several others stand in a wide circle around us. And a woodpecker hammers on my skull.

"Wha—?" I try to sit up, but the woodpecker turns into a jackhammer and I almost cry out. I grip my head with both hands and feel something warm on my scalp. One hand comes away red and I stare at it like I've never seen blood before.

"Easy, Jace," says Connor, helping me lie back down. "She's a doctor." He nods at the woman across from him. "From Saskatchewan."

The woman lowers a hand in front of my eyes. "How many fingers am I holding up?"

She's wearing a one-piece swimsuit cut low at the neck, and all I can focus on is cleavage. "Two," I sputter automatically through another choking spell.

She frowns, and then I see she's holding up four. I tell her so, and her frown relaxes.

"You hit your head when you dove in," Connor explains. "A ledge just below the surface."

"You're lucky your friend was right here," the woman says. "He pulled you out before you took in too much water."

Still coughing, I vaguely wonder what *too much* would be, as water continues to trickle from my nostrils. I wipe my nose with my other hand and pull away a string of snot. Embarrassment washes over me and again I try to sit up, the jackhammer drilling into my skull.

The doctor gently pushes me back down. "I need to make sure of a few things first," she says. She asks me what day it is and, without thinking, I tell her it's my birthday. She looks at Connor, whose eyes widen, and he just shrugs. She tells me to follow her finger as she moves it back and forth in front of my eyes, then asks me to turn my head slowly, first left and then right. I feel the bones in my neck complain, but everything seems to be working okay. Then she asks me to move my feet. No problem there, either.

"I can't tell for sure without doing a CT, but everything checks out. You're lucky," she tells me again. "An older person might have broken his neck."

I remember the old guy with the canes and wonder where he is now. I picture him kicking steadily forward and wonder if he's made it to the ocean, imagine him passing whatever rope or buoy or marker that separates the lagoon from the gulf, propelling himself out to sea. Then I'm gritting my teeth against the jackhammer pummelling my brain.

Another face appears over me, a Mexican whose shirt bears the eco-park's emblem. "I am José Ortiz," he says to the woman, "Assistant Director of Xel-ha. I understand you are a doctor." She nods. "How is he?"

She repeats what she's already told me, and I can see relief soften his features. "I appreciate your help," he tells her.

"However, we will need to examine him ourselves. We have medical personnel on staff—"

"No," I say, and this time I manage to sit up all the way, wincing as the pain ratchets through my head. "I just want to get out of here."

"I'm afraid that will not be possible until—"

"It's my fault." I point at the "No Diving" sign by the water's edge, which I've just now seen. "No one's responsible. I'm fine. I just want to go—" I almost say *home*. "I want to go back to my hotel." A wave of nausea swirls over me and, although I want to lie back down, I struggle to stand. I feel Connor's hand under my arm, and he pulls me easily to my feet.

"You sure you're okay?" he asks.

The circle around us dissolves as people return to their lives, and I desperately want to do the same. "I'm fine. I just need something to put on this," I tell him, pointing to the cut on my scalp.

"Here," says Ortiz, pulling plastic packages of sterile gauze from a first-aid kit. He hands them, along with a pair of rubber gloves, to the doctor. "I must insist, though, that you—"

"He says he's fine," interrupts Connor, and I'm grateful for his hand still under my elbow, steadying me. "We're staying at the same resort. I'll make sure he gets back there and sees the hotel doctor."

Slipping on the rubber gloves, the doctor looks at Ortiz. "My name is Sandra Payne." She spells her last name for him. "I can give you my contact information and verify that he refused treatment here. He's probably better off getting back to his family." She turns to me. "You *do* have family at your resort?" she asks.

"My mother and my aunt," I reply, all the while thinking how, if I had her last name, I'd have changed it, made the *P* into an *L* or a *W*. Who'd want to see a doctor with a last name like that? The things you think about when you hit your head. That and cleavage.

Ortiz takes out a notepad and writes down the doctor's name and the place she's staying, then asks me for the same information. I tell him, as another wave of nausea washes over me. Now the world around me starts to move, and again I'm grateful for Connor's supporting hand. "Thanks," I tell the doctor.

"You be sure to get yourself checked out," she warns.

Before I can nod, Connor says, "I'll make sure." He lowers me onto a bench. "You stay here while I return our gear and get our stuff, okay?"

"I will stay with him," says Ortiz, who sits down beside me. I can tell he's still reluctant to allow me to leave, but he's resigned himself to it.

The doctor tears open one of the packages and dabs with the gauze at the cut on my scalp. "You're lucky," she says for the third time. "I thought you'd probably need stitches, but it's not that deep. You must've just grazed the ledge."

I thank her again. "If you're ever in Halifax, come to the Parthenon Grill. My family owns it. I'll make sure you get meals on the house."

She smiles. "I may hold you to that." She drops the bloody gauze into a plastic bag that Ortiz holds open for her, then tears apart the second package and places the fresh gauze on the cut. "Press on this. The bleeding's almost stopped."

I do as she instructs and then tell her she should go, that she's done more than enough already.

Pulling off the gloves and dropping them into Ortiz's plastic bag, she looks around her. "I have a husband here someplace. I'd better see if I can find him." She looks at me again. "You're sure you're okay?"

"Nothing a fistful of Tylenol won't take care of."

She grins. "Remember what I told you—"

"I'll get it checked out," I say, more for Ortiz's benefit than for hers.

She moves off and I watch her go, trying to ignore the way her body moves in that swimsuit. But I can't, and a familiar warmth stirs in my groin. Even getting knocked unconscious hasn't affected that. *Am I some sort of pervert?* I wonder, then mentally shrug. No. What I am is a virgin. And to make matters worse, I'm now an eighteen-year-old virgin. With only five days left to do anything about it in Mexico.

I look at Ortiz, who is writing something else on his notepad, and then at the blood-stained gauze in the plastic bag at his feet. Then, sudden and unbidden, images rise from my memory. Bloody image after bloody image. I look down, gripping the wood of the bench I'm sitting on with my free hand, feeling the raised grain beneath my fingertips, and I see the two canes lying on the ground. Despite the images in my head, despite the blood in the bag and the continual throb that sets my teeth on edge, I smile.

Ortiz smiles back at me. "You're feeling better?" he asks hopefully.

"Much better," I lie.

=====

"Were you kidding before, about your birthday?" Connor asks.

We're riding in the back of a very small taxi. A Fiat, I think. An *old* Fiat. The driver bangs his palms on the battered steering wheel to the beat of a Rolling Stones song I haven't heard in years, Mick Jagger's tortured voice shredding my eardrums.

"Can you turn that down?" I ask the driver, then add, "*Por favor?*"

He looks in the mirror and grins at me, then turns up the volume. The sound chainsaws through my head.

Connor leans forward over the seat. "No, he said *down*." He makes an exaggerated turning motion with his fingers.

The driver's smile vanishes. He punches a button on the dash and the wailing stops. "*Perdóname,*" he says. "*No entendía.*"

I think he's apologizing but I could care less. I settle back against the ripped seat and savour the silence. That is, if you don't count the laboured roar of the motor and the howl of nearly bald tires on pavement. I was skeptical when we found the taxi waiting in Xel-ha's parking area, but Connor told me to get in anyway. "It'll get us there," he said. I had my doubts. I still do. But at least it has air-conditioning.

I feel really bad about Connor missing the second half of the day he's already paid for, but he said he was ready to go back to the resort anyway, that Tulum was the place he'd most wanted to see and he'd done that. But I still feel like a world-class wimp. And on top of that, I'm not sure if I have enough money on me to pay for the taxi. We were supposed to take the bus back, but it isn't scheduled to leave the park for another four hours. Connor didn't think we should wait that long.

"Were you?" he asks.

"Was I what?"

"Kidding about today being your birthday."

For a second, I consider lying, but what's the point? Would I be any *less* a loser if it *weren't* my birthday?

"No."

"Which one?"

"Lucky eighteen."

He chuckles, the sound like rocks rolling around in his chest. "Jace," he says, "this calls for a celebration, man."

"Some other time, okay?" Right now, all I want to do is crawl into bed.

"Yeah, sure." More pavement howls beneath us before he asks, "What'd you want?"

I turn my head to look at him and 220 volts zither up my neck, exploding in fireworks behind my eyeballs. "What d'you mean?" I manage to ask when the pain finally lessens.

"For your birthday."

I ease my head back so I'm facing forward again. I plan to stay in that position for a very long time. "Believe me, you *don't* want to know."

I hear the rocks roll around some more. "Did you get it?"

I let my silence answer for me.

Then I remember something I haven't done. "Thanks, Connor."

"For what?"

I'm embarrassed, but it needs to be said. "For saving my life."

I can feel him shrug beside me. "No big deal," he says, and I can hear embarrassment in *his* voice now. "What are friends for?"

Friends. Was it only this morning that I thought he was a total asshole?

I look at the meter on the taxi's dash that marks elapsed time in pesos, the numbers slowly increasing. Without intending to, I think about Stefan and wonder if there was ever a time he thought of me as a friend, if he ever once considered telling me what was wrong, what was so bad that he'd look for a way to halt that increase, to keep those numbers from counting up, forever freezing them in a single display.

I want to turn toward the window, but my neck won't let me. I yawn noisily and pretend to rub my eyes with the back of my hand, all the while wiping away sudden tears. Only the driver sees me do this, his puzzled eyes studying mine in the rearview mirror.

11

"Wow. This is some room you got here. Barn's and mine doesn't look *anything* like this."

Connor stands in the doorway looking at the plush leather furniture and the flat-panel while I swallow three Extra-Strength Tylenols, then pull down the covers on the bed. As usual, a towel folded into the shape of an animal—a lizard this time—sits in the centre. I knock it onto the floor, kick off my sandals, then pull off my T-shirt and trunks and slide between the sheets. Their crisp coolness feels good against my bare skin.

"You can hang around if you want," I tell him, drowsiness slurring my voice. No fake yawning now. My mouth feels like it's going to swallow my face, and I hear the bones beneath my ears pop. A white-hot needle stabs into my head and I moan without meaning to.

He moves toward the nightstand. "I'm calling the hotel doctor now," he says.

I reach out and put my hand over the phone. "Don't," I say.

He frowns. "The woman at the park said—"

"I know what she said." The needle stabs me again, then a third time, and then finally eases up a bit. "I'm fine. I just need to sleep for a while."

"Bad idea, Jace."

But already I'm beginning to drift off.

My eyes spring open as something jars the bed. Connor is sitting beside me. "You could have a concussion," he says, leaning over me. "It's dangerous falling asleep if you have one. Everybody knows that."

I can't imagine sleep ever being dangerous. It feels like the best thing imaginable right now. Even better than sex.

I have to grin at this last thought. If I weren't so tired, I might be concerned by that unexpected revelation. Clearly, I'm dying. My eyes close anyway.

A hand prods my shoulder. "Why don't you want me to call the doctor?"

I open my eyes again, considering his question. I suppose I could tell him about Lucas, about all the doctors he sees in the run of a year, doctors who probably know what they're doing but never fail to scare the living shit out of him. Each time he finishes their battery of tests, he looks less like my brother and more like the stranger who lives inside his head.

Or I could tell him about Mr. Greenberg, one of Pop's regulars, who stopped coming to the restaurant last year when he had his gall bladder removed, about how the surgeon nicked his bowel during what was supposed to be routine surgery and Mr. Greenberg died six months later, his guts rotted away from the inside out by the poison they couldn't stop seeping into his belly.

Or I could tell him about Stefan.

But I say none of these things.

"I don't want my mother finding out what happened. It'll totally screw up the rest of our vacation."

He nods. This he understands. "Okay, but I still don't think you should be sleeping. You gotta get up."

I moan again. I can't imagine leaving these sheets.

Connor pulls the covers back and tosses me my trunks. "Put these on. We'll sit on the balcony and watch chicks."

Despite the lead on my eyelids, I look at him and grin. This I can do. I have trouble sitting up and Connor reaches to help me, but I wave him away. If I don't want my mother finding out, I'd better fend for myself. I look at the digital clock on the nightstand and see I've only got three hours until the tour bus is supposed to return. She'll expect to see me after that. Three hours to look normal. It's a good thing my hair hides the cut on my scalp.

I manage to sit up and pull on my trunks, trying to keep my head elevated. If I lower it, the pulse in my ears threatens to blow the top off my skull.

I stand up and point toward the cabinet containing the bar. "Get yourself something, if you want," I tell him.

He opens the cabinet and whistles. "The restaurant business must pay well."

"My parents couldn't afford this place," I say. "My aunt's paying for it." I meant to say my uncle, but my mouth is out of sync with my brain.

"You be sure to introduce me to your aunt," he says, pulling out two Coronas. He hands me one. "Happy birthday."

I look at the Corona in my hand, feel its icy surface in my palm, then hold it to my forehead. Already droplets have condensed on the bottle, and the wet feels good against my skin. Better than sheets. Way better.

=====

Two hours later, I've had only the one Corona—I don't need *that* battle with my mother right now—and I'm on my second Coke and feeling a little better than I did before. Connor, too, is feeling better. Or, as Pop would say, "feeling no pain," which is how he describes customers who stagger out of the Grill after too many ouzos. I look at the empty Coronas by Connor's chair and marvel at how many he's been able to put away. But he's got all that body mass on his side.

He's been talking non-stop, keeping me from nodding off. And not just about the girls walking below us on the path to the beach. He's told me about his family, how he's the youngest of six kids, his siblings all sisters. He's told me his dad played hockey for the minors when he was younger, before he blew his knee out, and how he's convinced there's an NHL career in Connor's future. Which is what Connor wants, too. More than anything.

Which brings Connor back to the question of what *I* want. For my birthday. "You *gotta* tell me, man," he slurs. "I saved your goddamn *life*, 'member?" He leans forward and puts his hand on my shoulder, shaking it. "You owe me *that* much." Spray from his lips spatters my chest.

I sigh. It isn't as if no one knows. After all, I've told Rod. And now Connor's played the "lifesaver" card on me, which, when you think about it, trumps the hell out of the "pussy" card. I finally relent. "I wanna get laid."

He grins, opening yet another Corona and bringing it to his lips. "Don't we all, man. Don't we all."

I shake my head. "You don't understand. I *need* to get laid."

He looks at me, realization slowly dawning, and he pauses in mid-swallow. Wiping his mouth with the back of his hand, he says, "You never swiped your V-card? Good-lookin' guy like you?"

I shrug.

He leans back heavily in his cushioned chair. "Jesus."

"Make me feel like a loser, why don't you?"

He shakes his head. "Sorry, man. It's just I don't meet many virgins."

"Tell me about it," I say. My bladder is bursting and I welcome the opportunity to sidestep this particular topic of conversation.

I get up slowly and make my way to the bathroom to take a leak. When I return, Connor is sitting forward, his elbows on his knees, his chin in his hands. I think he's staring at the ocean, but then I discover otherwise.

"How 'bout *that* one?" he asks, nodding toward a woman approaching on the path below us. She reminds me a little of the doctor at Xel-ha. But with less cleavage.

"Please tell me you're not checking out women for me," I say.

It's his turn to shrug. "Just tryin' to help."

"Thanks, but I'd prefer someone born the same decade as me."

"What about her?"

I follow his gaze and see long, tanned legs emerge from beneath the palm leaves below us, followed by a white bikini and long, blond hair. Kate Townsend.

And just like that, I feel my heart hammer against my ribcage.

I hear Connor chuckle beside me. "Bingo!" he says.

I turn to him with what I hope is nonchalance. "What?"

But he's grinning and, even though he's drunk, I can tell he's seen right through me. "Hey, sweetheart!" he roars, pulling himself up to stand by the railing.

"Connor!" I hiss. "Don't!" But it's too late.

Kate stops and looks up at the balcony, one hand shading her eyes from the sun.

"Yeah, you!" shouts Connor. He waves his beer at her. "How 'bout you come on up here for a visit?"

I slouch down in my chair, but it's no use. The Plexiglas offers zero protection. I may as well be sitting in a fishbowl.

"I got a friend here who wants to hang out with you!" Connor calls down to her.

Kate drops her hand and continues walking. "Tell your friend I don't hang out with assholes," she says as she disappears around the corner of Ocean 1. She hasn't said it loudly. In fact, I could barely hear her.

But she may as well have screamed it at the top of her lungs.

And I suddenly wish Connor hadn't pulled me from that lagoon.

| 12 |

The knocking doesn't stop. "Hey, Jace! You up?"

I want to ignore him, but he's been rapping on that door for over a minute now. Persistent son of a bitch, that Connor. I pull the pillow off my head and look at the clock on my nightstand: 9:26 a.m. Sighing, I swing my legs over the edge of the bed and ease myself to my feet.

On the way to the door, I grab a towel from the bathroom and wrap it around my waist. My head doesn't feel too bad—I was up around four o'clock and took some more Extra-Strength Tylenol—but my reflection in the bathroom mirror looks like shit.

Apparently, the assessment is unanimous. "You look like shit," Connor says when I let him in. He, on the other hand, looks like a billboard for Dalhousie's Athletics program—both the muscle shirt and the shorts he's wearing bear the obligatory Torrents insignia.

I don't say anything, just head back to my king-sized bed and sprawl across it. I have absolutely no intention of ever leaving this room.

Connor, it appears, has other ideas. "It's almost 9:30, man. You're wasting the day!"

I bury my face in a pillow. "Don't you have someone else's life to ruin?" I mutter into the goose down.

The bed rocks as Connor drops onto it. "I didn't know you had your eye on her, Jace." When I don't respond, he continues, "Anyway, I bet she's forgotten all about it." I turn my head and give him a withering glance, but he's impervious. "Look, I'll make it up to you, okay?"

"Where are your buddies?" I ask. I'm hoping he'll inflict his help on someone else. After that scene on the balcony yesterday, I intend to spend the next four days with room service and my flat-panel.

He lies back, fingers laced behind his head, biceps bunching into baseballs. "They're around somewhere," he says.

That's profound, I want to tell him. *Almost existential.* But I don't want to encourage him with conversation. I just want him to leave me the hell alone.

He doesn't. "Your family ask you anything about yesterday?"

I sigh. He isn't going away.

I roll over and, staring at the ceiling, tell him about the events of last night.

Mom, Lucas and Mara came to my suite about an hour after Connor staggered out. I was no longer sleepy—humiliation can be a real bucket of cold water—and I was still sitting on the balcony feeling sorry for myself when they arrived. I told them all about Tulum and manufactured some interesting stories about Xel-ha, then said I ate as soon as the bus got back so they should go to the dining room without me. Mom commented that I looked wiped, but she accepted my explanation, that I was worn out from the day's activities. They were taking Lucas to Playa del Carmen that evening to do some shopping and wanted me to come—"To celebrate your birthday," Mara said—but I begged off, told them the birthday boy just wanted to relax, maybe watch a little TV and go to bed early.

I don't bother telling Connor what I *really* did last night: lay on my bed replaying that moment with Kate below my balcony over and over again in my mind. *Tell your friend I don't hang out with assholes.* The worst part—even worse than her calling me an asshole—was her obvious assumption that I'm Connor's new best buddy. I'm not just *any* asshole now. I'm a card-carrying member of the Eternal Brotherhood of Assholes.

And here I am beginning another day with Brother MacPherson. I pull the pillow over my face.

Connor punches me lightly on the arm. Except Connor's "lightly" still packs a wallop.

"Ow!" I whip the pillow back and glare at him.

He props himself up on one elbow. "Don't be such a pussy. There's no point in moping around here all day. How about we get you some breakfast and then go windsurfing? Or maybe parasailing?"

"You go."

"No fun alone."

"I'm sure your buddies'll go."

"They're occupied today."

"Occupied?" I picture a beach volleyball marathon, complete with babes in bikinis. I'm not far off. Except minus the marathon.

"They met some girls a couple days ago," he says, which appears to be all the explanation necessary.

"So did you," I remind him.

He shakes his head. "Not my type."

Now *that* surprises me. I remember those girls vividly. Both pretty, all boobs and bums. Not movie-star gorgeous, but pretty nonetheless. I guess when you're Connor MacPherson, though, you can hold out for movie-star gorgeous. *My* standards aren't quite so high. At this point, I'd settle for a pulse.

But who am I kidding? I don't even have the guts to step outside for fear of bumping into Kate. And unless the Empress's room service includes a side order of girls, Connor is my only alternative to solitary confinement. There's always homework, I muse momentarily, but *that* thought is enough to bring me to my senses. I'm in *Mexico*, for Christ's sake.

I sigh. "Let me get dressed."

=====

Jesus! I've never experienced *anything* like this.

Beside me, Connor shouts, "Like it?"

The wind whips our words away almost immediately, but I shout back, "*Awesome*, man!" We're maybe forty metres in the air, the parasail we're hanging from is tethered by a metal line to a powerboat that plunges through the surf below. Before us, the roofs of the resort's many buildings poke above a canopy of royal palm leaves. On the beach, tanned bodies glisten on loungers arranged with what appears from the air to be mathematical precision, while, beneath us, snorkellers thread the surface of water that's a dozen shades of green and perfectly transparent. Sea plants and coral outcroppings dot the sandy bottom, and I feel as if I'm seeing Earth from space, remote yet solidly there and beautiful. I wish I'd brought one of those disposable cameras with me. Instead, I try to take pictures with my mind, freezing each detail in my memory.

Suddenly, the powerboat cuts its motor and we're no longer being towed, supported now by the air beneath the parasail rather than the forward motion of the boat. And except for the occasional flap of the cloth and creak of the metal clips tied to the parasail's main line, it's almost completely silent. It's as though we've somehow stepped outside ourselves, our minds freed from our earthly forms. I could stay up here forever.

"Glad you came?" Connor asks me.

I turn and grin at him.

After eating breakfast—my first and Connor's second—we

went down to the beach and found my mother with Lucas on the sand. She bought him a boat in Playa del Carmen last night, and he was hard at work digging an elaborate system of lakes and canals to float it in. I introduced Connor to both of them, but Lucas didn't even look up, completely absorbed in the water world he was creating. Connor floored me when he dropped to his knees and offered to help. Lucas said nothing, but he allowed Connor to work beside him for a while, the two of them creating a network of channels that funnelled the surf toward Lucas's lake. When the boat was finally afloat, Lucas rewarded Connor with a smile he rarely gives strangers. Of course, strangers rarely get down on their hands and knees and dig in the sand with him.

I'd joined them for a while, but Connor's efforts made my help unnecessary. Besides that, the Tylenols I'd taken were wearing off and my head was beginning to throb again, so I just sat with my mother watching the rest of the excavation. It was weird seeing Connor in my own big-brother role. He's twice Lucas's size, and lots of people walking by—most of them girls—paused to watch him working beside Lucas. Once in a while he'd look up and smile at them, but most of the time he seemed as absorbed as Lucas in their work. Twice I had to shake away a memory of Stefan and Lucas at Crystal Crescent Beach, and, glancing at my mother out of the corner of my eye, I guessed she was seeing the same memory. She made a production of wiping sweat from her face with a towel, but not all of the wet was perspiration. I let on I didn't see—I've gotten good at that in the past year.

Watching some of the girls eyeing Connor, I thought of Kate again, and, for the first time, I wished she'd wander by. Maybe if she saw Connor playing with my brother she'd forget what a jerk he was on the balcony. And, more important, she'd forget that she lumped me in with the rest of that fraternity.

And the Empire Room will be serving barbequed Band-Aids for lunch. What an idiot I am sometimes.

After the lake was finished and he'd washed off the sand in the surf, Connor chatted with my mother for a few minutes about going to Tulum, about how amazing the place was. I was afraid he'd make up some story about Xel-ha that would contradict the one I'd already told her, but he only talked about Tulum. And if I'd doubted his interest in history before, I certainly didn't now. Even a day later, his observations about the ruins were just as enthusiastic.

Mara came down to the beach while he was talking to my mother, and Connor was an even bigger hit with her. The moment my mother introduced him, Mara stopped acting like my aunt and began behaving disturbingly like those girls on the beach the other day, all coy and tittery. I was embarrassed—and I could tell my mother was, too—so I interrupted their conversation with this big production about all the things Connor wanted to do that day. Mom was quick to tell me I should go too, that she and Lucas were perfectly fine with Mara and I should just enjoy myself.

And, surprisingly, I am.

Parasailing is a lot easier than our earlier activities. After I'd taken some more Tylenol, we spent most of the morning windsurfing. At least, I *tried* to windsurf. I've done some before at Stavros's and Mara's summer home in Chester, but their place is on a small cove, so the brunt of Atlantic breezes is blocked by a forested arm of land that separates it from the ocean. There's no such buffer here, and, to compound the problem, the wind strengthened as the morning wore on. Although I could manage to get myself up on the surfboard, I couldn't pull the heavy, wet sail up fast enough, and I'd end up falling forward into the water every time. Connor, of course, hauled his up effortlessly, and, in moments, he was slicing through the surf like one of those guys you see on ESPN, the board leaping high in the air each time it caught the crest of a wave.

My self-esteem got a much-needed boost on the catamaran. Because of his larger size, Connor found it hard to manoeuvre quickly on the tiny craft, so I took over and had us rocketing across the waves in no time. It was when we got beyond the reef that parallels the Empress beach that I finally saw a chink in the MacPherson armour.

"You think there might be sharks out here?" he asked me as the catamaran listed sideways and warm spray erupted over us again and again. We had to lean way out over the water in the opposite direction to keep the craft upright, and he continually scanned the waves for triangular fins.

"*Now* who's being a pussy?" I laughed.

He grinned sheepishly, but I could tell he was really worried, so I turned us around and sailed back in.

And now we're high above that same water.

"Aren't you worried about sharks?" I ask him as the parasail dips and glides, but he just grins, the brightly coloured cloth above us billowing in the breeze. The wind has eased up somewhat, and there are fewer windsurfers on the water. Below, the guy on the powerboat starts up a motor and the winch begins to wind us in. I'm disappointed. I could stay up here forever.

When I say so, Connor just shakes his head. "We should head up to lunch anyway," he says. "I'm hungry."

I think of his two breakfasts. "Are hockey players ever *not* hungry?" I scoff.

"Are virgins ever *not* horny?" he returns.

I laugh, but it's actually been hours since I've thought about my objective. Maybe there *is* more to life than getting laid. In Mexico, anyway.

| 13 |

The afternoon turns out to be even more fun than the morning—in the beginning, anyway. Because my head is feeling much better, Connor coaxes me to join him in an impromptu beach volleyball tournament organized by the Empress's activities director, and our team comes in second out of eight. There's one other guy on our team—a commodities broker from New Jersey named Scott—and the rest are women. One of them, a tall redhead from Minnesota, clearly doesn't understand the concept of friendly competition and plays like it's the Olympic semifinals, delivering blistering serves that few people are able to return. With her deadly accuracy and Connor's height and stamina, we easily eliminate most of our competition, beginning with a team made up of six guys from Oregon who look—and play—like accountants. Four of them are carrying more weight than they should be and all six have sunburns, but they're obviously there to have fun, and they do. Shaking hands with us afterwards, one of them hits on Minnesota and, to my complete surprise, gets her room number. Even an overweight accountant from Oregon has more luck with women than I do. How pathetic is *that?*

Easy victories aside, it feels great to be playing on a team again.

I've missed it since soccer ended in November. And although volleyball isn't my strongest sport, it's fun playing barefoot on the sand. It's not like a court, though—I often misjudge my footing and end up on my ass. But so does everyone else, and, before long, we're all laughing like idiots.

We lose the trophy—a tin tray someone crudely scratched the image of a volleyball on—to Kate's team. I'd forgotten all about her until she suddenly appeared across from me on the opposite side of the net—wearing a black bikini this time—and I missed three easy drops before I managed to get my mind back in the game. But by that time her team had the momentum and they rolled right over us, despite some impressive last-second saves by Connor, the kind you see on slow-motion television replays where players dive face first into the sand just in time to bump the ball back over the net. It's like there's no sport that he can't do well. I could really hate the guy if he hadn't turned out to be so decent. It's like he's this completely different person, so *not* the asshole I saw at the airport. He can still be a jerk when he's drinking, but there aren't many people I know—even close friends like Rod—who would have gotten down on their knees and dug in the sand with my little brother. Especially not when there are girls to cruise.

After Kate's team beats us, we all line up to shake hands and I look for my moment. I hold back and manage to shake hers last, gushing, "Great game!" She smiles and I suddenly lose the ability to speak. Her blond hair frames her face like a painting, and I get lost in her eyes as I stand there pumping her hand up and down like a moron.

Luckily, Connor performs another miraculous save, slapping me on the back and jarring me back to my moment. "So, who's your friend?" he asks.

Grateful, I release her hand and turn to him. "Um, Connor," I begin, "this is . . ."

And I completely forget her name.

Not moments before, it was pounding pulse-like in my brain, but now I can't even remember what letter it starts with.

"I'm Kate," she says, a sudden coolness in her voice. Not directed toward me, though, I'm relieved to realize.

"I saw you on the plane from Halifax," says Connor.

"I saw you, too," she tells him, each word like a staple in the air. "And yesterday on your balcony."

"Oh, that wasn't *mine*," Connor explains, seemingly unaware of the change that's just occurred. "That was Jace's balcony." And it's here that he claps a huge hand on my shoulder.

And it's here that my moment shrivels and dies as Kate turns to me and says, "Your balcony." I think she intends it to be a question, but it sounds more like an observation. Like *You're toxic.*

I feel my head nodding, but I'm mentally kicking myself, thinking how I wasted all last night worrying about Kate thinking I was an asshole. Because she hadn't recognized me on the balcony after all. To her, I was just another one of Connor's happy Torrent troop.

Not now, though. No, Connor's taken care of that little misunderstanding, clarifying the situation perfectly. How can I tell? By the set of Kate's shoulders as she pivots and walks off, that's how. She might even be *storming* off, but that's really hard to do on sand.

====

"Don't even *try*," I mutter. I'm doing a little storming of my own right now, my bare feet kicking up sand as I stride down the beach. I have to manoeuvre around Empress loungers and the occasional person sprawled on the sand, but I don't slow down. The more distance I can put between Connor MacPherson and me, the better.

Unfortunately, I can't outpace him, and he effortlessly dogs me down the beach. I start to jog, but he's right beside me all the way, and, after a few minutes of this, he's not even winded.

I finally stop and face the water. We're well beyond the Empress grounds now, standing on a stretch of undeveloped beach. Behind us, a tangle of vegetation stretches to the edge of the sand, and all around us are debris and litter that no one here is paid to clean up. What a difference the lack of an all-inclusive resort makes.

"I *said* I was sorry. What more do you want?"

I offer a suggestion that involves two different parts of his anatomy.

"C'mon, man, don't be a jerk."

I grunt. *Me* a jerk? Like *I'm* the one who can't keep my foot out of my mouth.

We stand watching the water some more. Or, more accurately, he watches the water while I seethe. I know he thinks all this is about me being a virgin, that I'm just looking for an easy way to score and he screwed it up for me—no pun intended. But it's more than that. After getting dumped by Cynthia, I meet the one person that I'd *really* like to get to know, and *twice* he manages to drive her off.

Of course, a more rational part of me realizes that since she didn't recognize me the first time, it's technically only once, but *twice* heightens the injustice, so I'm sticking with that.

"I know what you're going through," he says.

Right. I think about how he can have any girl he wants, with the singular exception of Kate, and I want to punch him. Instead, I drop to the sand, pulling my legs up and folding my arms on my knees. I rest my chin on my forearms and imagine all the times some girl must have told Connor MacPherson she wasn't interested in the Dalhousie Torrents' star right wing who's been having a love affair with the media all season. Poor him.

He sits down beside me. "I mean it," he says, his hands making circular tracks in the sand. His fingers close around a shell and he tosses it into the water.

"Yeah," I reply. "Sucks to be you."

He doesn't say anything for a moment. Then, "What are you *really* pissed at?" he asks.

"At *you!* Who d'ya *think?*" I wave my hand around me at the deserted stretch of beach.

"Seems to me you're pissed at yourself."

I look at him, my mouth twisting into a sneer. "And how'd you arrive at *that* brilliant conclusion, Sherlock?"

"I didn't see you try to explain yourself to her. You could've blamed *me,* for Christ's sake, but you didn't say a damn thing. You just let her walk away."

I look down between my feet and watch an insect I don't recognize crawl over the hot sand. The hills formed by my footprints must seem like Everest to it, impossible to get over, to move beyond. Something like the truth I find myself facing right now.

Because he's right. I *am* pissed at myself.

"Why didn't you say something to her?" he asks.

"It's not easy to say what's . . ." I stop, surprised I've said even this much.

I look out across the water and see a thin brown line on the horizon. When I first noticed it the day we arrived, I thought it was Cuba or Florida, but both are too far from here to see. According to a brochure in the Empress lobby, that brown line is the island of Cozumel, another resort area on the Mayan Riviera that's a short ferry ride from Playa del Carmen. It looks a lot farther than that, though. It's weird how distances across water are hard to judge, how what you think you see may be very different from the way something really is.

Like my relationship with Cynthia. I certainly didn't see the whole Corey thing coming.

And Stefan. I didn't see *that* coming, either.

I *should* have, though. Despite the fact that no one else did. I was his brother. I *should* have seen it coming.

And now, my own private Everest: I *did*.

Not what it led to, not that. But I knew something wasn't right. I knew. And I didn't say anything. Didn't know *what* to say. Like always.

There are moments when I fear my mother knows. I think I see it in her eyes sometimes, in the way she looks at me and then looks away, as if she can't bring herself to face it. Can't bring herself to face *me*.

"*What's* not easy for you to say?" asks Connor.

I think of what she's been like this past year, how she often stares at nothing, the story of Stefan stencilled on her skin. I catch her up late at night sometimes when everyone else is sleeping. I'll get out of bed to get a drink or take a leak or, more often, just to quit studying the ceiling, and I'll see the glow from a light downstairs. Know she's sitting in the recliner in the living room, which was Stefan's usual spot when he lived at home. The first time it happened, I went down and found her sitting there, her fingers moving over the leather arms as if pulling from them everything that remained of him. She'd been crying softly, the sounds more like sighs than sobs, and I saw the tracks her tears had left on her face. I asked if there was anything I could get her but she just looked at me, her fingers still travelling the soft surface, and told me to go to bed. I left her there and lay staring at my bedroom ceiling again, listening to the sounds resume and subside in the living room until, finally, she came up an hour later. It was the last time I went downstairs at night. But each time I woke to see a light on, I knew she was down there, her fingers endlessly moving.

And I couldn't help wondering if sometimes she wished it had been me instead of Stefan who'd died.

Stefan was the son most like her, even though I physically resemble her more than either of my brothers. In his final two years in high school, he'd grown unbearably moody at home, ping-ponging from monumental highs to days when he'd barely speak, his bedroom door closed to all of us. He was only two years older than me, but we seemed centuries apart. "He just needs his space," Pop would explain when Stefan raged if I entered his room, picked up the phone when he was talking on it, or dared to ask him about his latest girlfriend. They came and went like music videos—no sooner would I get used to one than another would enter our lives. I envied him his easy ability with girls, the way he carried with him only what he seemed to need.

So I gave him his space: avoided him when he sat in the recliner staring at nothing, asked him nothing, asked him *for* nothing. I felt like we were opposite ends of the same magnet, joined more by circumstance and situation than any common ground, and it was almost a relief when he started university last year. Although he could have lived at home and ridden the bus to the Saint Mary's campus, his scholarship included a single room in a residence that was a five-minute drive from our house. But it might as well have been in Vancouver. Distance isn't just measured in kilometres.

People often talk about how siblings grow closer when one of them moves out, but that wasn't the case with us. We sometimes had easier moments, visits when he'd arrive pumped and talkative for no apparent reason, but just as often he'd be sullen and withdrawn, slumped in the recliner, staring off into space.

I still see Stefan in that recliner sometimes. I'll be walking past the living room and suddenly he'll be in there sitting, his face turned toward the doorway and me. As if waiting. As he must always have been waiting. For me to . . .

When I think of what I could have said, *should* have said . . .

And then I'm sobbing. There on that empty beach with Connor MacPherson.

I struggle to laugh, to make some joke out of it, but the sobs just keep coming, my shoulders shaking as I press my face into my arms. All I can do is let it come. It's been a long time in the making. Nearly a year.

Connor doesn't say anything. I can't even imagine what he's thinking. Guy loses a volleyball game and doesn't get laid.

Instead, he puts a hand on my shoulder, lets me cry.

And I do. It's a couple minutes before I finally get myself under control, finally stop sobbing, choking. I reach back, pull my T-shirt off over my head and wipe away the tears and the snot. Before coming to Mexico, I'd never been knocked unconscious, and I gave up crying a long time ago, yet I've done both in twenty-four hours. And Torrent star Connor MacPherson has witnessed them both. I feel like such a goddamn loser.

I get to my feet. "It's not what you think—"

"I know," he says.

"You *don't* know," I tell him. How could he? No one knows. *No* one.

He stands up too. "Wait here. There's something I want to get," he says.

———

Later, holding it in my hands, I wonder what Connor must have thought when he first saw it. First read it. I open the cover and look again at what I wrote:

I wonder how the barrel of the gun felt in your mouth.
Was it cold and smooth?
Did you notice it was round, a circle with no beginning or ending?
Your life had an ending.
I still don't understand why.
You didn't tell me.
And you left no note behind.

We're sitting on the sand, Connor having jogged back along the deserted beach only moments ago with my notebook, the one he found beneath the other silver thatch palm the night I lost it.

"Why didn't you give me this before?"

He shrugs. "I was going to, but I didn't see you again that day. I didn't know what your name was or what room you were in. I didn't have it with me when I saw you on the bus, and it didn't seem like something I could just tell you about then. I thought you might be embarrassed."

"And today was so much *less* embarrassing," I say. He grins, which takes the edge off my humiliation. "Why didn't you just give it to me this morning?" I ask.

He sighs. "So much time had gone by, it seemed weird that I hadn't said anything about it earlier. I guess I was waiting for the right moment."

I look at my notebook again, read my words once more.

"I heard about your brother," he continues. "I remember seeing it in the paper. I didn't connect you right away with the name, even when you told me about your parents' restaurant. But then I met your family this morning and I remembered he was survived by . . ." He stops, embarrassed now himself, then finishes, "He had two younger brothers. Until then, I thought this was just a poem. Something you were writing for school."

I close the notebook. "How'd you remember something that happened nearly a year ago?"

"You don't hear about many . . ." His voice trails off, but I can guess what he was about to say. Canada's not like the States—or Mexico, for that matter—where firearms are a lot easier to come by. You don't hear about many young Nova Scotians using a gun to off themselves. Plenty of overdoses, carbon monoxide poisonings in sealed garages, a few hangings, bridge-jumpings. Some wrist-slicings, too, although that's not as effective a method as some people think. I should know. I've read a lot on the subject this past year.

"Do you want to talk about what happened?" Connor asks, and somehow I know he isn't being nosy, like he's dying to hear all the gory details. There were lots of people like that afterwards, but Connor hasn't asked me to *tell* him anything. He's asked me if I want to talk.

I haven't. Not to anyone. Not Rod, not my parents, not the psychologist they arranged for me to see. Not even Cynthia, who gave me every opportunity.

No, I haven't wanted to talk. Not before this.

But, for some reason, I feel like talking now.

| 14 |

I was the one who found him.

Until that moment, it had been a great day. A broken water main had unexpectedly shut down the school mid-morning, so I suddenly had several hours all to myself. Cynthia had decided to work on her *Macbeth* paper, which was due the following Friday, and with both his parents at work and his younger sister still at her junior high school, Rod had gone home to enjoy some uninterrupted porn-surfing. I decided to do something I wouldn't ordinarily do during the week—take in a midday feature at the Bayers Lake Cinemas before picking up Lucas. The film wasn't great—another remake of a Japanese fright-flick, horrible to the point of hilarious—but since Cynthia had repeatedly refused to go see it with me, I really didn't care. I enjoyed sitting there in the dark and tuning out the world: no classes, no helping out at the restaurant, no feeling guilty for making Cynthia watch something she hated. Quality "me time."

As usual on Tuesdays, I picked up Lucas following his after-school program, brought him home and got us something to eat. Although Mom worked every other weekend and some mornings and evenings, Tuesdays were the only weekday afternoons that she was at the restaurant, and she and Pop always ate at the

Parthenon on those days. She'd usually bring something home for dessert, but since Stefan had moved out, it had been my job to prepare a meal on Tuesdays that Lucas would eat. If I had a lot of homework, I'd fall back on tried-and-true favourites like Kraft Dinner or hot dogs, but if it was a slow night, I'd make something more ambitious. Like Shake 'N Bake chicken. The cooking gene had skipped a generation in the Antonakos family.

I was surprised to find Stefan's ancient Honda Civic, which he'd bought cheap from a friend at the end of the previous summer, parked in front of our garage when Lucas and I got off the Metro Transit bus. I called his name when we got in the house, but there was no answer. He'd probably stopped by to pick up clean laundry and then phoned one of his buddies who still lived in the neighbourhood—Owen, maybe, or Jeff—and gone out to grab a bite to eat. His residence had washers and dryers in the basement, but he was forever dropping off a green garbage bag filled with dirty clothes for Mom to wash. She didn't mind. I thought he was taking advantage—after all, he was nineteen and technically, living away from home—but she never complained. "You'll understand when you have children of your own," she'd tell me when I'd find her in the laundry room sorting his clothes into lights and darks. But I knew it was more than that. I'd lived with it all my life. Stefan was the oldest, special because he was first.

Lucas was special, too, of course. And not just because of his CDD. He was the youngest. Their baby.

I occupied the space between first and last.

I had a French oral to prepare for and some Physics questions to do that night, so I fried us both some wieners while Lucas watched his video. It was a program on Nova Scotia boat-builders that Mom had recorded earlier that winter, and although he'd seen it dozens of times already, he'd call it up on the recorder's menu and replay it as often as we'd let him. Boat porn.

After we ate, I loaded the dishwasher and pulled out my books. I had almost finished my Physics when I realized that Stefan still hadn't come home. Standing at the sink getting a drink of water, I saw his Civic beginning to collect a thin dusting of March snow. And then I saw the light on in the garage.

The people my parents bought our small colonial from had added the garage later, an afterthought built apart from the house and tucked into the corner of the backyard at the end of the driveway. We never parked vehicles in there. The garage had a heavy wooden door that rose out and up when you yanked on it, not like those lighter aluminum doors in newer constructions that roll up easily on tracks. It had a window in it, too, which added to the weight, and you really needed a strong back to heave that door upwards, so my parents never parked their car in there. The garage was just a place to store things like the lawn-mower, hedge trimmer, garden tools, bicycles, bags of garbage awaiting pick-up day, tires, plastic ice cream containers filled with every kind of nail and screw imaginable, piles of wood for projects my father began but invariably left unfinished and so on. More of a large storage shed than a garage. Not a place where anyone spent a lot of time. Someone had obviously left the light on by mistake.

I finished drinking my water, added the glass to the dishwasher and then turned it on. Pop had replaced the dishwasher just before Christmas and there were dozens of electronic settings on this one's control panel, but we always used the "Smart Wash" program, as if we'd be "Stupid" not to. Then I headed out to the garage.

As soon as I got the door up, I saw him. At first, I thought he was asleep. He was sitting in one of the white vinyl lawn chairs our father had stored at the back of the garage last fall, his head leaning slightly forward, hands folded in his lap.

"Jesus, Stefan!" I said as I wove my way around the various

obstacles piled between us, nearly tripping over a rake. "What the hell are y—"

And then I saw his brains on the wall behind him.

I didn't know that's what they were at first. They looked like wet globs of grey asbestos I'd seen in a film my Geology teacher had shown us earlier that semester, and for an odd moment I worried about cancer. Worried my family might get it if they touched that wall. Thought about that "Smart Wash" program. Wondered how you got rid of asbestos safely. And then I saw the blood.

If it had been summer, there would have been flies.

I placed a hand on his shoulder. "Stefan," I whispered, but I didn't expect an answer. I knew he was beyond hearing.

His hands were folded around the barrel of the rifle my father used to hunt deer every November, the stock having slid from his fingers to the floor. His mouth was partially open, as if in surprise, and there was a dark smear on his lips. Gunpowder. And more blood.

I don't know how long I stood there looking at him, trying to make sense of what I was seeing. Probably would have continued standing there if not for the car horn that blared on a nearby street, making the moment real again. I removed my hand from his shoulder, then moved slowly back toward the open door and followed my footprints in the snow across the yard and into the house. I called 911 and my parents, then stopped Lucas's boat-builder video and restarted it from the beginning. Then I returned to the garage.

His torso had slumped forward, my touch having altered the delicate balance of his body, and the back of his ruined head now gaped at me. I vomited, liquid and chewed bits of fried wieners spraying the concrete floor beside him, and the room whirled around me. I reached out for support, my fingers closing on what remained of Stefan, and he fell forward into me.

My legs crumpled and I ended up kneeling on the floor in my own vomit, Stefan cradled in my arms. It was somehow important to me that his head not touch the floor, that as long as I could keep him off the concrete, things would be all right again, everything would be okay. I didn't want him losing any more of what was already gone.

The paramedics found me there like that, the red lights on top of their ambulance stabbing the night and my eyes.

My parents arrived moments later, and my mother's screams seemed somehow distant, like the car horn I'd heard earlier. Seemed, in fact, part of a different moment, far removed from the one that closed around me now. She tried to pull Stefan from me, but my father and one of the paramedics stopped her, spoke to her in low tones, did something that softened her screams. Didn't stop them, but made them less shrill somehow as the paramedic helped my father lead her to the house.

The other paramedic was busy with Stefan, and I was surprised by his urgency. "Everything's all right," I tried to tell him. "I kept his head up. Everything's okay."

"What's your name, son?" the paramedic asked me as he continued to work over my brother.

I told him, my legs cramping under me as I knelt on the cold concrete.

"You did good, Jace," he told me. "But it's our turn now. We have to take him with us. You can let go of him now."

I looked at him, confused, and hugged Stefan tighter. "I can't let his head—"

"It's okay," he said. "I'll make sure to keep his head up."

I looked down at my brother asleep in my arms. "You're sure?" I asked. "You can do that?" Stefan's eyes were open.

"I can do that, son," he said quietly. "You can give him to me now."

Suddenly I wanted more than anything to do just that. To give

Stefan to someone else. I was tired. Now my arms were cramping, too, and I clenched my teeth to keep from moaning. I needed to lie back on that concrete for a moment. Just for a moment.

"You're sure?" I asked again.

But I didn't wait for him to answer. I let go of my brother then. I just let him go.

———

The days leading up to the funeral were a blur of faces and meals that went to waste. Everyone—relatives, friends, neighbours, people I'd never even met before—brought food that my mother heated up and put on plates every meal, then later scraped off into our green compost bin in the backyard. Only Lucas was able to eat, slowly spooning food into his mouth while my father, my mother and I shared the terrible silence around our table. For the first time, I envied my younger brother the world he was lost in, a world that now made perfect sense if it filled that silence with distraction. I longed for my own distraction, something that could help me forget what I'd found in the garage, what I'd seen and done in there—and what I'd seen and hadn't done the night before.

But the only distraction at our table was the soft scrape of forks and knives against china as we cut up pieces of chicken or beef or lamb or fish we didn't eat, just moved from one side of our plates to the other. At one point, I remember thinking it might make more sense to take the food that people brought us and dump it straight into our compost, but my mother seemed to feel this middle part was important. As if sitting at the table gave meaning to the day and made what lay ahead somehow easier to bear.

My father closed the restaurant but he couldn't stand being home. Couldn't handle the endless parade of people who dropped by to offer their condolences and their help, their murmured words a meaningless blend of vowels and consonants. *If there's anything you need . . . If there's anything we can do . . . If there's anything, anything at all . . .* He'd thank them and promise to call if he thought of something, but I knew that what he needed they couldn't give him. They knew it, too.

After they'd leave, I'd sometimes catch him standing in front of the garage. He never went inside, never even looked in the window, just stood staring at that wooden door as though watching a movie on its painted surface.

Once I went out and stood beside him for a bit, but he didn't say anything. The whole time, though, I could hear him swallowing thickly, the sound like something clotting in his throat. I glanced up at the bare limbs of the oak that leaned over the garage, and I thought of the family tree I'd drawn in Grade 7, thought of the website that said my dead brother's name meant "constant." Watching my father stare at the garage door, listening to him make those sounds in his throat, I suddenly longed to share that definition of constancy with him, wanted him to find the meaning in it for me, but he turned and went back into the house without saying a word.

He reopened the restaurant the following day.

———

Stefan's funeral was colourful.

Greeks are big on black when it comes to mourning. I know of Greek women who've lost husbands or children and have worn black every day since. Four of Pop's older regulars, in fact, look as though they're forever going to or coming from burials, their grey heads perpetually covered in black lace as they pore over the Parthenon's menu.

Lucas has a thing about black. We first noticed it the Hallowe'en he turned five, when our mother dressed up as a witch to hand out treats. He clung to me and shrieked himself hoarse until she took off the black dress and pointed hat and put her regular clothes back on. We thought it had to do with witches, that *The Wizard of Oz*, which I'd rented for him earlier that month, had scared the shit out of him.

But it wasn't witches. It happened again in the restaurant the first time he saw Mrs. Mouskouri, one of Pop's regulars-in-mourning, sitting at her usual table. I remembered then about the crayons that always went missing from the large bucket in Lucas's room. The black ones.

Mara was on the phone for hours making sure everyone knew what not to wear to the funeral home and the church. Someone asked her, "Wouldn't it just be easier to keep Lucas home?" Mara never told us her reply, but I could fill in the blanks myself. Mara isn't one to mince words.

So, despite another skiff of snow that had fallen before the funeral, the cemetery was filled with blues and yellows and pinks and greens the day we buried my brother. We looked like human Easter eggs huddled beside the open grave, and I hoped Stefan could see us, hoped he was looking down from wherever he'd chosen to go and was enjoying the spectacle.

And I prayed that no one would learn the part I'd played in his death, that I'd practically loaded the rifle, given him the bullet that tore the brain from his skull.

15

"Jesus!" Connor breathes when I finish. He seems about to say something more, but then he shakes his head. "Jesus," he repeats more softly.

I mop my face with my T-shirt again, as much to cover it as to wipe away the last of my tears. I'm embarrassed as hell. If I'd had any idea when I woke up this morning that I'd be sitting on the beach spilling my guts to someone I've only known a couple days—and who I thought was the biggest asshole this side of a hemorrhoid commercial—I'd have pulled that down-filled duvet over my head and force-fed myself a breakfast of feathers. I can't imagine what he's thinking. But then I don't have to.

"That's a lot to carry around," Connor says. "You're one strong guy."

Looking at the damp T-shirt in my hands, I snort. "Yeah, I'm a rock."

He puts a hand on my shoulder again. "Look, man, we all carry loads. You got stuck with more than your share."

I turn to look at him, surprised by his generosity. It makes what I have to say next even harder. "Connor, you won't . . . you know . . . tell anyone about . . ."

He shakes his head. "I've got this condition," he says, grinning. "Selective amnesia. Just kicked in."

I must have been holding my breath because suddenly I'm conscious of exhaling again. "Thanks."

He claps me on the shoulder once more, then points toward the ocean. The waves still roll toward us, but the water is dark, no longer luminous. While I was telling him about Stefan, a thick canopy of black cloud from the west blanketed the sky, shrouding the beach in premature twilight. I've already felt a fat raindrop on my shoulder.

"We should get back," I say, too late.

A fiery ribbon arcs between the clouds and the sea, followed almost immediately by a tremendous crash, and I can feel the hair on my head and arms drawn toward it. Then the sky opens up. Walnut-sized raindrops hit my face, and I reach for my notebook and stand.

"We'd better run," I call, shouting now above the roar of new thunder and the rising hiss of downpour against sand, but Connor just sits there, his face turned toward the sky. Warm sheets of water slap our bodies, and I hunch forward, trying to shield my notebook from the rain.

Connor is laughing.

"We'd better run!" I repeat, louder this time, but he shakes his head.

"Too far," he hollers, pointing down the beach.

He's right. The Empress isn't even visible in the distance through the downpour, and the only refuge is the tangle of forest behind us. I vaguely recall a warning about standing under trees during a lightning storm. We're probably safer on the beach.

I sit back down and watch as the storm unravels around us. Most of the lightning strikes the water, but a tremendous bang suddenly makes us both jump as one bolt hits somewhere to our right. I turn, expecting to see fire, but there is only the rain. For a moment, I smell something separate from salt and sea. Something acrid. Ozone? But then the rain drowns it and there is only the storm again.

The deluge stops almost as quickly as it began, as though someone flipped a switch. One moment we can barely see through the water rivering down our faces, and then it's over. Already the dark mass to the west of us is breaking apart, and broad shafts of sunlight pierce the clouds.

Connor nudges me. "Look," he says, and I turn in the direction he's pointing. About forty metres away, a thin tendril of smoke coils upward from the sand. He rises and jogs toward it, and I follow.

He reaches the spot first and kneels down. "Watch out," he warns me. "It's still hot." He points at a section of sand that has congealed into something liquid-like, yet solid.

"What's that?" I ask.

"Glass," he tells me.

I think of the empty Coronas I saw his buddies drop on the sand a few days ago. "Did the lightning hit a bottle?"

Connor shakes his head. "Hit the sand. Fused it into glass."

And then I remember what glass is made of. Silica. Which is found in sand. I suddenly want to record this moment, but my English notebook drips between my fingers—it'll be a long while before that dries out. I wish I had my camera with me.

The piece of glass isn't large, not more than twenty centimetres across. It looks something like a tree, a central trunk with branches flowing away from it. More star-like than tree-like, I realize now, but I'm thinking again about that diagram I drew in Grade 7.

Connor pulls off his wet T-shirt and folds it twice around his right hand. I can hear the cloth sizzle as it touches the glass, as he uses it like a potholder to lift the object. A shower of sand falls from it, and I find myself marvelling at this beach. Marvelling at how some of it has become glass while some has remained sand. I find myself wondering how often this happens, this transformation from one thing to another.

As Connor lifts it up, the sun suddenly reaches us again, lensing through the object in his hand and turning it golden. It becomes in that moment both the ugliest and the most beautiful thing I have ever seen. And for the first time in nearly a year, I feel something different move inside me. At first, because it's so foreign to me, I don't recognize it.

Hope.

———

The Empire Room is crowded by the time I finally get there. After the storm, Connor and I returned to our rooms to get dressed for dinner, agreeing to meet at the entrance to the dining room. Before that, though, I had another stop to make. Something I'd forgotten to do on my birthday.

I find Connor already waiting for me, and it's weird seeing him in a shirt with sleeves, black slacks and dress shoes. I notice he's not wearing socks, and I wonder if the maitre d' will comment on this subtle act of rebellion. He doesn't.

I see my mother, Lucas and Mara at our regular table, and I bypass the buffet and head toward them, Connor trailing me.

"Hey, Lucas," I say as I bend down beside him, "Connor and I found something really cool on the beach this afternoon. He'll show it to you later, okay?"

Lucas acknowledges my presence with only the faintest of smiles. I know he hears me, but his eyes are transfixed. A glass of white wine on the table across from him refracts the light from one of the chandeliers like a prism.

"You're welcome to join us, Connor," says my mother, "but there's only one chair here." She points to my usual place. "Maybe Nabor can bring another—"

"That's okay," I tell her. "Connor and I'll just sit at his table. There's no one else there."

Connor nods toward a section on the opposite side of the dining room. "My buddies went into Cancun for the day and won't be back until late tonight."

"So, Connor," Mara says, "Jace said you two found something on the beach?"

He briefly tells her about the storm and the beach glass, and my mother, of course, is horrified. Turning to me, she scolds, "You might've been *hurt*, Jace." I notice she hasn't said I might have been *killed*, and I find myself wondering if this is intentional. I wonder too much. I know this.

Mara's reaction, however, is quite a bit different. "Connor, maybe you could bring that glass thingy to my suite later. I'd love to see it." Then, almost as an afterthought, she adds, "Mine is the door before Jace's. You know which one I mean, don't you, honey?"

Thingy? Honey? What's gotten into her? And then I see. Her wine glass is nearly empty, and I'm certain Nabor has refilled it several times already. They've finished their appetizers and entrees and are now eating dessert, Mara's a single wedge of fresh pineapple.

Connor seems as embarrassed as I am. "Um," he stumbles, "I'll, ah, make sure you see it."

"Don't you forget now," she warns him, the smile on her face broader than any she's worn since we arrived.

I prod Connor's back, nudging him away from the table. "We're getting something to eat now," I say, moving toward the buffet. "See you guys later."

"Have a nice evening," Connor says over his shoulder.

"You too, Connor." Mara smiles, then does this little wave thing with her fingers. "You too."

"Like *that* wasn't weird at all," I tell him as we stand at the seafood station. I ask the server for the calamari and Connor chooses the tiger shrimp. The aromas of both are indescribable. "Sorry about that."

He raises and lowers one shoulder. "Family," he grins. "Can't live *with* 'em—" He stops abruptly, coughs and watches with sudden interest as the server dishes up his shrimp.

I finish his thought in my head: *Can't live without them.* Sometimes you just have to, though. The tough part is figuring out how.

The server places generous portions of calamari and rice on my plate, and we move toward a large table where Connor says he and his friends have eaten dinner at later sittings. A waiter who looks quite a bit older than Nabor pulls out chairs for us and we sit down.

"Good evening, gentlemen," he says, filling our water glasses. "Will you be having wine?"

I see he's noticed my all-white bracelet, which I picked up earlier at the front desk, in exchange for the one with the orange dot. My day-late birthday gift to myself.

"Sure," Connor tells him. "White, please." He looks at me as the waiter moves away. "White okay with you? I just figured since we're both having fish—"

"White's fine," I say, surprised he knows anything about wine. I figured all he drank was beer and hard liquor.

While we wait for the waiter to return, I tell Connor about some of the drinking customers I wait on regularly at the Parthenon. "One guy always asks for rum, no matter what he orders off the menu. A double with his appetizer, another with his entree, and one more with dessert. My father usually has to pour him into a cab when he leaves."

"Must have one strong liver," Connor observes.

I think about the booze I've seen him put away in the last few days and wonder if he ever worries about his own liver. But, then, I don't really know him, don't know if he drinks like that all the time or if this is just Winter Break Excess. And who am I to question his drinking habits, anyway? Tonight I'm fully prepared to celebrate my brand-new bracelet.

The waiter returns and fills both our wine glasses. I've had white wine before, usually when there's just a little left in a bottle at the Parthenon and Pop won't notice I've drained it, but one taste of this tells me it's quite a bit better. Very dry. And very expensive.

Connor approves. "Wine's good," he says after swallowing more than half his glass. "This, too," he says, pointing at his shrimp. "How's yours?"

I put a forkful of the calamari in my mouth and savour the taste of squid fried to perfection. Pop serves it at the restaurant made from a recipe my grandmother gave him, and it's the best I've ever had. Until now. "Great," I tell him. "Want some?"

He looks at the slender pieces of fish on my plate and shrugs. "Never had octopus before."

"Squid," I correct him.

"Yeah. Big difference," he says, pointing at the rows of tiny suckers lining the underside of the tentacles.

"It's good. Try some," I tell him.

He stares at my plate for a moment, shrugs, then reaches across the table, stabs a piece with his fork, puts it in his mouth and chews. Then he grins. "Thought it would be rubbery," he says, "but you're right. It's good. Think I'll get some of that next. Here, try my shrimp."

I reach across and take a shrimp off his plate and pop it in my mouth, where it seems to explode. I reach for my water glass as Connor laughs and, after four gulps, I'm finally able to speak.

"Whew. Hot."

"I like spicy food," Connor says. "This stuff is great."

As I eat another forkful of calamari, I look around at that incredible buffet stretching the length of the dining room, the waiters moving efficiently from guest to guest anticipating every need, and I shake my head in wonder, remembering what Kate said that first morning on the beach. Just as I'm about to repeat it, Connor says it for me.

"Life doesn't get any better than this, does it?"

I grin. "You bet," I tell him.

Then, to our left, a waiter hurrying to clear a table drops a tray, and the sound of metal striking marble echoes like gunfire overhead. Startled, Connor and others around us turn to watch the embarrassed server stoop to collect what he's dropped, but I look away, my mind echoing now with a similar sound that no one heard last March.

And I'm reminded just how quickly life can change.

16

"I didn't think discos even *existed* any more," I mutter. My head's a little fuzzy from the wine, but I've only had two glasses. I don't plan on getting drunk and, as a result, getting sick. I've already lost half a day of this vacation, and I don't want to spend tomorrow—Wednesday, already!—with my head in a toilet.

Connor, however, is not as cautious. Because he's bigger than I am, he can put away a lot more booze. And he has. He isn't staggering, but his eyes are glassy as he points toward the entrance of the Blue Parrot, where a driving beat pours out each time someone opens the door. "Don't be a *pushy,*" he says, then laughs. "You know what I mean."

I know what he means, all right. What I can't understand is why he'd want to go in there. As nice as the Empress is, it surprises me that its owners would want to have something as tacky as a disco on their property, like displaying dollar-store keychains beside Armani suits. But apparently most resorts have them. I guess they cater to older guests trying to recapture their youth, because I've already seen some guys who look to be in their fifties going in. Alone. Probably men who've come to Mexico on business without their wives. Or divorced guys looking to get laid. Which, of course, reminds me of my primary objective. I reconsider. With only four days left before we fly home, maybe the Blue Parrot is exactly what I need.

"Okay," I tell him. "You win."

"Attaboy," he says, clapping me on the back and propelling me toward the door. I couldn't stop him even if I wanted to. There's over two hundred thirty pounds of muscle behind that hand.

Inside is pretty much what I expected, right down to the flashing lights and the mirrored ball hanging from the ceiling. The dance floor isn't much larger than our living room at home, and there are only about thirty tables scattered around it, but there are people sitting at several of them and more standing by the bar. I'm surprised that most are women. I guess my earlier assumption about business people or divorced spouses doesn't apply just to men. Most of the women in here are at least my mother's age, and a few look quite a bit older. It's hard to tell, though, because it's fairly dark, even with the flashing lights and mirrored ball. In fact, that's probably the point.

I see that no one's on the dance floor yet. Everyone looks to be sizing up everyone else, seeing what their options are. Your basic meat market, all right. Unfortunately, all the meat on display is rapidly approaching its expiration date.

Connor guides me toward a table and the two of us sit. The wooden chairs have backs that curve out around their seats, and Connor has to wedge himself into his. Almost immediately, a waiter comes over to take our order. I see him discreetly checking out my bracelet, but I only order a Coke. Connor asks for a Corona and tells the waiter to keep them coming, and I remember Mara's instructions to the Air Canada flight attendant in First Class. There's no question that the service in this place is First Class too, because the waiter returns in seconds with our drinks.

I try to place the song we're listening to, some Latin remix of a recent Top 40 tune, but it quickly throbs into another one that's equally familiar and unidentifiable. I lean over to ask Connor if he recognizes it and my head bumps into boobs.

"Hi, sweetie," says a woman standing by our table. She looks to be Mara's age, but that's where the similarity ends. She's poured herself into a very short, low-cut, strapless dress that sparkles when the light strikes it. It's at least two sizes too small for her, and parts of her seem to be trying to squirm out. "Care to dance?"

I'm about to say *No, thanks* when I realize she's not talking to me.

Connor looks at me and winks. "Sure," he tells her, and he gets up and follows her onto the floor. The song is fast, but she immediately grapples him as if it's a waltz, and they make quite a pair out there by themselves. Even in ridiculous stiletto heels, she doesn't even come to his chin, but she's gazing up at him as though she's found her soulmate. Connor looks over her head and winks at me again. He's clearly enjoying himself.

It's like they've opened a floodgate because the dance floor quickly fills with people. I see several other mismatched partners, one clearly older or younger than the other, but I also see two couples who have obviously come here together. One's a man and woman a little older than my parents, and they're having a ball doing some dance that involves a lot of ass-bumping. They gyrate around the floor like teenagers, and I try to remember the last time Mom and Pop enjoyed each other like that.

The other couple is quite a bit older, late sixties maybe. Like Connor's partner, they've decided to waltz, and they stare into each other's eyes as though they're the only people out there. I feel a tug in my chest as I remember looking into Cynthia's eyes that way. She's probably staring into Corey's right now.

I turn away and find myself looking at Kate, who's looking at me. She's standing by the bar with a girl not much older than she is, and she leans over to say something to her now. Likely giving her an Asshole Alert.

It's probably because of the wine I've had. Or maybe because I see Connor out there enjoying himself with Two-Sizes-Too-Small. Whatever the reason, I push my chair back, stand up and saunter over.

"Come here often?" I ask. After everything else that's happened, my slob-in-a-seedy-bar line seems weirdly appropriate. What do I have to lose, anyway?

She actually smiles. She's holding a glass with something dark in it and I think I can smell rum, even from where I'm standing.

"Your friend looks to be having fun, as usual," she says, pointing at Connor.

"Look, about that. I'm sorry. He's actually not so bad."

"Right," she says, the word like scissors.

I don't know why I feel I need to defend him, but I do. "He doesn't mean half what he says."

The girl beside Kate raises her eyebrows. "I wouldn't mind hearing the half he *does* mean," she says.

Kate rolls her eyes. "Alicia, this is Jake. Jake, Alicia."

"Jace," I say.

"What?"

The music seems louder all of a sudden, and I lean toward her to make myself heard. "My name's *Jace*." I can smell her perfume, and I get a sudden image of spring in my head. Flowers. Meadows. Soft breezes. Corny, right? But I can't get enough of it.

"Jace?" she asks. When I nod, she says, "Never heard *that* name before."

"It's Greek," I offer automatically, leaning toward her again just so I can breathe her in.

"Your friend," interrupts Alicia. "Think he'd mind if I cut in?"

"Only one way to find out," I tell her, but I really don't give a damn what she does. I just want to stand right here. And breathe.

Kate, however, has other ideas. "See you around, Jace," she says, setting her untouched drink on the bar as Alicia moves onto the dance floor. Kate's already heading toward the door.

I follow her. "You're not staying?"

She shakes her head and continues walking.

"What about your friend?"

"She isn't."

"Isn't what?"

"A friend. I barely know her."

We reach the entrance and I realize there's no stopping her. "Then how—?"

"I met her on the beach this afternoon. She dragged me here against my better judgment." She pushes through the door with me behind her and, outside, the night and the palm trees swallow up the Latin throb. Once the door closes behind us, all I can hear are soft bird sounds and the murmur of distant waves on the beach.

It's perfectly still. A thumbnail moon hangs over the palm trees, its arc nearly horizontal, so different from the vertical crescent I'm used to seeing in Nova Scotia's night sky. I don't want to lose this moment and I struggle for something, anything to say.

"You don't like to dance?" Like that's going to stop her headlong rush from the Blue Parrot and me.

She reaches down and takes off her shoes, carrying them as she continues along the path, barefoot. I feel a little like something stuck to those shoes—a wad of gum, maybe—because I'm somehow wedged between her and the night, unable to do anything except continue along beside her, breathing in her scent. To her credit, though, she doesn't look at me like I'm a stalker who's suddenly—and freakishly—into smells.

"I like to dance," she says. "I just find the whole meat market scene creepy."

My eyes widen at her use of the expression. "I know what you mean," I tell her as I match her stride.

She turns to me, a wry smile on her lips. "Yeah, right. You and Igor back there must really hate it."

I flush, imagining what she thinks. "I've never been in there before. He dragged me."

I suddenly realize how pathetic *that* sounds, but she must think I'm joking because she smiles. "There's a lot of that going around," she says, and I smile too.

We walk in silence for a bit, and I think of all the things I could say that might make this moment last. It's like I have another chance here and I don't want to blow it. But then we reach a building called Garden 3 and she says, "This is me. Thanks for the company, Jace." She turns to go in.

"Kate?"

She hesitates. "Yes?"

I take a deep breath, catch that amazing scent of spring again, and then blurt, "I'm really not the kind of person you think I am."

"And what kind of person is that?"

I sense she's teasing me, but I don't care. At least she's still standing here. "I'm not an asshole." It sounds stupid saying it like that, but there doesn't seem to be any way to say it plainer.

She frowns, and I think I've blown it after all.

But then, "Good," she says. "Because I really don't like assholes."

———

We walk for hours, first along the paths that wind through the resort grounds and, later, down on the beach. We aren't the only ones who think it's a perfect night for walking because we meet lots of other guests, some of them couples, some of them obviously friends or family members. At one point we pass two women who look to be in their seventies standing at the top of a path that leads to the beach. They're holding hands, their voices low as one points out constellations to the other, and, as we walk by, I see one of them lean over and plant a kiss on the other's cheek. This surprises me. I've seen lesbians before, but none of them as old as these two. I'm used to the lesbians that come into the Parthenon sometimes, the obvious ones, anyway—hair buzzed off, wearing baggy fatigues and army boots. Real butch. Either one of these women on the beach could be somebody's grandmother.

I'm about to make a comment to that effect when Kate leans over and whispers, "Sweet, huh?"

I shrug. "Kinda old to be doing that, don't you think?"

She looks at me. "That's what makes it so terrific. That they've been together so long and still have those feelings. It couldn't have been easy for them."

I think then of what she's told me about her parents. About her mom leaving when she was four, her dad raising her by himself. There was almost a stepmother once, but she didn't last, either.

I look back at the two women, their bodies silhouetted against the lights of the resort, their arms around each other now. I shrug again and think of Pop's line: "Live and let live."

Hearing him say it, you'd think Pop was this progressive New Ager who embraces diversity, but it has more to do with good business practice than tolerance. At a conference that Stavros took him to a while back, one presenter pointed out that homosexuals are fast becoming a "target market" because many are professionals without kids, which translates into lots of disposable income. There's even been talk of establishing Halifax as a gay-friendly destination for cruise ships, because they could be a real boost for the area's economy. So, whenever a customer at the restaurant makes some off-colour remark about gays, Pop is quick to reply, "Live and let live," because his very best customers at the next table might have a gay son or lesbian sister, or, for that matter, might be gay themselves.

Back in the kitchen, though, Pop isn't so liberal-minded, his pasted-on smile evaporating the minute the door closes behind him. Whenever he comes to me on a Saturday night and says, "You take table nine, Jace," I know Louis and William have arrived, two aging queens who eat at the Parthenon every Saturday evening before going to the nine o'clock show at the Oxford Cinema. Pop doesn't use the word "faggot," but he doesn't need to. He says it with his eyes.

Kate says a lot with her eyes, too, and as we walk I watch a thousand different expressions flicker through them. We talk endlessly. At first, I tell her about school and my teachers and the homework Bradford and Sanderson gave me this week, and she tells me about her school in Dartmouth and all the stuff she has to do while she's away. I tell her about my friends, some of the funny experiences Rod has had at the video store, and she tells me about her best friend, Kyleigh, who works at the Old Navy store in MicMac Mall keeping shoplifters from double-dressing in the changing room. I tell her about my parents and about working at the restaurant, and she tells me about her dad's job as an insurance underwriter and how she works part-time at the Alderney Gate Library. I tell her about Lucas and his CDD, about the way he used to be and how he is now, and she tells me what it's like to be an only child.

I don't bother telling her about Cynthia, and I'm really glad when she doesn't mention another guy. I want to ask if there's someone waiting for her back in Dartmouth, can't imagine how there couldn't be, but it seems like that's something she'd say if there was.

I'm surprised when we find ourselves back at Garden 3. I don't want the night to be over yet, but it is. A faint glow in the east hints that dawn isn't far off, and I tell her I hope she doesn't get into trouble with her dad. But she tells me he isn't even at the resort right now, that he went to Cancun on business and won't be back until tomorrow. Which is now today.

Standing in front of the entrance to Garden 3, I want desperately to kiss her goodbye. But I also want desperately to see her again, and I don't want to do the wrong thing here, don't want her thinking I'm that asshole she assumed I was before. So I just say, "Maybe we can do this again." A deaf person could hear the longing in my voice. I could not sound more like a loser.

But, apparently, she doesn't think so. She puts her arms around my neck and draws me toward her, presses against me as her mouth meets mine, her tongue a warm tangle between my lips. It's all I can do not to tremble.

"I'd like that, Jace," she says as she steps back, her voice husky, her face flushed. Then she turns and is gone.

I can't stop humming as I make my way to Ocean 1. Music bubbles up from somewhere inside me, everything from Top 40 songs to Latin tunes I don't recognize. At one point I even start singing, and I laugh out loud at my foolishness.

I'm still humming as I take the stairs to the third floor and make my way down the marble hallway toward my suite. As I reach into my pocket for the magnetic key card, I hear a door open to my left. Mara's door. I turn, surprised that she's up already, but eager to tell someone about my night.

It isn't Mara I see, though. It's Connor. Tucking in his shirt and zipping his pants as he turns and heads toward the stairs.

17

"You son of a *bitch!*"

Connor whirls to face me. "Jace! Buddy!"

"Don't buddy *me*, you prick!" I close the distance between us in a heartbeat and, without thinking, take a swing at him. I must have the element of surprise on my side because my fist connects squarely with his jaw and he goes down in a heap against the wall. My hand feels like I've slammed cement, but I ignore the pain, relishing instead the blood that begins to drip from Connor's mouth, staining his shirt. I've never been so angry.

"Jesus!" he moans, shaking his head and reaching behind him, trying to push off the wall and get to his feet. "What'd you do *that* for?"

"She's my *aunt!*" His feigned innocence only fuels my rage, and now I'm shouting. "My mother's *sister!*"

"Jace!"

I turn and see Mara in her open doorway, an Empress bathrobe wrapped loosely around her. Her lipstick and makeup are smudged, and her hair is a mess. I've obviously gotten her out of bed.

By now, Connor has managed to stand and he's holding his mouth with one hand, blood seeping through his fingers.

"You *hit* me," he says, almost matter-of-factly. As if he's just now realized it.

"And I'll do it again if I ever catch you—"

"Jace!" says Mara, her voice a hoarse whisper in the hallway, but I doubt we have to worry about waking anyone else. No one could still be asleep after all this.

I'm right. I hear my mother's door open behind me. "Mara? What on earth—?"

"It's not what you think," Mara says, more to me than to her sister.

"Sure it's not," I tell her, my voice a snarl. "You were just giving him the goddamn five-star tour, right?"

"Jace!" This from my mother, who hurries toward us. "Don't use that language with your aunt!"

I look at her and suddenly feel like laughing. My aunt is cheating on her husband with someone half her age, but I should watch my language. That's perfect. It all makes so much fucking sense.

We hear a groan and the three of us turn to Connor, who is staring at his bloody hand and wavering on his feet. His shirt looks like Exhibit A from one of those cheesy crime shows.

When my mother sees him, her eyes widen and she cries, "Oh! *Look* at you!"

He *is* looking, and it's immediately clear that Connor MacPherson, star right wing for the Dalhousie Torrents, can't stand the sight of blood. His own, anyway. He releases another groan just as his knees buckle and he pitches forward into me with the force of a freight train. I go down with Connor on top of me.

It's like a sitcom with no laugh track. I lie on the marble tile gasping for air, the wind punched from my lungs, while my mother tries to push an unconscious Connor off me. No luck. He's a dead weight. Mara gets into the act now, tugging on one arm while my mother shoves on the other, and they finally manage to roll him to one side. I'm still gasping, but at least I can draw air into my lungs again.

"What's going on here?" my mother asks, her face flushed. She leans against the wall panting.

It takes me a moment, but eventually I suck in enough air to answer her. "It's pretty obvious, isn't it?"

She looks at Connor sprawled before her and seems, finally, to notice the untucked shirt. And the time of day. And the open door we're standing in front of. Now *she's* the one who moans, the sound full of hopeless resignation. Like the sounds I hear her make at night in the living room recliner.

I turn to look at Mara, but she's disappeared. I hear her voice, though, coming from inside her suite, and I realize she's on the telephone. Calling for help.

=====

The hotel doctor doesn't seem to mind being summoned so early in the day. At least, he doesn't let on he does. "It looks worse than it is," he tells Connor, who lies on the leather sofa in Mara's suite, the end of a cold, wet towel between his teeth.

My mother has gone back to her suite to be with Lucas, and Mara is in her bathroom getting dressed. I'm the only other person in the room, and I want to be just about anywhere but here. Actually, what I want is to kick something. Connor's ass, for starters.

"You gave your tongue a bad bite," the doctor continues. "But at least you didn't hit your head when you fell." He turns to me. "It was quick thinking on your part to catch him."

I grunt, if for no other reason than to keep from bursting into what would surely be, for the doctor, an inexplicable guffaw. Mara and I haven't told him the whole story, just that Connor bumped his jaw, saw blood and fainted. I don't give a shit if he believes us or not, but he doesn't ask difficult questions. Just enough to get the job done. Working as a hotel doctor, he's probably seen more than his share of unusual events over the years.

He straightens and begins gathering up his equipment. The tongue depressor made sense, but I thought the thermometer and stethoscope were overkill. I have to hand it to him, though— he's thorough. All part of the job, I guess. First Class all the way.

"Please come see me if you have any further problems," he tells Connor. And then he leaves.

I've heard the saying *you could cut the tension with a knife,* but I've never been in a situation where it actually applied. Until now. Connor is staring at me like I've just beamed down from the mothership, and I'm praying to God that Mara will hurry up and finish dressing. I told her I'd wait until she comes out, but then I'm out of here.

"*Ithithinwhaoothink.*"

"Huh?"

Connor says it again, but talking around a towel mucks up the message. I can guess what he's saying, though.

"If it isn't what I think, why don't you tell me what it *is,* asshole?"

"There's no need to be upset with Connor, Jace."

I turn to see Mara, fully dressed now, step down into the living area, and I get up. "Don't worry," I tell her, "I'm plenty upset with you, too."

At least she has the grace to seem embarrassed. "Look," she says, "he *did* spend the night with me—"

I wave my arms over my head, cutting her off. "Spare me the details." I brush past her, take the steps in one stride and head toward the door.

"Jace!"

I stop, my hand on the doorknob, but I refuse to look at her. At either of them.

"Connor spent the night on the sofa. Right where he is now."

I roll my eyes at the door. "Like I'm supposed to believe *that*."

"I don't care *what* you believe right now. You seem to have your mind all made up anyway. But it's the truth."

I turn and stare at her, then at Connor, who nods.

"Mind you, I won't say I didn't *want* something to happen," she says, her voice nearly a whisper, "but he was a perfect gentleman."

I try to process this new information, but it's too much to handle at one time. I decide to go with the second part. "If he was such a gentleman, why didn't he go back to his own room?"

"*Ipathoh.*"

Mara translates. "He passed out."

"*Thoomuththoothrink.*"

This I understand. There's a pattern here, and I can't help wondering if Connor sees it yet. I also can't help feeling foolish. *And the Emmy for overreacting goes to . . . Jace Antonakos!*

Mara clears her throat. "I want to talk to you about this, Jace. I think you deserve an explanation." She nods at Connor. "But there's no point in putting *him* through this. He heard it all last night."

Connor slowly gets to his feet. He's pretty unsteady, but I can tell by the look on his face that Mara's right, that he really doesn't want to hear again what it is she has to say. He rubs his jaw, then pulls out the towel and rolls his tongue around his mouth, wincing a bit, and I see he's being very careful not to look at the towel itself. I don't blame him. All that blood is starting to unsettle my stomach, too.

"We okay?" he asks as he approaches the door.

I feel like such an idiot. I've punched two people in my entire life, the first one Davey Greenough in Grade 4 when, as a joke, he smeared snot on my recess snack. Connor is the second. I still have no regrets about Davey, even though I got three lunch-hour detentions for doing it, but I'm really sorry for hitting Connor. I tell him so.

"First person ever to take me down with one punch," he tells me. I know he's trying to make light of it, and I'm grateful for that, even though it doesn't make me feel any better.

He yawns and then grimaces, so I can tell it must hurt him to move his jaw. But he sticks out his hand and we shake. "I'll see you later, okay?" he asks.

"Later," I tell him.

He leaves, and I turn to Mara.

Sitting across from me on the leather loveseat, Mara takes her time explaining everything. She begins by telling me her marriage is in trouble.

"No shit," I respond. Call me crazy, but I figure inviting guys half your age to spend the night with you isn't one of the "Top Ten Ways To Please Your Man." Cynthia was forever reading dumb articles like that in those stupid women's magazines, but I certainly never saw any payoff. Neither, it would appear, has Stavros.

"Don't be crude, Jace."

I think about her earlier comment—"I won't say I didn't *want* something to happen"—and now I'm pissed. She tries to screw around on my uncle—in the hotel room that *he* paid for, for Christ's sake—and then she has the nerve to criticize *my* behaviour. Which makes about as much sense as Cynthia screwing around with Corey Salter and expecting me to understand. Is it just me, or is the world getting wonkier every minute? I push out my next words through clenched teeth. "Mara, I don't think you're in any position right now to tell anyone *else* how they should act."

Her eyes do this little down-and-up thing, and her perfectly manicured fingers fold and refold themselves before she speaks.

"I guess I deserved that," she says, "but you don't know everything, Jace."

"Really?" I ask her, the word more a challenge than a question. "Then why don't you *tell* me what I don't know."

So she does.

She begins with the affairs. My uncle's, not hers. Stavros, she says, has been sleeping around for years and has had lengthy relationships with at least half a dozen women, probably more. Mara's gotten phone calls from a couple of those women, their way of getting back at Stavros for dumping them and moving on. She tells me about the first phone call, how she confronted Stavros and he told her he was sorry, begged her to forgive him, promised it would never happen again. And she believed him.

But it did happen again. And again. And then it got to the point where Stavros stopped asking for forgiveness, even stopped pretending he was sorry. Instead, he told Mara there were plenty of women who would gladly switch places with her to have what she had: anything she wanted whenever she wanted it—with, of course, the exception of her husband. He was there when he felt like it and gone when he didn't.

Ten seconds into this, I don't want to be listening to it, don't want Mara telling me all that I don't know. It's been so long since I've heard someone in our family talk about how they really feel, actually put into words what's going on in their heads, that I have no idea what to say to her. I think of my father in the restaurant with his tidal wave of words, the way he greets people with his booming voice, the way he pumps customers' hands or slaps them on the back. So different from the silence that settles around our dinner table at home every night. I think of all the times I've sat across from him moving the food around on my plate with a fork, willing him to say something, anything at all. How sometimes he'll clear his throat and shift in his chair and

I'll think *Okay, this is it,* then he'll ask me to pass the salt. And I do. Like father, like son.

Not that Mara's ever been one to talk about personal stuff, either. I think about that blank Home Depot expression she wore in the limousine on our way to the Empress. I've seen that expression on her face lots of times before, but it's only now that I realize how useful something like that could be to hide what you're really feeling. That and the booze.

She's not hiding anything now, though. I asked her for an explanation and I'm getting it, whether I want it or not. The genie's out of *that* bottle. *Way* out.

As she talks about her lousy marriage, Mara's voice grows stronger somehow, which surprises me. It can't be easy for her, either. To admit that your whole life is a lie.

She tells me how, in the beginning, she blamed herself for Stavros's infidelity. More than anything, he wanted children. But after two years of trying, they went to doctors who put them both through test after test and eventually discovered that Mara couldn't conceive. Devastated at first, she began urging Stavros to consider adoption, but he wanted nothing to do with someone else's kid. Even when close friends of theirs brought back infants from China and told them of the thousands of babies who desperately needed homes, he wouldn't budge on that point. As if his own genes were so remarkable, somehow beyond reproach.

So Mara looked for other ways to please the man she'd married, despite his sleeping around on her every chance he got. She tried getting involved in his business, but he made it clear he didn't want a working wife. She tried redecorating their house, but he was seldom there to appreciate or even notice the results of her efforts. Then she focused on her body, believing that by making herself look younger, more attractive, she could reignite the passion they'd shared when they first met. But that, too, failed. They are, she tells me now, two people who occasionally occupy space in the same home.

I'm embarrassed to hear her say this. It's like watching someone expose a wound, pull back the ragged edges so the pus can ooze out. Rather than look in her eyes as she speaks, I watch my hands form fists on my knees, the hollowness of her voice almost more than I can bear.

I don't know what to think. I'm angry, sure, especially since my uncle comes across to everyone as being such an upstanding guy. Believe it nor not, he's the sort of person who'd do anything for family. In fact, my father might have lost the restaurant if Stavros hadn't stepped in and helped him out. After Stefan died, business dropped off drastically. Many of the regulars stopped coming in, probably because they didn't know what to say to us. It's funny how people tend to handle the grief of others. Most want absolutely nothing to do with it. *If there's anything you need . . .* I swear to God, the unspoken end of that sentence is *don't expect me to be around to do it for you.* What everybody really wants is for you to just get over it, to get back to being the person you were as fast as possible so they don't have to feel so goddamn awkward any more. I know now that the most sympathy a person can expect after any tragedy is a couple weeks of casseroles and sandwiches on tinfoil platters that don't need to be returned.

So when Pop missed three of the Parthenon's mortgage payments and the bank sent the first notice of foreclosure, Stavros gave him the cash to stay afloat and to renovate the interior. "Nothing like a reno to get customers coming back," Stavros told my father. And he was right. People think that if your place suddenly looks different, then *you're* suddenly different, too—if, by "different," you mean "back to normal." The renovations weren't much more than a couple coats of paint, new upholstery in the booths and a mural on the entrance wall, but they were enough.

Within four days of our "grand reopening" the regulars were back, and they'd brought a few friends with them.

Yeah, Stavros is quite the saviour. I look around at the suite he's paying for—Mara's and my mother's are mirror images of my own—and I can't help feeling guilty for some reason. As though, by accepting this trip, I have no right to be angry at my uncle, that we're all obligated to keep our mouths shut.

"Why do you stay with him?" I ask Mara during a moment of silence. I'm not sure if she's finished or if she's just paused in the telling, but I can't handle the sudden stillness. Besides the hum of the fan whose blades whir ceaselessly overhead, the only sound I hear is the wash of waves beyond her balcony. And my own breathing.

Mara turns toward the wall of windows and scans the turquoise water as if seeking the answer to my question. Unsuccessfully. She turns back to me, and this time I return her gaze, seeing something in her eyes that reminds me of Stefan sitting in our living room recliner. Resignation, maybe. A sense that this is really all there is. "I love him," she says simply.

I can't help wondering if love can really be blamed for the things we do to ourselves. I loved Cynthia. Told her this, in fact, many times. And I still love her, to some extent. There's still a heaviness in my chest when I think of her, still a rush of warmth when I remember her face, her touch, her smell. Still a sense of loss and longing. All this despite the fact that she cheated on me with Corey.

I force my fists to unfold, and I see I've skinned the knuckles of my right hand, the one that struck Connor's jaw. I must have grazed his teeth. My hand no longer throbs, but the fingers move stiffly as I unclench them. I turn my palm upward and notice the contrast between the pale undersides of my fingers and the sun-bronzed skin of my left arm. Light and dark. Right and wrong. As if things could be ever be so simple. So straightforward.

I realize now that I have to let this go. This thing with Cynthia. To be fair, she never once told me that *she* loved *me*. I just filled in the blanks for her, mentally inserted the appropriate, expected response each time I told her that *I* loved *her*.

When I consider this, when I really stop to think it through, I wonder if maybe I'm the one who's been unfair. Can you really cheat on a person you haven't made a commitment to? And the flip side of that: can assuming that a person loves you justify blaming her because she doesn't?

I want to ask Mara this question, but I suspect I know her answer already. There's something I'm curious about, though. "You invited Connor back here?"

She nods, reddening. "I ran into him on the path. He said you were with him at the disco but then you disappeared. I told him you'd probably just gone back to your suite, so we came to find you." She looks down at her hands, inspects those manicured fingernails. "When you didn't answer your door, I told him he could wait for you here." She nods toward the sofa I'm sitting on. "We talked for a bit and then he passed out. He'd had quite a bit to drink."

She's being kind. I suspect Connor was plastered. "Did you mean what you said?" I ask.

"About what?"

I don't know how to say this, don't know if I even have the right to ask after all she's told me, but I say it anyway. "About wanting something to happen between you and him."

She does something then that surprises me. She smiles. "Nothing would have happened," she tells me.

"How can you be sure?"

But she just smiles at me again.

18

I can barely keep my eyes open. Even if the sunlight weren't bouncing off the water directly into my face, the morning heat is already oppressive, sapping what little energy I have. And since I was up all night with Kate and then Mara, there isn't much left to sap. I consider dragging my lounger into the shade of a palm tree, but even that seems like too much effort. I yawn. Loud. So loud, in fact, that two people walking past on the sand turn and stare.

"Why don't you just go to bed?" my mother asks.

"No way," I insist, shaking my head. "It's Wednesday already. Over half our vacation is gone, and I don't want to waste any of the time I have left."

"And you're making such good use of it now," she observes dryly. She's obviously referring to the fact that I've done little more than lie here yawning for the better part of an hour.

I don't know what her problem is. After all, I took Lucas boogie-boarding right after breakfast. So what if I spent nearly the whole time lying face-down on my board while he chased every wave this side of Cuba? He had a great time. I kept dozing off and getting water up my nose.

But something isn't right. It's like she's annoyed with me.

Not in that I'm-*so*-grounding-your-ass kind of way, though; it's more like the silent-suffering-mother routine that can go from bubble to full boil in seconds. At first I think it's because of last night—she could obviously tell I was just getting back to Ocean 1 when all that commotion with Connor started—but she hasn't said a word about it. Not that I'd feel obligated to tell her, of course. I *am* eighteen. But I'm surprised she hasn't asked me where I was.

And then there's this thing with Stavros. She must know by now that Mara and I talked about him, but she hasn't once brought it up, which would have been easy to do since Mara hasn't come down to the beach yet. Of course, there's probably an easy explanation for that. They're sisters, after all. She's probably known about Stavros for a long time.

This little brainwave sends a more unsettling thought corkscrewing through my head. If she *knew* what a two-timing asshole my uncle has been, why would she agree to come on this trip in the first place? I can't imagine she'd want to do Stavros any favours. If he were *my* brother-in-law, I sure as hell wouldn't.

I turn to face her. "Mom?"

She doesn't look at me. Behind her sunglasses, her eyes are fixed on Lucas in the waves. "Mmm?"

How do I ask the question? *So, Mom, how long have you known that Stavros is a scumbag?* A part of me wants to believe she didn't know, yet even if she isn't aware of all the details, surely she's guessed before now that things aren't quite what they seem. After all, how does a woman suffer through years of her husband's affairs without her own sister knowing something is wrong?

And then, from nowhere, I hear a voice in my head. Stefan's voice. Hollow and distant. *How does a guy get to the point of killing himself without his own brother knowing something is wrong?*

I can't breathe. Someone has punched me in the gut, the fist forcing its way up under my ribcage, bruising parts of me I didn't know I had. I suck in air but it enters someone else's body, someone else's lungs. *How does a guy get to the point of—*

I sit up, swing my legs over the side of the lounger, try to focus on the feel of sand beneath my feet. But instead of the shift and give of warm grains between my toes, I feel only concrete. Cold and unforgiving.

Waves that roll toward the beach have receded in my head, replaced now by other waves. Waves of images that come from nowhere and everywhere, shuddering through me as they rise up and over the space I've made for myself. The space between fearing and knowing.

"Yes, Jace?" my mother prompts again from far away.

"Nothing." I stand, surprised my legs can still support me, can still carry me as I move across the cold concrete that only now becomes sand again. I head toward the water's edge, picking up speed, jogging by the time my feet make the first splash. I keep running as the surf slaps my shins, then my thighs, then my arms and chest. I continue ploughing through the water but, neck-deep now, I'm no longer running, just going through the motions of lifting my legs and forcing myself forward.

As the next wave washes over my head, some part of me marvels at how good I've gotten at this during the past year. Going through the motions. Forcing myself forward.

———

I'm nearly waterlogged by the time I finally leave the surf and collapse on the lounger again. I'm exhausted, but it feels good to be drained, to have every part of my body match my brain.

My mother has pulled her lounger into the shade and continues to stare at the water. At first I think she's watching Lucas, who—amazingly—continues to bodysurf, riding a wave to the sand and then racing back out to catch the next big one. Watching him myself now, I begin to count and realize he's riding every sixth wave. Six is his new favourite number. It used to be eight because of the two closed loops, but now he prefers six, a loop with a handle. Everyone needs something to hold on to.

But my mother isn't watching Lucas. Not exactly, anyway. He's in her field of vision, but I can tell from the tilt of her chin that she's looking beyond him. I shade my eyes and try to see what she sees, but there's only the thin brown line of Cozumel, whose distance from us is impossible to judge. I think again how distance over water always fools people, and I remember Ms. Granter, my Grade 9 Science teacher, explaining how it's all about proximity of known landmarks. It's why we think the moon looks larger when it first rises. Seen behind a skyline of trees or buildings, the moon dwarfs those recognizable things and, as a result, looks enormous. As it rises, though, it seems to shrink because, alone in the night sky, there's nothing to compare it with. Funny how the same isn't necessarily true of people. Even in the empty landscape of memory, Stefan still looms over all of us.

"Hey, Jace."

I turn to see Connor loping toward us over the sand. Somebody else who looms over the rest of us. Although I'm still embarrassed about slugging him, I'm really glad to see the guy. Anything to get my mind off Stefan.

Connor says hi to my mother and waves at Lucas, who, amazingly, smiles back at him. You can never predict when Lucas will respond to a greeting. More often than not, he'll look right through you, so part of my brain registers surprise all over again at the effect Connor has on my brother.

Connor has an entirely different effect on my mother, who suddenly stands and gathers up her towel and beach bag. "Jace, would you watch Lucas for a bit? I want to check on Mara." It's like she can't leave fast enough.

"Sure," I tell her, but she's already walking away.

Connor sprawls on the sand beside my lounger, and now I see the dark flower of a bruise on his jaw. I feel like a jerk all over again.

"Connor, about last—"

"Forget it," he says. "Honest mistake."

"Does it hurt?"

"Only when I eat."

"So, pretty much all the time."

"Funny," he says. He looks in the direction my mother has gone. "I guess she's pissed at me, huh?"

I shrug.

"Your aunt told her nothing happened, right?"

I nod. "After I left Mara's suite, she went to my mother's." At that hour, when everything's quiet, conversation filters through those connecting doors. So does the sound of someone crying.

"But she's still pissed."

I shake my head, looking down the beach toward Ocean 1. "This stuff has been going on for a long time. She can't blame you for . . ." I stop.

"What?" Connor asks.

I feel the frown on my face before realizing what it is. *She can't blame you.* I think about my mother's behaviour this morning, these past few months, the past year. *She can't blame you.*

"Jace?"

I turn to him, try to hear his voice above the blood rushing in my ears. Try to focus on Connor's face as I feel the heat in my own.

"If she doesn't blame me," he says, "what's she so pissed about?"

I look again at the line that is Cozumel. "Nothing," I reply, amazed at how easily I say this word.

We've gone even farther than Connor and I went yesterday, beyond the rocky outcropping that forms a point at the southern end of the beach. Behind us, the people lying on Empress loungers look like smudges on the sand. Ahead of us, there is only sea and more sand.

And shells. Hundreds of them. Lucas and Connor are each carrying several, some of them in their hands, the rest cradled in arms folded against their chests. It's my job to collect the shells they drop. I think about how naturally I assume this role. It's so much easier than making my own choices, actually selecting what I'll keep and what I'll leave behind.

"You guys must have enough by now," I offer. We've been beachcombing for over an hour.

"Don't ask me," says Connor. "Check with the boss."

I have to grin. "Boss" isn't a word I'm used to hearing applied to my brother. Usually, Lucas functions on the periphery of everyone else's world, a kind of human equivalent of Muzak, present but apart. For the last hour, he's been more excited than I've ever seen him, scurrying back and forth across the sand and holding up the various treasures he's found for us to inspect and respond to. And we do. Connor and I have used more variations on *nice, great* and *terrific* than I thought existed, and I've decided to list some of those adjectives in Bradford's notebook to help me with my word count. That is, if it ever dries out. It's been airing on my balcony since the rainstorm yesterday, but it's still pretty damp.

As much as I appreciate all Connor's doing to help me entertain Lucas, I'd really like for us to head back. For the past thirty minutes, my mind's been mostly on Kate, and once more my thoughts return to the evening we spent together. For the tenth time I wonder what she's doing, wonder if she's even out of bed yet. Although the breeze off the water is filled with smells of the sea, all I can think about is the scent of her hair when we kissed this morning. The taste of her lips. The feel of her body against mine. The way she—

"—there, Jace?"

I look at Connor, who's staring back at me, an odd expression on his face. "What?"

"I asked if that was a beach metal detector you've got there." He grins broadly and then continues, "Or are you just glad to see me?"

I look down and see the result of my daydreams straining against the front of my trunks. I grimace, mortified. "Yeah, it's all you, big guy," I tell him, grateful my embarrassment has the sudden effect of a cold shower. I notice his hands are empty, and I turn to see Lucas down by the water, his hands empty, too. "What happened to all the shells?"

"You didn't see? Where *were* you the last few minutes?" he asks.

No way am I going down *that* road again. "You guys get tired of carrying them or what?"

Connor glances toward Lucas, who turns and begins walking back in the direction of the resort. "I don't know. I think he just decided they needed to go back where they came from. He dropped all his in the water so I did the same with mine."

I look at the shells I'm still carrying and let them fall to the sand. "It's about time," I say. My stomach rumbles and, looking at my watch, I see it's already 11:45. I think of the Mayans at Tulum and their monumental efforts to track time. Me, I've got my stomach. "You hungry?"

"Starved."

"So what else is new?"

He punches me in the arm. There's no real force behind it, but I figure I'll end up with a bruise anyway. Now we're even.

That's what I think at the time, anyway. But I'm wrong.

Twenty minutes later, the three of us are in line at the lunch buffet loading up our plates. At least, Connor and I are. Lucas is with us in body only, his eyes constantly returning to the waves visible through the palm trees. We've chosen to eat at the Beachside Café rather than walk all the way up to the Empire Room, but maybe this wasn't such a good idea. When we returned to the resort, Lucas immediately wanted to go back in the water, and I had quite a struggle getting him to come to lunch. Since Mom and Mara were nowhere around, it wasn't like he had a choice, so I had to use the behavioural technique my parents showed me, holding his face between my hands to ensure eye contact and then enunciating slowly: *"First lunch, Lucas, then beach. Lunch. Then beach."* I'm always amazed when it works, when I see acceptance surface in his eyes.

So we got him to the self-serve section of the café that many of the beachgoers use, but judging from the way he's watching the water, I doubt he'll eat anything. Give the kid a second week here and I swear he'd grow gills.

I tong a slice of pepperoni pizza onto his plate, repositioning it in his hands so the pizza doesn't slide off onto the floor.

"Careful there, Lucas," says Connor. "You don't want to wear it."

But my brother isn't listening to us. He only has ears—and eyes—for waves right now.

I see Connor piling another slice on top of the four already on his plate, and he shrugs. "Hey, I missed breakfast," he says.

"Yesterday's too?"

"Comedian," he says, jabbing me in the ribs and nearly making me drop my own pizza.

I move around to the other side of the buffet and reach for some raw vegetables, more for Lucas's benefit than my own.

He's always liked food that makes a sound when he eats it, so I pile on some carrot sticks that look fresh enough to crunch. I'm reaching for some sliced green peppers, too, when the place fills with another kind of sound.

"MacPherson!"

I turn to see Connor's missing teammates charge toward the buffet table, assorted bikini-clad babes in tow. Heads throughout the café turn to watch the spectacle that unfolds: lots of high-fiving, back-slapping, arm-punching. It's like they haven't seen Connor for days.

And then I realize: they probably haven't.

"Where ya *been*, buddy?" demands the Torrent called Barn, who has a well-endowed woman fastened to his hip. Her burgundy-coloured hair is the exact shade of her swimsuit, and up close I notice that she's older than he is. By at least ten years, I figure, but that doesn't stop her from squealing and giggling like someone half her age. Nor does it stop the Torrent from draping an arm over her shoulder, his hand elaborately squeezing her right breast. Which triggers another round of squealing and giggling. I suddenly want to get Lucas away from this group. Far away.

"Yeah, Connor, whatcha been doin'?" This from a Torrent with a woman on each arm. Like a Doublemint Gum commercial.

"More important, *who* ya been doin'?" A series of guffaws sprays from a third Torrent, who has clearly been into the Coronas all morning. "I see you didn't make it back to the room last night, you dog!" More guffaws, followed by even more high-fiving and arm-slugging.

"Didn't I see you going into one of the Ocean units with some woman last night?" asks the burgundy giggler.

Two of the Torrents grunt obscenely, and the whole bunch emits a group whoop. Connor just stands there grinning foolishly.

"Got quite the bruise there, Connor," Barn observes. "She put up a fight?" This comment elicits an even louder whoop.

I wait for Connor to say something to these goons, anything to set the record straight. This is my aunt they're talking about, my aunt he's letting them trash. But he just shrugs his shoulders and the assholes guffaw again.

I'm disgusted by all of them, but I'm fucking pissed at Connor. He knows it, too. I can tell by how he looks away, pretending he doesn't see me. Which is probably a good thing. I want to Frisbee my plate into his goddamn grin. Instead, I put my hand on Lucas's shoulder and prod him toward the soda fountain on the far wall. More forcefully than I intend, though, because he looks at me and whimpers, but I want to be out of here. Now.

After getting a root beer for him and some water for me, I turn to see that one of the Doublemint women has attached herself to Connor, her hands fluttering over him as the group describes what they've been up to for the last two days. None of them is at all reluctant to describe—at full volume—the coke they've been snorting and the Cancun bars they've been thrown out of. It's like a performance, and I wonder if all of us here at the Beachside Café are supposed to applaud. Glancing at the faces around me, I can tell several of the onlookers are as unimpressed as I am.

"C'mon, Lukey," I mutter, nudging him forward. "We'll eat this on the beach."

At the mere mention of the B-word, Lucas grins. "Beach," he says, the word like a marshmallow in his mouth. It's all I can do to keep up with him as we leave the café.

═══

"Had enough?" I ask Lucas. His chin is covered with tomato sauce from the pizza he's eaten, and he looks a little like a vampire after a late-night feeding.

But he ignores me. His eyes are glued to the water that rolls endlessly toward us, and I might as well be talking to the palm tree we're leaning against. He points to the water, his food forgotten, and the plate on his lap slides to the sand. Along with his pizza. "Beach?" he asks me.

I sigh. I haven't eaten more than a couple of mouthfuls of my own pizza. Those jerks in the café ruined whatever appetite I had. I've been sitting here seething at Connor, but I realize I'm even angrier at myself. I knew from the second I laid eyes on him that Connor MacPherson was an A-plus asshole, but I allowed myself to forget that fact. I was so surprised that he liked history that I completely bought the sincerity shit he's been shovelling the past couple of days. As if appreciating the past is the mark of a great guy. Hell, even Hitler was a history buff.

What I don't understand—and what's really pissing me off—is why he'd do all this in the first place. Why hang out with me all this time when he's got buddies and bimbos to occupy his time? Of course, they've been off enjoying *la vida loca* the past couple of days. Were my family and I just a weird diversion for him while they were gone? Or *were* they gone? Didn't one of them comment on Connor not being back at the room last night? They seem to know where he's been most of—

I freeze. *They seem to know.* Is that it? *Do* they know? Has all this been some kind of sick joke? My mind does a quick rewind, remembering the Torrents that first morning on the beach betting on everything. Did Connor lose a bet? Was payback having to hang out with some loser and then report back to his buddies at night?

My guts clench at this last thought, and for a moment I feel like I'll puke. I think of the things I've shared with him about my family during the past couple of days, all the stuff he knows about my parents, and now this business with Mara and Stavros. I think about the things I told him about me, too, how he read my stupid poem, watched me bawl on the beach yesterday.

During all this time, has he been cracking up inside, dying for the opportunity to share everything with those dickheads?

And then, of course, I remember telling him I'm a virgin.

They must have laughed their goddamn asses off over that little detail. They're probably laughing about it all over again right now. How could I have been so stup—

"Beach?"

I'm in mid-cringe and all but groaning when I realize what Lucas is asking me. I look at him and suddenly envy his ability to seal himself off from what the rest of us call life.

I nod. "Okay, Luke." He can't eat more anyway, now that his pizza's covered with sand. And besides, I could use a few waves myself right now. My Hilfiger trunks sport a bright red circle of tomato sauce from a wayward slice of pepperoni, so I look like the victim of enormous crotch crabs. Which only reminds me of my Viagra moment with Connor earlier, and I'm seething and cringing all over again.

Lucas is already on his feet, but before he can run for the water I grip his arm. "Let's clean up this mess first, okay?" There are large baskets under several of the palm trees where Empress guests can put glasses and dishware they've brought to the beach. Every fifteen minutes, a resort employee discreetly replaces each with a fresh basket lined with white linen before carrying the full basket away.

But before I can make him follow through on cleanup, Lucas twists away from me and races for the waves, and all I can do is watch him go. I sigh again, stooping to collect our dishes and then carrying them to the nearest basket. I'm on my knees depositing them when I hear, "I like a man who knows how to clean up after himself."

I turn to see Kate grinning down at me. Even after being up all night, she takes my breath away. She's wearing a bikini I haven't seen before, this one a tan colour matching her sun-darkened skin so perfectly that, for a moment, it looks as though she isn't wearing anything. I silently curse the stain on my trunks. "Hey," I tell her.

"Been up long?" she asks, and for a weird moment I think she's referring to my crotch.

"Too long," I tell her. Which is the absolute truth.

19

Mara and Mom show up right after Kate, and I introduce her to both of them. Mara asks all the appropriate questions: where are you from, where do you go to school, yadda-yadda. The kinds of things that aunts ask girls who are introduced by nephews. My mother, however, barely says hello. She nods, murmurs something that, with a huge leap of the imagination, might be considered a greeting and then moves down by the water to watch Lucas, her hand to her forehead shading her eyes from the glare. Her ramrod-straight back all but screams *Get lost.*

I couldn't be more embarrassed. Both for me and for Kate. I'm tempted to confront my mother about her rudeness when, suddenly, I realize what's been eating her.

Cynthia.

I still haven't told my mother about the breakup.

She probably knows that I was out all night with Kate, and she can see how pleased I am that Kate's here now. I realize how all this must look to her, especially since I'm sure she knows about Stavros cheating on Mara. And there's another thing: she and Pop really like Cynthia. "That one's got a good head on her shoulders," they've said more than once. *That* one. As if, like Stefan, I've brought home dozens of girlfriends. Well, *that* one probably has her head on Corey Salter's shoulder right now. Which suddenly makes me more pissed than embarrassed.

I know I should walk down to the water and quickly tell my mother about Cynthia, make her understand what's happened, but I don't. Part of it has to do with Connor having fun with his buddies at my expense, making me feel like an even bigger loser than the one who got dumped for a choir director's son. After that colossal kick in the nuts, I really don't feel like explaining myself to my mom right now. But there's something else, too, something more that makes me think I shouldn't have to justify my actions to her or anyone else.

Stefan.

My brother never once explained to our parents why he stopped bringing one girl home and began seeing another. It was just something that Stefan did, something we all accepted. Because that's who Stefan was. A girl was lucky to last a month before he moved on. Some didn't make it to the end of the week.

Why shouldn't *I* get to be that kind of person? At least while I'm in Mexico.

I turn away from my mother and back to Kate.

I can tell that Mara is embarrassed by my mother's coolness because she kicks into overdrive and begins asking Kate even more questions: what she uses for sunscreen, what she does to keep her skin from drying out, things that mean nothing to me but that women seem to obsess over. It's like a completely different language. Rod calls it "skin-speak." "Ask a girl what moisturizer she uses," he says, "and she'll talk non-stop for hours." I tried it on Cynthia once, and he was right. My eyes probably glazed over, but she had a birthday coming up, and it gave me an idea. I went to the Body Shop at the Halifax Shopping Centre and bought her three kinds of scented creams and something called Mango Body Butter. She loved it all. Cost me an arm and a leg, but she let me get all the way to second base that night. Big deal.

As soon as there's a split-second pause in the lotion lecture, I dive in. "Uh, Kate. You got any plans for the rest of the day?"

She turns to me and nods. "Yeah, I kinda do," she says.

Disappointment hits me like Body Butter. Cold and clammy.

"I planned on spending it with you," she continues. "If that's okay."

I nearly cartwheel on the sand, but I force myself to be cool. My brain goes groping for some witty comeback like *Let me check my calendar* or *I'll have my people talk to your people.* But I've never been much in the comeback department—they don't get much lamer than the calendar line—and I suddenly wonder, what's so terrible about being honest? And then, for the very first time, I find myself wondering how honest I ever was with Cynthia. How often did I tell her exactly what I was feeling? Did I ever?

My silence says exactly the opposite of what I intend. "If you'd rather not—" Kate begins, but I interrupt her.

"There's nothing I'd rather do," I tell her.

And there really isn't.

———

Kate and I end up nursing virgins most of the afternoon.

After leaving my family, we walked up from the beach with plans to check out the afternoon activities, but music drew Kate to the open-air piano bar by the pool. I like music as much as anybody, but I wasn't thrilled with the idea of listening to lounge performers when there were so many other things I'd rather be doing. With Kate.

Following her into the bar, I had a hard time—pun absolutely intended—keeping my eyes off the rear view of that tan bikini. And an even harder time trying to ignore the mental movie of me getting her *out* of that bikini. By the time we sat down and the waiter brought us our drinks—non-alcoholic Bahama Mamas—I had to hold my glass on my lap. You don't have to go to medical school to know that ice reduces swelling.

Holding my second Bahama Mama now, I'm glad I didn't order a real drink. I was going to—Kate has an all-white bracelet too—but she ordered first so I just asked for the same. Early afternoon isn't a great time for getting a buzz on anyway. Of course, the idea of an afternoon buzz gets me thinking about Connor and his crew of idiots, but I immediately shrug this thought away. That slimy son of a bitch actually did me a favour. If I'd been hanging out with him again, I would have missed this moment with Kate.

I can't get over how beautiful she is. And it's the kind of beautiful that doesn't even try. Rod is forever whipping out *Penthouse* and *Hustler* magazines from under his mattress and moaning about how gorgeous their models are, and he gets no argument from me—my own mattress covers a fair-sized lending library of recent issues. But you'd have to be blind not to realize how manufactured those women are, how they're made up and siliconed and airbrushed into people their own parents probably wouldn't recognize on the street. If they were wearing clothes, that is.

There's nothing fake about Kate, though. She isn't wearing a trace of makeup and her hair still falls breeze-blown over her shoulders from our walk up the beach, yet there isn't a guy who's walked through the bar who hasn't turned and given her the eye as he passed. But she's completely indifferent to all the attention. Her long legs tucked up under her in the leather chair, she just taps her glass and nods her head to the music as if she and I are the only two people here. I have to physically force myself to look away from time to time and focus on the performers.

Three musicians were playing some heavy jazz when we arrived, and we listen now as they move effortlessly through another intricate riff. I'm surprised by how good they are. And by how much I'm enjoying them, because I don't even like jazz. At least, I *thought* I didn't like it, but suddenly things don't seem quite as clear any more. There appear to be a few things that I don't understand as well as I thought I did. Like that stuff with Cynthia. And now jazz.

When the group takes a break, I discover that Kate knows a ton about jazz, and about lots of other kinds of music, too. Me, not so much. I always have music on at home, either on my iPod when I'm out jogging or on my computer in my room, but I'm usually listening to whatever the latest file-swapping software has hauled off the Internet. I'm your basic download kind of guy, one of those pirates the recording industry makes all those commercials about: *You wouldn't steal a car, so why steal music?* I guess because it's so easy. If it was harder, I wouldn't do it. At least, that's what I tell myself. And Kate.

It turns out that Kate has some pretty strong opinions about the whole downloading thing. She actually pays for what she gets off the Net using only sites that sell legitimate recordings, something she tells me has a lot to do with her father. He's a musician himself—in his spare time, when he isn't underwriting insurance policies for car manufacturing companies—and he plays bass guitar in a band made up of four guys who jammed together in university and have remained friends ever since. She says they're as good as these guys in the bar, and, since I have no reason not to believe her, I'm impressed. I'm also impressed by her description of her dad's music library. He has what sounds like a museum-quality collection of recordings that include work by jazz greats like Duke Ellington and Ella Fitzgerald—people even I've heard about—as well as recordings by John Coltrane, Sarah Vaughan and Billy Strayhorn, names that mean nothing to me until Kate tells me about them, describes their contributions to the music scene.

I ask her how she got to know so much about all this and she explains that when other dads were reading bedtime stories to their kids, her father was playing her recordings and talking about where the music came from and how it all connected. I think about what it must be like to share an interest like that with your father. I can't imagine.

When the musicians return, they're joined by a tall woman with ebony skin, a brilliant smile and a voice that flows like chocolate through the bar. The group switches gears and moves from jazz into some contemporary R&B, then hiphop, and then something that sounds like a cross between North American aboriginal music and European *über*-pop. Not that I'd really know, of course. I've never heard anything like it before, but I can tell Kate has, and her expression mirrors her appreciation.

All four performers are far too good for this after-lunch Empress crowd. They should be playing at some funky nightclub to hundreds of people, or at a concert hall to thousands, not to the nine of us in beachwear nursing tropical drinks with names that rhyme. I wonder if the group has their own CD, even consider finding out their names so I can download some of their stuff when I get home. But it's something I consider only briefly. These people I'd actually pay for.

Near the end of their set, the group moves seamlessly from that weirdly beautiful mix of sounds into a song that's vaguely familiar, and then my memory makes the connection. "You have this on your iPod," I whisper to Kate. "You were listening to it on the beach the morning I met you."

"'Never-Ending Empty,'" Kate murmurs in return. "It's an old Leah Delaney song." She frowns at me. "Don't tell me you haven't heard of Leah Delaney, either."

I grin. "Never downloaded her but, yeah, I've heard of her. They play her sometimes on the FM station my father pipes through the restaurant."

Kate rolls her eyes. "Delaney as background. Criminal."

Smiling, I turn to the singer and lose myself in that choco-late voice, listening for the first time to the lyrics that Delaney wrote:

There are stories in our silences
The things that don't get said
speak louder than we ever dream they can
They echo through the space between
the place I long to be
and this never-ending empty where I am

I suck in my breath. It almost hurts to hear these words, to lis-ten as the singer describes my life for everyone in this piano bar. I turn toward the sunlight beyond the entrance, try to focus on the blue of the pool and the green of the palms, but all I can see, all I can think about are the silences in my own life and the space I occupy, the space between my brothers: Stefan, who haunts me still, and Lucas, who lives in a world as distant as anything Stefan might inhabit now. I think about the never-ending empty of the last eleven months and all the things that haven't been said. That won't get said. And then the song is over.

Everyone around me applauds, even the bartender, who sets down the glass he's been polishing. I turn and begin to applaud too. It's then that I see Kate dabbing at the corners of her eyes. Grimacing, she says, "Sorry. Can't help it. Music can do that to me."

I put both my hands over one of hers. "Nothing wrong with showing how you feel," I tell her.

And then I remember someone else saying those same words to me: Cynthia.

It was right after Stefan's funeral. We'd just returned to the house from the cemetery, and the two of us were alone in my room. I was standing in front of my open closet, looking at the bag on the floor under the hanging clothes, thinking about his final gift to me. Not the gear. The gore. He must have known I'd be the one to find him. Did he hesitate for even a second, his finger on the trigger, picturing me in those first moments of discovery? Did he care?

Cynthia came over and stood behind me, put her hands on my shoulders. Said nothing, but seemed to be waiting.

I shut the closet door and turned to her. Shrugged. "What d'ya wanna do?" I asked her.

She frowned, placed one hand gently on the side of my face. "Jace," she said.

I pulled away. "What?"

"It's okay."

I looked over her head at the poster above my bed. Two grizzlies snarling at each other by a river, their claws gripping the same salmon, the caption short and to the point: "Fuck off!" I wanted to tell Cynthia this. Instead, I asked her, "What's okay?"

"Jace, you just buried your brother. There's nothing wrong with showing how you feel."

I wanted to believe her, wanted to tell her how I felt. Wanted to tell her what had happened, what I'd done. And what I'd failed to do. Instead, I took her home.

"I see it got to you, too," Kate tells me.

I'm in the bar again, looking at her hand in mine. "What?"

She reaches up and wipes at something wet on my cheek. Her fingers like Cynthia's on my face that afternoon in my bedroom. But this time I don't pull away.

"Just something in my eye," I tell her.

But we both see the fiction in that. She laughs, and in a moment, as incredible as it seems to me, I'm laughing too.

20

"We call them Kevin and Joanne."

I look at Kate across the table from me, her blond hair pulled back in a clip, and I have to concentrate hard on what she's saying. All I can think about is how much I want to reach out and touch that hair, run my fingers through the soft wisps that curl around her neck. But her father is sitting beside me.

"Kevin and Joanne?" I force myself to ask.

Mr. Townsend grins at his daughter. "That's what *you* call them."

"Okay, but don't they *look* like a Kevin and Joanne, Jace?"

I turn, relieved to see that Connor and his merry band of assholes aren't eating in the Empire Room tonight, and I glance at the couple three tables over from us. They look like they could be anyone. They also look like they've never been introduced. Although they're seated opposite each other, both are turned slightly to one side so their eyes focus somewhere over the other's right shoulder.

"They really don't talk at all?" I ask.

"Not a word," Kate replies. "Every night's the same thing. They come in, sit down, eat their meal and look everywhere but at each other."

Mr. Townsend chuckles. "Leave it to my Kate to notice. I wouldn't have looked twice at them." I hear it in his voice when he says *my Kate*, how important she is to him.

"You make me sound like a pervert," says Kate, making a face. But she's already midway though her story. "They must've arrived at the resort around the same day we did. They've sat there every night we've been here, but they never even touch."

"Maybe they're just friends sharing the same room," I offer.

"Friends at least talk to each other. They're just too weird."

"Kate's created entire histories for them," her dad says. "Arranged marriage for immigration purposes, CIA operatives doing surveillance—"

"Hotel inspectors preparing a report on staff efficiency," Kate interjects, "paparazzi waiting for the million-dollar shot."

"A different story every night," says her father. "How about you, Jace? Your turn tonight. Who are Kevin and Joanne?"

I turn and look again. Kate's right, they don't touch. Even when Kevin passes her the basket of bread, Joanne's fingers don't come close to his. "One of them has a contagious disease. Kevin, I think. Something venereal. Maybe chlamydia." It's out of my mouth before I remember there's a father sitting at this table. I flush, the heat sudden and searing, and I begin studying the crumbs on my dessert plate with exaggerated interest.

"Of course!" says Kate, and I can hear the approval in her voice. "He caught it when he cheated on her! And now she's making him pay. You're good at this, Jace." She turns to her father. "Isn't he, Dad?"

I look up to see Mr. Townsend grinning. "You guys are too much."

No, *they're* too much. I can't remember the last time I sat at a table with my parents and talked such terrific nonsense. Did we ever?

I look now across the dining room to where my family is sitting. Mara, as usual, holds a glass of wine—probably her fourth or fifth—and she's chatting non-stop about something while my mother listens, nodding occasionally. I briefly wonder what they were like as children, wonder if they were always so different, if my mother always appeared years rather than months older. I've wondered more than once how they can be so close when they're so unalike. Why did Stefan and I never find that common ground?

I finally told my mother about Cynthia. I went to see her before dinner, surprised that, despite how I'd felt earlier, I needed her to understand, after all, that I wasn't fooling around with Kate behind my girlfriend's back.

My mother was disappointed. "I always liked Cynthia," she said, as if the breakup was somehow my fault, as if I'd thrown her into Corey Salter's outstretched arms. I don't know what I expected. A little sympathy, maybe? Who am I kidding? I'm not Stefan.

When I told her Kate had invited me to have dinner with her and her father, and that the two of us were planning on going into Playa del Carmen later, she just nodded. As I was leaving, she said something else, but it was too soft to catch, and I didn't ask her to repeat it. She might have told me to have fun, but I can't be sure. Not that it matters. I'm having fun anyway.

"Well, I don't know about you two, but I can't eat another bite," Mr. Townsend says, pushing his chair back from the table. He's done a great job trying, though. He matched me dessert for dessert, all the while fending off Kate's warnings about his cholesterol and blood sugar. I could tell he was used to hearing it, and that she was used to saying it. They're obviously both used to taking care of each other.

"So what are you two doing tonight?" he asks. "Watching the show?"

I'm surprised he's so casual about his daughter spending the evening with a guy she barely knows and that he's only just met himself. Cynthia's dad wouldn't let her go out with me until I'd been to their house a few times and proven I wasn't an axe-murderer. It's nice to be taken at face value for a change. Reaching for my water glass, I'm about to tell Mr. Townsend our plans when Kate does it for me.

"We were thinking of going into town," she says. "That is, if it's okay with you. Jace has been off the resort but I haven't. And we'd both like to see what Playa del Carmen is like before we leave. Maybe even do a little shopping."

"Hmm," he says. "Life beyond a conference room. Interesting concept."

"You can come with us, if you want," she offers.

I turn to gape at her in mid-swallow and nearly choke on water that goes down the wrong way. They both watch me cough and sputter into my napkin, and Kate asks if I'm all right. I give them a strained smile to show them I'm fine. Surprised as hell, though, that she'd ask her father to join us, and relieved when he turns down her invitation.

"I'd love to," he says, "but I'll pass. I've got a ton of work to do tonight."

"Is the company still calling this a vacation?" Kate asks.

He sighs. "*Working* vacation. How's that for an oxymoron?" Standing, he says, "I'm going to check out that group in the piano bar first, though. Sign says they're on again at eight. Are they really as good as she says, Jace?"

Kate and I stand too. "I don't know much about music," I reply, "but I think they're great."

"Good enough for me," he says. "Maybe I'll take my laptop to the bar and work there."

"Like *that's* not pathetic," observes Kate.

He grins at me. "She's my reality check." He holds out his hand to shake mine. "Jace, it was very nice to meet you. Please don't keep Kate out too long, okay? A father worries."

"*This* one does, anyway," she affirms.

"Don't give me reason to, okay?" he tells her. "You two be careful. This isn't Nova Scotia." He leans over and kisses her.

As he says goodbye, I'm thinking about that gesture, the simple pressure of lips against cheek, the gentle intimacy of it. And I wonder how it stops being part of what some people do. What some families do.

======

The cab ride to Playa del Carmen doesn't take more than five minutes. We could have walked, but when we asked Raoul in the lobby for directions, he recommended a taxi. "For your safety at nighttime," he explained. "Empress bracelets sometimes draw the attention of people whose motives . . ." He let his words trail off, but we understood the implication.

Moments away from the resort, we see poverty everywhere, and I find myself thinking about what it must be like to labour for a few pesos each day while privileged people from other countries enjoy the very best that Mexico has to offer. Then I remember my Global Geography notebook back in my room, remember that this was the observation I wanted to record for Sanderson that morning on the way to Tulum, but Connor MacPherson interrupted. I feel a jagged pulse of anger in my chest, but I shrug it off. Kate's here beside me. Life is good.

Playa del Carmen is swarming with people as the cab driver drops us at Fifth Avenue, a street lined with trendy, upscale stores, their facades a broad expanse of white stucco. Even at night, Fifth Avenue is ablaze with illumination from store windows, street lamps and what seem to be kilometres of rope-lights coiled around the trunks of trees in the little square. For the next hour, we wander in and out of stores like Bershka, Pull and Bear and half a dozen others that cater to consumers with lots of cash. The Mayan Riviera's answer to the New York avenue with the same name. Minus the limousines.

Raoul was right. Our Empress bracelets attract a lot of attention, most of it positive in this part of the town. Security guards seem to snap to attention as we pass, and salespeople take one look at the white straps on our wrists and immediately offer to help, nearly stepping over each other in an effort to get to us first. I know they'd be disappointed to learn I'm only carrying twenty American dollars in my pocket—I hate souvenirs, and it's not like I have a girlfriend at home to buy for—so I pretend I'm interested in everything they show us. Kate tries on a few pieces of gold jewellery, but she doesn't buy anything. That is, until she sees a dress on a mannequin in a window we pass. It's red, backless and cut low in front, and I can't help but imagine what she'd look like wearing it.

"Go in and try it on," I tell her, and she doesn't need much coaxing.

When she comes out of the changing room, she looks even better than I imagined, and I turn to see I'm not the only one who's noticed how amazing she looks. The guard at the door practically drools as he stares at her, and a guy wearing an "I played at Playa del Carmen" T-shirt ogles her out of the corner of his eye while his girlfriend models a new pair of jeans in front of another mirror.

The salesclerk who helped her find the right dress size now comes to stand behind her at the mirror and, to Kate's surprise and my own, reaches up and unfastens her hairclip, allowing her blond hair to fall to her shoulders. "*Muy bonita, señorita,*" he tells her, stepping back.

Her face crimson, she turns and asks me what I think.

I can't tell her what I *really* think, what the guard and that guy with the girlfriend would both agree—that she's the hottest thing this side of the sun in that dress. Instead, I just say, "He's right. *Muy bonita.*"

The clerk beams and hands her the hairclip, and she disappears into the dressing room again. When she returns, she's carrying the dress in her hands. "How much?" she asks him.

It's more than either of us would have guessed. "Sorry," says Kate, "I don't have that much," and she hands it to him.

"But, *señorita*," the clerk says, looking at her bracelet, "we deliver the dress to the Empress, yes?"

"No," she replies. "Sorry. I can't afford it." I follow her toward the exit.

Before we reach it, though, the clerk is by her side again. "*Por favor, señorita . . .*" And so it goes.

Ten minutes later, Kate leaves the store with the dress in a bag under her arm, and I whistle. "Shrewd shopper. Remind me never to haggle with Kate Townsend."

She grins. "I really wasn't *trying* to haggle."

"Right," I tease her, nodding at her package. "You did him a *favour* taking that 70 per cent discount."

She swipes at me with the bag, and we're laughing like idiots as we turn the corner and enter another world.

The Playa del Carmen that stretches before us now is only a few steps from Fifth Avenue, but it may as well be a universe away. Gone are the upscale shops with uniformed security guards and salesclerks in designer clothes. Lining the streets ahead of us are small bars and hole-in-the-wall eateries interrupted frequently by dozens of narrow, open stalls jammed with every Mexican souvenir imaginable: sombreros, T-shirts emblazoned with "Riviera Maya," blankets, paperweights in the form of Mayan temples, kites, necklaces strung with seashells and beads, cigars, baseball bats stamped with images of the country's flag, beer mugs, chess pieces chiselled from stone, ashtrays, seascapes painted on soft canvas, sandals, and on and on and on. In front of every stall a person clamours for our attention, calls for us to come look, come see, come buy, all of them staring at our bracelets.

It's much darker down these narrow streets. The crowds press closer to us, and fingers brush repeatedly at my back pocket containing my wallet until I clamp my hand over it. Raucous music shatters the night air as people enter and leave the bars we pass. Stall owners rant at us to stop, those closer to Kate calling "*Muñeca!*" and "*Mamacita!*" while those on my side of the street shout, "You buy for pretty *señorita!*" It's a little unnerving, and I feel Kate's hand slip into mine. I think of Sanderson's notebook again and wish I could record details about the faces in those stalls. Determination lines each of them as their eyes lock on any-one who might be willing to part with a few pesos. I can't help but imagine behind each face, unseen, a family: children to feed, to clothe, to care for. And then, without intending to, I'm seeing us—Kate and me—through *their* eyes, our white-braceleted hands clinging to a bag with a designer's logo and each other. And I won-der if they resent us, resent the necessity of us.

As we and other tourists move farther down the street, the cries for our attention, our business, our money grow more insistent. Kate and I walk faster, avoiding the outstretched, beck-oning hands, until we turn a corner and pass a stall lined with wooden figurines. Sitting on a stool in front of them is a girl about Kate's size but younger, maybe thirteen or fourteen, and she looks up at us hopefully as we pass. Kate, on the other side of me, doesn't see her, so I touch her shoulder and gesture toward the girl. Kate's eyes widen and we stop.

The girl's hair is the colour of coal, and her flawless, cop-pery skin almost glows in the harsh overhead light of her stall. I imagine her Mayan ancestry, imagine the generations of people before her whose hands carved and transformed wood into objects like those around her, and I let my eyes pass over the shelves filled with figures of all shapes and sizes. Some are large and intricate, carvings of torsos with limbs intertwined, the bare wood sanded and polished to a glossy sheen. Others are smaller, delicate, painted with images that seem almost three-dimensional.

I move into the stall and pick up a wooden figure the size and shape of a large thimble. On its smooth surface is a picture of a long-haired man, the features painted as realistically as any I've seen at the Art Gallery of Nova Scotia in Halifax. The girl glances at me shyly, reaches out and takes the figure from my hands, twists it, and it separates into two halves. Inside it is a smaller thimble-shaped figure, with a smaller but otherwise identical image painted on its surface. She passes it to me and motions with her hands, and I take it from her and twist. It opens to reveal a still smaller but identical figure.

The noise and commotion around us seem to recede as I continue to twist figures and remove from their hollow insides ever-smaller but equally perfect carvings. When I finish, there are five in my hands.

"Jesus," I murmur, impressed.

"*Si, señor,*" the girl tells me. "*Hay-soos.*"

I look at her, confused, and then recognize her Spanish pronunciation. *Jesus.* I look again at the painted figures and smile. So it is.

I turn to Kate, whose face reflects my own astonishment. "Wow," she breathes. "It must take forever to make those."

I look at the shelves around me and then back at the girl. "Who did these?" The girl's raised eyebrows reflect her uncertainty, and I make carving motions in the air with my hands, nodding at the figures. "Who made all these?"

Her face relaxes as she understands what I'm asking. "I make," she tells us. She turns and gestures around her. "I make," she says again.

I can't believe it. She's so young. "How much?" I ask her, pointing to the Jesus figures she's nesting inside each other again. She tells me an amount in pesos that I mentally calculate to be about ten American dollars. I take out my wallet and give her fifteen—we'll need the remaining five for the cab ride back.

She looks at the money in her hand, frowns, and then holds out one of the fives I've given her.

I shake my head. "No," I tell her. "Keep it."

She lowers her eyes and I can barely hear her when she says, *"Gracias, señor. Gracias."*

A few moments later, Kate and I are heading back along the stall-lined street, but this time the cries of vendors seem less insistent, as though we're hearing them from farther away. In one of my hands is a paper bag containing the nesting Jesus. My other hand is holding Kate's tightly. And we're both grinning like idiots.

"What you did back there . . ." I begin, my voice filled with an emotion my brain hasn't fully registered. Awe? Admiration?

She looks up at me, shrugs. "It really doesn't change anything, does it?"

"Not a thing," I tell her. But I know both of us are still seeing the face of that girl clutching the bag with the designer logo that Kate gave her, her copper-coloured fingers feeling the soft red fabric of the dress inside. Her dark eyes as large as the sea beyond the town.

"Not a damn thing," I repeat. Except maybe us.

—————

We're almost back to Fifth Avenue when a commotion catches our attention, and we turn and see several people pour out of a bar to our right. Music blares from the open doorway as one of them, a tall man, staggers and falls forward into the dark street, his body hitting the pavement heavily. Others stand over him with raised bottles, hooting and cheering, while one of them, a woman, tugs on his arm. I watch the man roll slowly over onto his back and, as the light of the street lamp strikes his face, I see his eyes focus slowly on mine before glancing away. Connor.

"That's your friend," Kate says, and I'm surprised to hear concern in her voice.

"Forget him," I mutter, then tug her hand, moving us quickly past them. The sound of the group's harsh laughter disappears behind us as we turn into Fifth Avenue.

Moments later, in a cab heading back to the Empress, Kate turns to me. "So what was that all about?"

"What?" I hope she can't hear the pretense in my voice. I'm embarrassed all over again by what happened this morning, what's been happening all week without my knowing it, and I have no intention of explaining myself.

Kate, apparently, has other ideas. "Igor looked like he could've used your help back there."

"Yeah, well, looks can be deceiving."

She frowns. "Something happen between you two?"

My elbow on the doorframe, I look out the window and focus on the Mexican countryside morphing into Caribbean opulence once again. "Your first impression was right. Total asshole."

"I seem to remember someone saying he's actually not so bad."

I grunt at the window. "That someone was wrong."

She doesn't say any more about it, and I'm grateful for that, as the cab driver signals and guides the taxi through the Empress gates. I haven't seen the resort's entrance at nighttime before, but pools of light washing over fountains and flower beds don't provide nearly the distraction I need right now.

Getting out of the cab, I'm surprised to see it's only a little after ten o'clock. "What d'you feel like doing?" I ask Kate.

She stifles a yawn, then flushes. "Sorry. It's not you, Jace. I guess last night is catching up with me."

Her yawn is contagious because, before I know it, I'm expos-
ing molars even my dentist hasn't seen. Definitely not what you'd
call my classiest moment, but then we're both yawning—and
laughing—at the same time.

"Walk you home?" I ask when I finally get my mouth under
control.

"I'd like that," she says, and I slide my hand into hers.

The lobby is almost empty and, now that we've seen those
vendors' stalls in Playa del Carmen, it's never appeared larger.
Cavernous, in fact.

As we pass between the curving staircases and out onto the ter-
race overlooking the pool and the grounds beyond, Kate says, "I
wonder where she lives," and I know she's thinking of the wood-
carver too. It's almost eerie how our thoughts coincide, how so
often she seems to know exactly what I'm thinking. Walking
beside her, I recall images of her in that red dress, and I cross my
fingers that she doesn't know what I'm thinking right now.

"That was a nice dress, though, wasn't it?" she asks, and I nearly
stumble.

"Yeah," I say. I don't trust myself to say more.

"Do you think she'll actually wear it?"

"Sell it, more likely," I tell her.

"I hope not. With that hair and skin, she'd look gorgeous in
it."

"*You* looked gorgeous in it." I have no control over my mouth
tonight. First the yawning and now this.

She lowers her head. "Yeah, right."

I stop and, because I'm holding her hand, she does too. I turn
toward her, raise my other hand to touch her hair, brush a lock
from her eyes. "You *are*," I tell her.

"Are you looking to get laid, Jace Antonakos?" she asks.

I nearly choke, and she throws her head back and laughs, the
sound like the fountain spray behind us. We walk again in a

comfortable silence and, all too soon, we're at Garden 3. This time, it's her hand that reaches up, pulls my head toward hers. Our lips meet and I can no longer hear the fountains, the breeze through the palms, the waves on the beach—only the pounding of my heart, the quickening blood-pulse that drains strength from my legs. When we pull apart, she looks at me through half-lidded eyes that suggest she's felt at least some of what I did.

"If I *was* looking to get laid . . ." I begin. Like an idiot.

She grins. "Yes?"

"I have a suite all to myself." All one headlong rush of words.

She pats me on the shoulder, and I immediately know whatever moment we had is now behind us. A squeeze suggests possibility. A pat is a squeeze with the life sucked out of it. "You enjoy your suite, Jace. I'll see you tomorrow." She turns away.

What do I have to lose? "If you change your mind, I'm in—"

"I know where you are," she says. And then she's gone.

I stand there for a moment in the darkness thinking it can be no accident that "Jace" and "jerk" both have four letters and begin with a J. I wonder if I was born a jerk, had the jerk gene implanted, or if I've cultivated my own unique jerkness over time. I give new meaning to the phrase "just jerking around." I could teach seminars for guys who aspire to jerk greatness.

If it were possible, I'd kick myself in the ass.

———

I'm lying in bed flicking through channels at light speed, searching for anything that will keep me from thinking about what a screw-up I am. But there's nothing that comes remotely close to distracting me from that realization.

And then there is.

A knock on my door.

And some part of me guesses it's Kate on the other side of that door. Who *did* feel what I felt. Who has come here after all at, according to the clock on my nightstand, 11:44. While her father is sleeping.

I fling back the covers and leap up, but in the process, my feet tangle in the sheets and I fall straight to the floor, banging my knees and elbows on the marble tiles. "Just a minute!" I call in a strangled voice and wrestle with sheets and duvet, dragging them behind me in my plunge toward the door. "Be right there!"

And then I am. I fling it open. But it isn't Kate I see in the hallway.

It's Connor. Covered in blood.

21

I try shutting the door but he stops it easily with the palm of his hand, pushing it open.

"What are *you* doing here?" I growl.

"Jace," he moans, leaning against the doorframe, the smell of Mexican rum and something else wafting off him in waves. "I gotta sit down."

"Try the hallway," I mutter, shoving my shoulder into the door, which doesn't budge.

"Please, Jace," he says, "lemme in."

I look down to see his foot in the doorway, and I'm tempted to slam that door with everything I've got. Unfortunately, what I've got is a duvet wrapped around my legs, which makes the whole slamming thing problematic. If I throw all my weight forward, I'm likely to land on my face.

"Please," he says again, but I don't have much choice anyway. Movable object—door—meets immovable force—Connor MacPherson. I'd probably end up having to pay for something. Damage to the door.

Reluctantly, I shuffle aside, kicking the duvet away. All I'm wearing is the shorts I sleep in, and I move to the closet and begin pulling out clothes.

"Goin' somewhere?" he asks.

"Anywhere you aren't."

"Jace—"

"*What?*" I shout. "What the hell do you *want?*"

"I wanna 'pologize," he begins, but then he's retching and lunging toward the bathroom. I hear him heave into the toilet what sounds like a litre of booze and most of a lung. By the time he finishes, the contents of my own stomach are shifting uneasily, and I head out onto the balcony for some fresh air.

I'm still breathing deeply when he joins me, stands unsteadily by the railing and takes a few deep breaths himself. Then he groans and I'm suddenly worried he'll start puking here, too. But, apparently, he just needs to sit. Which he does.

I turn and see the blood that covers much of his face is dry, caked on from a cut on his forehead. From his fall into the street? Why the hell hasn't he cleaned himself up?

And then, *Why the hell am I even wondering about this?* The guy is a total *prick.* No amount of apologizing can change that.

I turn to go back into the room, intent on dressing and getting out of here as fast as I can. It's not yet midnight. Maybe that group is still performing in the piano bar.

But before I can leave the balcony, Connor slides the door shut, and I see he's planted his shoe in the track.

"Move your foot." It's been a long day. I am so *not* putting up with his crap right now.

"You wan' calm down?" he slurs.

"What I want is for you to move your goddamn foot. After that, I don't care what you do. Take a flying leap off this balcony for all I care."

"Thought about it," he murmurs.

I'm torn between asking him if he's serious—*Don't you dare pull this shit with me!*—and throwing him off myself. If I could get him over the railing.

Then he's crying. Connor MacPherson is sitting on my balcony crying.

======

I manage to get him cleaned up, which is only slightly easier than pushing him off the balcony would have been. I help him to the bathroom, supporting as much of his weight as I can without my knees buckling, and tell him to get out of his clothes. I consider putting him in a cold shower to sober him up, but I doubt he'd be able to stand that long, so I run him a bath in the Jacuzzi. While he soaks, I gather up his clothing—besides the blood on them, they reek of booze and something else I'm guessing is dogshit, courtesy of Playa del Carmen pavement—and put them in a hotel laundry bag, which I hang in the hallway on the doorknob. According to the information printed on the bag, Empress staff will collect it during the night and return the clothes washed and dried by six o'clock tomorrow morning. I've already resigned myself to the fact that Connor is spending the night. He's in no shape to stagger back to his own room, and I can't get him there by myself.

But that's not the real reason, of course.

I can't take the chance that he meant what he said about throwing himself off the balcony. I'm pretty sure he didn't, despite the tears. Because he knows about Stefan, it makes sense that he'd try that tactic with me. And, because he knows about Stefan, he knows it's a risk I can't afford to take. Won't take. I have no idea what he's up to and I really don't care. I just want to get through this night and send him on his way in the morning. But, just to be safe, I lock the balcony door with my room key.

I check on him in the Jacuzzi a couple of times—I don't want him passing out and drowning on me—and in a few minutes I hear him getting out. After he's towelled himself off and, from the sounds of it, gargled half a bottle of Mayan Empress mouthwash, I give him one of the thick bathrobes hanging in the closet, and he makes his way out to the living room.

"Thanks, Jace," he says as he settles himself onto the leather sofa, the frame creaking slightly under his bulk.

I have no words for him. He's a complete mystery to me: asshole, pretend friend, suicidal repentant. I'm beginning to wonder if he's bipolar. Which would explain a lot of things. I throw the duvet onto the bed, crawl in under it and turn off the light.

"I'm real sorry," he says in the darkness.

I say nothing.

"'Bout what happened today."

I wince at the memory of this morning in the Beachside Café. Like I need to be reminded of *that* humiliation, being played like a piano for a few laughs. I roll over and bury my face in the pillow.

"Jace—"

"Just go to sleep!"

There's a moment that comes right after you hit your thumb with a hammer or bang your knee into a coffee table, that split second when the pain is suspended. You know the hurt is coming, but there's this reprieve just long enough to get your hopes up, to make you think that maybe, just maybe, this time you dodged it. But then it comes anyway. That's what this moment is like. And then it ends. I hear ragged intakes of breath in the darkness and I know Connor is crying again.

Jesus. I reach over and touch the panel on the wall beside the bed and two lamps slowly glow to life. No sudden eye-wrenching glare at the Empress. Like everything else at this resort, it could not be less like real life. Which, let's face it, is eye-wrenching by design.

Reluctantly, I toss the pillows out of the way and push myself up against the bed's padded headboard. The clock on the nightstand tells me it's been thirty-six minutes since I thought Kate had arrived at my suite. Which makes me think of multiple realities, how some scientist theorized that at any given moment the universe is splitting into alternate outcomes of every event. I wonder if in one of those alternate universes Kate Townsend actually appeared at my door. I, of course, get the universe that includes the drunk with the crying jag.

I sigh. Loudly. "What's wrong?"

The sounds continue, so I wonder if I'm mistaken, if maybe Connor is snoring rather than sniffing, but then he clears his throat and begins to talk. "Never thought my life would turn out like this."

His life. Hockey superstardom, adoring fans, media limelight and unlimited women. Yeah, a real bitch. But, of course, I know now that isn't what he's talking about.

"There are groups you can join," I tell him. "People trained to deal with this." I'm thinking of Alcoholics Anonymous, but the university probably has private substance abuse programs for athletes like Connor. They probably look after their own.

He says nothing for a long moment. Then, "You really think they can help me?"

I shrug, trying to remember TV shows I've seen that included AA meetings. "Depends on you. The first step is admitting it, right?"

There is another silence, longer than the first, and I begin to think Connor has dozed off. But he hasn't. "One Jesus big first step," he says. He makes it sound like Neil Armstrong planting the first footprint on the moon, and I want to tell him it's not rocket science, that people admit to being alcoholics every day. Or not. But I don't.

I fist the sheet in my hand, resenting what I'm about to do. I don't know why I think I should try to make him feel better, especially after what a prick he's been, but I can't help it. I think of the things I might have said to Stefan. Things I *wished* I'd said. "There are people like you everywhere," I tell him. And, thinking of his teammates' early-morning Coronas, I add, "I bet some of your own friends."

He doesn't say any more after that and, in a minute, I lean over and turn out the lights again. As my eyes adjust to the darkness, I think of Stefan one more time. Wonder if he had anyone to talk with toward the end. I'm still thinking this as sleep settles around me.

=====

I'm standing on the path in front of Garden 3 with Kate. Her arms are wrapped around me in the darkness, her lips pressed against mine. At first, our kisses are soft, tentative, like travellers exploring new territory. Then they grow more urgent, as though time is running out here on the path in front of Garden 3. I hear sounds come from inside me that I've never made before, sounds that begin as murmurs but grow into moans. I run my hands through her hair, trace the curves of her ears, draw my fingertips across the line of her jaw, feel the coarse stubble of her skin—

"What the—?" I jerk back, bump my head against the padded headboard. "What the *fuck* are you *doing?*"

22

Connor sits up on the bed. "I . . ." he begins, then stops.

I feel the wet on my lips, and realization hits me like high-beam headlights. "*Fuck!*" I leap off the bed and drag the back of my hand across my mouth. "What the fuck *is* this? Are you *crazy?*"

The clock says 6:37. The first fingers of dawn are reaching across the horizon beyond the balcony. In the dim light, I don't even recognize Connor's face. It's like one of those death masks people made in the Middle Ages, plaster-of-Paris impressions of the moment after someone croaked.

"Did you *hear* me?" I'm only vaguely aware that I'm shouting at him, and I force myself to lower my voice. I don't want to wake Mara or my mother in the rooms next door. "What do you think you're *doing?*"

When he finally speaks, his voice doesn't sound like his, either. I can barely hear him. "You really need me to spell it out for you, Jace?"

"Is this some kind of *joke?* Something else you're gonna tell your friends?"

He looks up sharply, his voice suddenly stronger. "What d'you mean something *else?* What d'you think I *told* them?"

I want to slug him for making me say it, so I don't. "They must've had a hell of a lot 'a laughs over the Antonakos family this week."

I see comprehension flicker across his face. "You mean about my night with your aunt? I didn't say anything about her."

"You didn't have to. They knew all about—"

"They didn't know anything. They just assumed I was with a woman in this building. It's a big building, Jace."

"Why let them assume at all? Why not just tell them the truth?"

"People don't *want* the truth," he says, his voice barely audible again.

"So what *is* the truth?" Even now, though, I'm beginning to understand. The wet on the back of my hand.

Connor draws a huge breath, releases it shudderingly. Says nothing.

So I say it for him. "Connor, are you . . . gay?"

He doesn't answer me. Doesn't need to. The look on his face is enough. It's like watching a jigsaw puzzle come apart, pieces of it pulling loose and falling away.

"Jesus," I tell him, if for no other reason than to make a word with my mouth, to give it something to do besides feel wet. "I sure didn't see *that* coming."

Then he says something else I didn't see coming: "I thought you were gay, too."

"*What?* You thought *what?*"

He shakes his head. "C'mon, Jace. An eighteen-year-old guy who's still a virgin? Who gets a hard-on walking on the beach with another guy? And who tells me last night I've got friends with the same problem I have? What was I *supposed* to think?"

My jaw drops. In a bizarre kind of way, his rapid-fire reasons almost make sense, and I'm suddenly on the defensive. "This is bullshit. What about Kate? You know how I feel about her—"

"I only know how you *said* you feel." He lets that line hang there for a few seconds, then continues, "I've said the same things about lots of girls. More times than I can remember. To keep people from . . ." He looks down at the sheet twisted in his hands, spreads his fingers apart and releases the soft cotton. "From finding out."

I'm going to wake up in a minute and none of this will have happened. Everything will be normal again. *I'll* be normal again. Not someone whose only chance to get laid in Mexico was with another guy! But I don't. Wake up, I mean. Because I already did. To some weird adult version of Lucas's disintegrative disorder. Where nothing is the same as it was before, and never will be. I don't know whether to laugh or get angry or just throw my head back and start baying at the sliver of moon that hugs the brightening horizon.

I'm still considering my options when Connor shakes his head. "Guess I was wrong about you. Sorry, Jace." He pulls the sheets back and I see he's naked, which is definitely not a picture I need in my head right now, and I'm grateful when he reaches for his bathrobe on the floor by the bed and pulls it on. Getting up, he heads for the mahogany cabinet that holds the refrigerator. "I need a drink," he says, reaching inside and pulling out a Corona.

"*That's* what I thought all this was about," I tell him, nodding at the beer.

Flipping off the cap, he shrugs. "This? This is the only thing that makes any of it bearable."

Before he can bring the beer to his lips, though, I cross the room and place my hand on the bottle. "Gay is one thing, Connor, but gay and *stupid*? It's not even seven o'clock yet."

His knuckles whiten on the beer bottle and, for a second, I wonder if he's going to slug me with it. But then he shrugs, hands it to me.

And begins to talk.

" . . . so I couldn't introduce you to them," he says.

We're sitting on the balcony and, because Connor is dehydrated from the booze, he's finishing his third orange juice while I'm still on my first. Hearing the events of the past twenty-four hours described through his eyes, I feel ridiculous for assuming what I did.

I try to sum up what he's telling me. "You mean, if they met your gay *friend*, then they might suspect *you* were gay, too." I should probably be pissed at this, but the whole thing is so much to digest that I'm more awed than offended. It's like we're talking about two people who aren't even in the room.

"Right," he says.

There is, of course, a question that's been circling around and around in my head since we sat down to talk. It's only now that I muster the balls to ask it. "So, do I *look* gay to you?"

"Do *I* look gay to *you?*" he asks in return.

I shake my head, thinking of those two old queens at the Parthenon. And then someone else. "There was this guy in one of my classes last year. Alex something. Parker maybe." I think for a bit. "No, Praeger. Alex Praeger. Definitely gay. A real flamer. *That* guy I could tell. But not you."

"Doesn't sound like you knew him very well."

I shake my head again. "He left school before the year was over."

"What happened to him?"

"Got into some trouble. Something to do with his family, I think. Someone said he ended up in a group home for a while."

He grunts knowingly. "Sounds like his parents weren't too keen on having a fag under their roof."

I'm surprised at his use of the word. "I don't know the details," I tell him. "But, no, I don't think they were."

Connor takes a final swallow of his juice and sets the glass on the balcony table. "It would kill my old man," he says.

"You don't know that."

He laughs, but completely without humour. "You don't know my old man. He kept pushing my mom to have kids until he got the son he wanted. He was working on an entire girls' volleyball team before I finally showed up."

"So what? Lots of fathers want sons."

"Not gay ones." He gets up and stands at the railing, looking out at another perfect Caribbean day. "You remember all those same-sex marriage debates in the media? Whenever my dad saw something about it in the paper or on TV, he'd say, 'Nothin' but perverts and child molesters. They should castrate the whole lot of 'em.'"

"Jesus, that's cold."

Connor turns to me. "You don't know the half of it."

"What about your friends?"

"What about them?"

"Why not tell them?"

He doesn't say anything for a bit, and at first I figure he's not going to answer me. Like there's no answer to this question. Then, "They're good guys. Jerks sometimes, but basically decent. They'd have real trouble with this, though."

"You sure?"

He takes a long breath, scans the horizon one more time as if looking for something that isn't there, and then sits down again. "They got talking about gay people one day, out of the blue. Jokes at first, most I'd heard before, some I'd even told myself. But then it turned serious. Ugly. How queers were sick, that anyone who'd choose to be gay *deserved* a good bashing now and then." He shakes his head. "*Choose* to be gay," he repeats. "Like anyone would *choose* this." He looks down and begins tracing invisible lines on his thigh, and I think he's spelling the word "gay" over and over again. "Barn sort of summed it all up when he said he'd rather go to prison than be gay. Everybody agreed." Connor pauses. "So did I," he says, then looks up at me. "I still do."

I try to make a joke. "Prison's probably not the place a guy oughta go to avoid being gay." But he doesn't crack a smile, and I think again about those three words—"I still do"—and what they really mean. And what it means to say them. And then about all the unspoken words beneath them. "Have you ever, you know, before . . . ?" And suddenly this is a question I don't want to finish. I take a swallow of my orange juice.

He stops his tracing and looks at me. "If you're asking have I ever slept with a guy, you would've been my first."

I'm in mid-swallow and I nearly choke. "Lucky me," I say when I finally stop sputtering.

I see something like a grin play at the corners of his mouth. "You know, for a straight guy, you're taking this a lot better than I would've thought."

I shrug. "I was so pissed at you before that this is actually kind of a relief. For me, I mean." I narrow my eyes. "You're not gonna try to kiss me again, are you?"

This time his grin is real as he shakes his head. "You know, it's kind of a relief for me, too. You're the first person I ever told. It actually feels good to finally talk about it."

"No one knows?"

"No one."

"So, who're you gonna tell now?"

"What do you mean?" he asks, his words suddenly acrylic, their edges hard and defined. "Nobody."

I blink. "People will find out, Connor."

"No one can find out, Jace. *No* one." Even though his voice is low, I can hear the heat in his words.

"*I'm* not gonna say anything, if that's what you're worried about." And I can tell by his face that he *is* worried about that. "Shit, Connor, who would I tell?"

He shrugs. "There's a lot of reporters who'd like to write *this* story."

I don't know how to say this, don't know if one way is better than any other, but I say it anyway. "Maybe they should." I'm thinking about what he said last night on this balcony. About jumping. And, of course, I'm thinking about people like Stefan. Who jump in a different way. "Maybe it would help somebody."

The acrylic becomes splashed acid. "Like a public service announcement, right? No thanks. I got enough problems living my own life. Let everyone else worry about theirs."

"And this life of yours is so great, right?" I don't mean that to sound like it does, but I remember him on the pavement in Playa del Carmen and then covered in blood and dogshit at my doorway.

He seems to know what I'm thinking because he reaches up and touches the cut on his forehead, which scabbed over during the night. "It's the only one I got," he says.

There are so many things I want to ask him now, so many things I want to know. But, again, it's like he knows what I'm thinking, because he answers my next unspoken question. "Yeah, I sleep with women."

This shouldn't surprise me, but, after the last few hours, it does. "How does *that* work?" I ask.

His tone softens and he grins. "I'm pretty sure even a virgin knows that."

My face suddenly feels like day-long sunburn. "You know what I mean," I tell him.

He nods. "I had a coach who taught us this visualization process. Helps you focus on the outcome, which on the ice translates into goals." He looks out at the water before he continues. "It can work *off* the ice, too."

"And when it doesn't?"

He looks at me. "There's advantages to being drunk. *Too* drunk, if you know what I mean."

And I do. Which suddenly explains a lot more about the booze.

We both watch the water for a while. A breeze has come up and, despite the early hour, already there are people windsurfing, and one of the catamarans is out beyond the reef. I expect someone will be parasailing before long.

I turn to Connor. "How'd you find out you were gay?"

He doesn't miss a beat. "I got the membership card in the mail."

I grin. "I *heard* you gays were funny."

"Great interior decorators, too."

It feels good to be joking around again, but I really do want to know. "So when were you sure?"

He leans back, runs both his hands through his hair. "It's not about being sure of anything. It's about feeling. Feeling that everything is different for you than for everyone else. But you're not sure." I can see him groping for something more, some way to make me understand. "It's like colours. Who's to say that the blue I'm seeing out there is the same colour you see?"

"Blue is blue. Period."

"But *is* it? Maybe all this time the colour you've been calling blue is the colour I see as red. But when I was learning my colours, everyone told me it was blue. Maybe the blue I see is what you call purple or yellow or orange."

I picture Connor seeing a red ocean right now rather than the electric turquoise that floors me every morning. "That's too weird."

"Yeah, or maybe it explains why we don't all have the same favourite colour. Maybe we do and just don't know it because we call it something else."

I let this thought hang in the air for a moment, consider what he's telling me, consider whether this stuff about colours is really so weird after all. It's a lot to take in. "So," I ask him, "when did you first have this feeling you weren't seeing things the same as everyone else?"

"Junior high. My friends were always talking about tits, wanting to cop feels, shit like that. Barn and I went to the same school, were in the same class together in Grade 7, and he came in from recess one day totally wired about getting Carla Henderson to show him her boobs behind the bleachers on the soccer field. I just didn't see what the big deal was. I was always more interested in what happened on the field than behind the bleachers."

"More into soccer than sex," I offer.

"That's what *I* thought. Later, though, I began to realize that what I liked so much about sports wasn't just the competition." He runs a hand through his hair again, shakes his head. "If Barn knew this, after all those showers we took together . . ." He doesn't finish the thought. Doesn't need to.

"So, you had a thing for Barn?"

He nearly spits. "Christ, no. He was my *friend*. Still is." I'm sure both of us hear the unspoken *as long as he doesn't find out* hovering above us.

"Was there anyone you *did* have a thing for?"

He leans forward toward the railing, his elbows on his knees, his chin in his hands. "You gotta understand that I didn't let myself think like that. I wasn't gay. Just a little mixed up. You hear health teachers and guidance counsellors talk about that all the time, how adolescence is all about discovering our bodies, about experimenting, shit like that. I told myself I was confused. At that age, Jace, who isn't?"

I'm pretty sure I know the answer to my next question, but I ask it anyway. "You dated a lot in school?"

"Sure. Saw my own share of boobs, steamed up a lot 'a car windows, action like that."

I find myself thinking about how much more action Connor has seen than I ever have. What a waste. "Tell me you liked *some* of it."

He shrugs. "Who wouldn't? I wasn't gay, right? I was a guy. That's what guys do."

"But?"

He starts tracing the word on his thigh again, absently. "But it never felt the way I expected it would. I always found my mind . . . wandering."

"Wandering," I repeat. I think about all those times with Cynthia, how it was never my *mind* doing the wandering. Or *trying* to.

"I thought," Connor continues, "maybe it was because I hadn't met the right girl, that it'd be different when I finally found her."

"Maybe that's it. Maybe you just haven't found her."

"That's not it."

"How can you be sure?"

He looks at me, says nothing for a moment, then shrugs. Nodding over his shoulder at the bed in the room behind us, he says, "Because what we were doing in there felt like what I've been waiting for all this time."

Whoa! I get up so fast I nearly knock over my chair. "Uh, Connor, you need to, uh, you need to know that—"

He holds up his hands as though surrendering. "I know," he says. "Now."

I stand there looking at him, my mind doing some complicated aerobics to avoid picturing what Connor is talking about. A little wetness on the back of my hand I can handle. I am *definitely* not ready for a high-definition replay.

I sit back down. "So you never even kissed a guy before?" I ask, careful to leave the word "today" off the end of that question.

He shifts in his chair, and I get the sense that there's a limit to the things I should be asking. A limit to the things Connor may be willing to share. But I'm wrong. "Never even touched a guy," he says. "Not in that way."

"Why not?"

"Because I wasn't a fag. I was *normal*. Just like everybody else."

I understand what he's saying. I have first-hand knowledge of what it means to deny something you know in your heart is true. But that's a thought I'm not ready to entertain right now. "So what you're saying is *I* made you gay," I quip.

"It's all you, big guy," he says, and I recognize the same words I said to him on the beach a hundred years ago. We both try to laugh, but the sound has no meaning, like the lie about the sea inside the shell.

| 23 |

Connor is changing into his freshly laundered clothes when there's a knock at my door. I'm surprised to see who's standing in the hallway—she's never up this early.

"Hi, Mara," I say. "Everything okay?"

She looks past me at Connor in the living room pulling on his shirt, then beckons me into the hall. When I follow her out, she closes the door behind me, pulls me down the empty corridor and into her suite. Once inside, she turns and looks me straight in the face.

"Jace," she says, "you know I love you like my own son."

What *is* it with the confessions today? After the last hour, I'm really not prepared for something this heavy, but I nod. "Sure," I tell her.

"Then you'll understand that what I have to say to you is for your own good."

I'm mystified. "What d'you have to say?"

She looks up at the ceiling, and I get the odd impression that she's going to recite something she's memorized. "I want you to promise me you're being safe. That you're taking precautions."

"Against what?"

She places a hand on my arm and squeezes. "It's okay, Jace. I know."

Now I'm *really* beginning to worry about an adult disintegrative disorder. Nothing's simple for me any more. Nothing makes sense. "Know what, Mara?"

She lets her gaze drop to the floor for a moment, then takes a deep breath, looks up and launches in. "That you're homosexual."

"*What?*"

"It's okay—"

"No! It's not! *I'm* not!" *Jesus!*

"Jace, please, there's no need to make this harder than it is. I just want to be sure you're—"

"Mara! Stop!"

She looks at me, her mouth open.

"Why do you think I'm *gay?*"

I can tell she's flustered, whatever resolve she had before now evaporating. When she speaks again, her voice is little more than a whisper. "I heard Connor in your room earlier."

Connor.

"*Much* earlier," she adds.

Oh.

Oh no.

"Mara—" I begin, but she doesn't let me finish.

"Jace, you shouldn't feel ashamed—"

"I'm not ashamed! I haven't done anything to be ashamed of!"

"You're right, Jace. You haven't. There are some people, though, who think—"

"Mara! You're not listening!" I remember what she said to me when I thought she'd slept with Connor: *You seem to have your mind all made up anyway.* Now I know exactly how she felt.

Pigheadedness must run in the family because I can't seem to get through to her, either. "I do *not* like guys that way. I do *not* have those kinds of feelings. Nothing happened between Connor and me. *Nothing.*"

She looks at me for a long moment before she speaks, as if weighing every word. Finally, "Connor told me how he feels about you, Jace."

"*Feels* about me?"

"That night he stayed here with me? Before he passed out, he talked a lot about you. He was drunk and rambled on and didn't make a lot of sense, but I could tell it wasn't *my* suite he wished he was in."

"Mara—"

"Jace, your parents aren't as open-minded about things as they could be. Your mother's not much older than I am, but she seems a *lot* older when it comes to things like . . ." Her voice wavers, but she presses on. "We just see the world differently, that's all. I know it's not my place to say so, but I don't want you telling her about this. She doesn't need to know. Not right now, anyway. She's had so much to deal with this past year. But as long as I know you're practising safe—"

"Mara," I say, putting my hands on hers, "you've gotta believe me when I tell you this. I am definitely not gay." She looks unconvinced, but before she can say anything else, I continue, "You're right, Connor *is*, but no one can know about that. No one." I squeeze her hands in mine. "He spent the night with me because he was too drunk to go back to his own room."

"Jace, these walls aren't as soundproof as you might think. I heard you arguing earlier."

"So?"

Her face flushes. "And before that, I heard you . . . moaning. Both of you."

Oh. My. God.

My face is on fire but I try hard to keep my voice low and even. "I'm going to say this once more, Mara. I am *not* gay. Now repeat after me: Jace is not gay."

She sighs. "Just be safe, okay?"

━━━━

"What was *that* all about?" Connor asks when I return.

"Mara knows about us."

His eyes widen. "Knows what? There *is* no us."

"Yeah, try telling *her*. Good luck with that."

"She knows I'm—?"

"—an interior decorator," I finish, but he's not amused.

He paces to the window and back. "How'd she find out?" he demands, clearly pissed.

"Don't look at *me*. Apparently, *you* told her."

He freezes. "*Me?*"

"That night you were drunk in her suite."

"Christ!" He turns and opens the cabinet refrigerator, pulls out a Corona.

Now I'm the one who's pissed. "That's what got you into this trouble in the first place."

Clutching the Corona, he glares at me. "What am I supposed to do now?"

"First, put that down." I nod at the bottle.

He scowls at me, then grudgingly returns it to the refrigerator.

"Next," I tell him, "you can't spend the rest of your life worrying about people finding out. You need to deal with this. It's not going away."

He slumps onto the sofa, runs his hands through his hair again, shakes his head. "You don't get it, Jace."

"What don't I get?"

He fastens his eyes on mine. "You ever heard of fan clubs for homo hockey players? People lining up to see fags on the offensive line?"

"Maybe you'll be the first." But even as I say these words, I don't believe them.

He gets up and walks over to the window again, looks out at the beach and the water beyond. "Ever heard of Muhammad Ali?"

"The boxer? Who hasn't?"

"Jim Brown?"

"One of the best running backs of all time, right?"

"Gordie Howe?"

"I think he holds the record for most games ever played in the NHL. Or used to, anyway."

He turns to me and I can see he's impressed. "I thought you didn't like hockey," he says.

I shrug. "You don't have to like the game to respect the players."

"What about David Kopay? Ever heard of him?"

I shake my head.

"Played pro football from '64 to '72," Connor says.

"I'm drawing a blank," I tell him.

"All-American running back in his senior year at the University of Washington. Leading rusher for the 49ers in his very first year. Also played for New Orleans, Washington, Detroit and Green Bay."

"Never heard of him."

"He was gay."

Now I get it. "Oh."

"I read about him online. One of the first professional athletes to come out of the closet."

I almost say *oh* again, but I don't.

Connor looks out at the water once more. "When he retired, he was considered a top contender for coaching jobs all across

the States, but no professional or college team would hire him."
Connor lets that sink in for a moment before turning to me and
continuing, "He ended up selling floor coverings."

"You're kidding," I say.

"Installed them, too."

Now it's my turn to look out at the water. It isn't red, but it
may as well be—it wouldn't be any more screwed up than what
Connor's been telling me. "But that was then," I reason. "Times
have changed. People have changed."

"You think so, huh? How many gay athletes have you heard
about in the last five years? Or even the last ten years?"

"Um . . . that Canadian swimmer who won the Olympic med-
als. Hawksbury."

"Tewksbury."

"Whatever."

"Name some others," he says.

I think some more, but my silence soon tells him what he
already knows.

"I Googled people who've come out to the public," he says.
"Lots of performers have done it over the years: actors, singers,
musicians. A few politicians, too. But athletes? Maybe a handful.
And most of them after they retired." He shakes his head. "They
all learned Kopay's lesson."

I remember what he said last night during his crying jag: *Never
thought my life would turn out like this.* Only now do I think I
understand what he meant.

―――

"I'll try to get it out farther this time, Lucas," I say. I make another
long cast into the surf and then hand the rod back to him. I'm not
sure he understands what we're doing, but he likes the repetition,
the safe predictability of it: I cast, he reels in; I cast, he reels in.
We haven't even gotten a nibble, but I'm not surprised—the guy

at the equipment hut who gave us the rods warned us that there's very little marine life near the shoreline. Most of the coral reefs near the resorts are dead, and people who want to catch anything substantial charter a boat to the barrier reef about a kilometre offshore. I don't care, though. It's just good to be out of that room, to put the morning behind us and try to enjoy the day.

Connor's line, of course, goes nearly twice the distance of mine. It arcs over the waves, the lure slicing into the water with hardly a splash. Despite his superior casting ability, though, Connor's no luckier than we are, and the lure returns fishless every time. But I can tell he's okay with this too, that the mindless pattern of casting and reeling in keeps his mind from dwelling on things that he'd rather ignore, like the awkwardness that has settled around us. Neither of us is quite sure how to move beyond his big revelation this morning. It's like there's this huge Goodyear blimp hovering directly overhead flashing "Connor MacPherson's gay! Connor MacPherson's gay!" while both of us pretend there's only blue sky up there.

We're far from swimmers and boaters on an empty stretch of sand, but it almost feels like we're in the middle of a crowd, sidestepping around each other to keep from saying the wrong thing, making the wrong move that'll be misinterpreted somehow. At least, that's the way *I* feel. We haven't said anything to each other for a while, and I'm beginning to wonder if maybe even Lucas can feel the tension.

I think back to everything that's happened in the last few days. Coming here was supposed to be a break. A chance to forget about Cynthia, to kick back, relax, have some laughs. And sex, of course. Quite a lot of sex, in fact, if the number of condoms in my sock drawer is any indication. Since every one of them remains in that drawer gathering dust, it's painfully obvious that having a clearly defined objective isn't worth shit. I consider writing *that* in Bradford's notebook.

I glance sideways at Connor and wonder what he's thinking. Or *not* thinking. When he returned to his room earlier, his buddies had already gone for the day, leaving a note about taking the ferry to Cozumel and telling him to meet them over there at an address they'd scrawled at the bottom. He didn't. When he realized they wouldn't be back until late this evening, he returned to Ocean 1 and suggested the two of us and Lucas go fishing, something he does a lot with his dad.

I suppose I could've been annoyed. Since I'm only "safe" to hang out with if his buddies are out of the picture, it's a sure bet *they* think I'm gay, too. In fact, I could get really pissed if I chose to think about it, but the whole thing is surreal, like it's happening to someone else. What did Connor say? *You know, for a straight guy, you're taking this a lot better than I would've thought.* To be honest, this straight guy doesn't know *how* he's taking it.

Watching Connor casting like a pro, I find it impossible to believe he could like guys the way I like girls. I have zero trouble picturing him surfing ten-metre waves off Australia's Great Barrier Reef, hunting big game on some African savannah, even hiking the Himalayas, but I can't understand how someone that testosterone-driven doesn't like sex with women. Which probably makes me a candidate for Stereotyper of the Week. But I've never seen a homo like him before.

Which makes me think of Alex Praeger again.

And then I'm thinking about something else: all the crap that guy had to put up with at school. Words like "Faggot!" and "Freak!" scratched into his locker weekly, jocks tripping him on the stairs, someone even tossing a dog turd at him in the cafeteria once. He had a couple friends—one of those Goth girls who look like they bite the heads off snakes, and a guy in a motorized wheelchair who could only communicate with a computer—but neither of them had the same schedule he did, so he was usually off by himself whenever I saw him. I remember Rod saying once how Alex manufactured most of his own grief, referring to how he dressed and acted—Alex wore lots of brightly coloured silk and tended to flail the air when he talked—and I remember thinking a couple times myself how it certainly wouldn't hurt him to tone it down, make himself less flamboyant, less a target. I don't think I ever spoke more than three words to his face. Most of what I said was behind his back.

"You'd think there'd be *something* out there," Connor says, pulling me from that memory.

I turn to see him getting ready to cast again, see how he plants his feet in the sand, see how he grips the rod in his right hand, his left loosening the line, creating the slack that will help power the snap. I can tell it's instinctive, that he knows what to do without even being conscious of it, and I suspect I'm seeing part of what makes him such a great hockey player.

"You wanna quit?" I ask.

He shakes his head. "Fishing isn't just about *catching* fish," he says, and I wonder if this is something his father told him. "Besides, Lucas seems to be enjoying himself."

If my brother's grin is any indication, Connor is right about that. Lucas has never fished before, so I don't even know for sure if he understands what we're doing, that despite Connor's philosophy on fishing, there really is a point besides casting out the line and reeling it back in. Not that I have any experience in the *catching* department, of course, which only reminds me again what a horse's ass I was with Kate last night. Although I met her only a few days ago, I know she's a person I'd like to get to know a whole lot better. After last night, though, I doubt there's much chance of that ever happening. I let myself relive that final moment again, this time seeing it through her eyes, and I'm embarrassed that I probably came across no better than Connor's happy troupe of teammates, who clearly share my single-minded objective. Except, of course, they actually *do* get laid. Frequently.

I feel a tug on my arm and see Lucas holding the rod out to me once more. This time I put everything I have into my cast, and I'm pleased to see the line sail a few metres farther than before. Which, for some reason, seems important. An omen of sorts. Maybe there's hope for me after all. If I'm destined to remain a solitary virgin, maybe I can parlay that untapped energy into angling excellence. Instead of returning to Halifax the day after tomorrow, maybe I'll just stay here and become a professional line-caster. Resorts the world over will clamour for me to stand on their sandy shorelines, flex their fibreglass rods and let their fishing lines fly.

And camels shit ice cream on Sundays.

There are too many things in my head right now: Kate and our moment last night, Connor and our moment later, Mara and our moment after that. I try not to think about any of them, but it's no use. All of them keep pouring back, including Mara's knowing look when Connor and I went to get Lucas this morning. She arrived at my mother's suite moments later and kept shooting me glances and nodding toward Connor. I'm sure she thought she was being discreet, but she reminded me oddly of those old black-and-white movies where a cigar-chomping guy wags bushy eyebrows the size of poodles to get someone's attention. I kept frowning at her but she didn't let up, so, as we were leaving, I leaned over and whispered that I'd be safe. I said it to get her off my back but, now that I think about it, I realize I was basically promising my aunt to have safe sex with a gay guy. Can my life *get* any more humiliating? I don't think so.

But then, of course, it does.

24

"Your aunt said I'd find you here."

I turn and see Kate walking toward us, and I feel warmth that has nothing to do with the sun wash over my body.

"Hey," I say, astonished that she's here. Astonished, as well, that someone can look that good this early in the day. She's wearing a blue bikini this time, and tied around her waist is a see-through yellow sarong that only draws more attention to the part it's supposed to be covering. More of *my* attention, anyway. Like waving a red flag in front of a bull.

Connor nods to her and then returns to his casting, his next toss even more powerful than the others. I half expect his line to run out before his lure touches water.

Kate comes to stand beside me and says hello to Lucas. Entirely absorbed in reeling in his line, he doesn't acknowledge her, but she seems to understand, and she smiles at him as he deliberately works the handle of his reel.

We make small talk for a bit—how fast the week has gone, how it'll be tough adjusting to winter again in forty-eight hours, stuff like that—and I can't believe she's chatting as though last night never happened. Or seems not to mind that it did. Whatever the case, I could care less. She's giving me a third chance here, and I do *not* intend to blow it.

I ask her if she'd like to try casting the line, but she shakes her head. "Do you think we could go someplace for a bit?" she asks, her voice suddenly so low I can barely hear her over the waves unfurling on the sand. "Just the two of us?"

I can't believe she's said this, and it's all I can do to keep from dropping the rod, grabbing her hand and dragging her down the beach. "Connor, would you mind watching Lucas for a little while?"

His back to me, he shrugs, but he winds in his line and goes to stand beside my brother, ready to take Lucas's rod for the next cast.

"Thanks," I tell him over my shoulder, because Kate and I are already walking away.

=====

"So. What'd you want to talk about?" I ask. I understand now that this is *all* she wants to do. I was going to suggest parasailing or taking out one of the catamarans later, any activity that would involve me being as physically close to her as possible, but before I could, she asked if we could sit at one of the outdoor tables at the Beachside Café. I really don't care where we are, as long as we're there together.

She takes a sip from a drink I don't recognize—something with lots of coconut and a pink umbrella—and then looks at me. "Jace, about last night," she begins.

So, it isn't behind us after all. "Look, Kate," I tell her, embarrassed, "I'm sorry for that. I shouldn't have—"

"No," she says, "*I'm* sorry."

I stare at her. "What are *you* sorry for?" My mind gropes for possible answers to this question, but there's only one that makes sense, only one I want to hear: *Sorry for not spending the night with you.*

Nothing could have prepared me for the answer she gives me, though. "For using you."

I blink. "You were using me?"

She twirls the tiny umbrella before taking another sip of her drink, and I get the sense she's stalling, delaying what comes next. And part of me is okay with that, wants her to take several more sips, delay all she wants. But she doesn't.

"I have a boyfriend, Jace."

I don't say anything. I'm suddenly numb. Too numb to make my mouth manufacture words that don't mean anything anyway.

"His name's Blake," she continues. "We've been going together for over a year now."

I look at my own drink, a *real* Bahama Mama this time. Not a virgin.

"You're very nice," she tells me, "and I've really liked getting to know you."

You're very nice. Cynthia said something similar the day she broke up with me, and anger flares in me now just as it did then. "And Blake doesn't mind you making out with other guys?"

She lowers her eyes, clearly embarrassed. "When you're this far from home, things seem freer."

"Freer." I say the word, but I have no idea what the hell it means. What the hell *she* means.

"It's like a vacation from yourself—a time away from the person you are. I came here to have fun, and I guess I let myself get carried away."

"You *guess?*" I ask, the question almost a snarl, my anger bubbling out of the same place I pulled all those things I said to Cynthia.

"I know I did," she says softly. "Twice."

Neither of us says anything for a bit, and during this pause a waiter comes and asks if we'd like to get something from the buffet. I shake my head. So does Kate.

"I know it was selfish," she adds when the waiter leaves, "and it probably sounds weird, but it's just that Blake and I've been together a long time. It felt good being kissed by someone different again. Even someone like you."

"Someone like me." I hear my voice repeat the words like they're Swahili or Chinese. Incomprehensible.

She shrugs, her cheeks pinking. "You know, like you and your friend."

"My friend?"

"The hockey player."

"What about him?" I ask.

"You two are gay, right?"

=====

Trudging back along the sand alone, I find myself trying to make sense of the past few hours. During that time, I've tried to persuade three different people that I'm not gay, and only one of them—a guy who actually *is* gay—believes me. Am I sending off some weird vibe to women? Could that have been part of my problem with Cynthia all along? It might actually be funny if it weren't so goddamn pathetic.

As ridiculous as Kate's reasoning was, I have to admit she made some compelling arguments. For two people who'd never met before, Connor and I were spending a lot of time together. She first suspected it the night she saw the two of us eating off each other's plates in the Empire Room. I didn't even know she was there that evening, but her knack for inventing histories for people kicked into high gear when she spied us sharing our seafood. Rod and I often snag food off each other's plates, but apparently if you do it in a fancy restaurant, you're gay. Kate's father must have reached the same conclusion, which explains why he had no problem with his daughter spending time with me. As far as he was concerned, I was harmless.

Later, when I was so on-again-off-again in my opinion of Connor, Kate just assumed we were boyfriends having relationship problems. Boyfriends! And seeing us fishing together this morning—after I'd assured her only last night in Playa del Carmen what an asshole he was—only confirmed her suspicion. I can't help feeling like I've been outed, and in my mind I hear Rod offering his two cents' worth: *Maybe there* is *something that turns chicks off faster than a dude doin' homework on the beach, Jace. Dude goin'* gay *on the beach.* This is one part of my Mayan Riviera experience that I won't be sharing—with Rod or Bradford or anyone else.

Whether I convinced Kate or not, I didn't feel much like hanging around after she dropped the Blake bomb, despite her invitation to go with her to the Empress's Internet lounge. She said she was going to e-mail some friends, but I figured what she really planned to do was write Blake about what she'd done, and neither of us needed me on hand for true confessions. I'd rather spend the rest of the day with my brother, one of the few people in Mexico who *doesn't* think I'm gay.

Grimacing now at the memory of our goodbye—both of us promising to call when we got back to Nova Scotia, and both of us lying—I scan the beach for Connor and Lucas, but I don't see them anywhere. Not that this surprises me. It's so like Lucas to switch off right in the middle of something that mesmerized him seconds before. I expect they're sitting under a palm tree resting, or else Connor has taken him to get something to eat.

But then I see the fishing rod on the sand ahead. A single fishing rod.

And I know something is terribly wrong.

25

"Lucas!" I holler, my feet kicking up sand as I run. I put my hand to my forehead to block the sun's glare as I scan the water, but I see only waves and a large seabird floating lazily on the breeze above them. I reach the fishing rod and recognize it as the one Connor was using, his lure clipped carefully to the reel. It's my rod that's missing. My rod and my brother.

"Lucas!" I shout again, and I scour the sand for footprints. Except for mine and Kate's, none lead away from this place. There are only prints leading into the water.

Without thinking, I plunge into the surf, and some part of my brain registers the size and force of the waves, recognizes them as higher and stronger than any we've seen this past week. Or maybe they're not. Maybe they're the same. Maybe it's just me that's different. Terrified.

"LUCAS!" I'm screaming now, and a wave flings water into my mouth and up my nose, making me sputter and cough. But I keep ploughing ahead, my arms and legs propelling me seaward.

And then, a few metres to my right, I see a head break the surface. Connor. Alone. I try shouting to him but salt water cauterizes my throat, reduces my words to a gargle. He pulls air noisily into his lungs and then he's gone.

I churn toward the spot where he disappeared and I dive. Sand swirling in the water stings my eyes, but I see him far below me, tugging on something. A bundle. A bundle that's snagged on dead coral, a bundle that rolls with each sweep of waves toward the shore but goes nowhere. My brother.

I shout his name and water rushes into my mouth but I ignore it, kicking downward, punching through the water that separates Lucas and me. I reach him and see that Connor is tugging at nothing. And then, seeing the rod beneath his feet, I know it's fishing line, invisible in the water. Fishing line that's caught around the reef and my brother. There are thin red threads rising from Lucas's flesh, places where the line is slicing his skin, blood seeping free on the ocean floor. His eyes are open, staring at me. Seeing nothing.

And I'm suddenly cold, frozen on another floor thousands of kilometres away.

I force myself not to cry out again, my air almost gone, and I reach out to where Connor is tugging, feel the line like piano wire beneath my fingers. I pull, yank, begin sawing the line back and forth against the coral, try not to see the water turning crimson. Some part of me remembers Connor talking of red oceans, and I yank again, harder.

Now the blood comes from me. From my hands.

My lungs shriek for air and my vision clouds, darkening at the edges. But I brace my feet against the coral, as Connor is doing, the jagged rock-like knives carving my soles, and together we pull one more time.

And then he's free.

Gripping Lucas's arm, Connor kicks toward the surface and, for a moment, I simply watch them go. My lungs like seared inner tubes, my heartbeat hammering against the backs of my eyes, I stare at the blood rising from my hands and wonder what it would be like to be finally rid of it. To have it all go away. To choose what Stefan chose.

But then I kick to the surface, too.

======

Lucas comes back to us all at once. One minute I'm kneeling over him on the sand, pushing repeatedly on his chest, pinching his nostrils, blowing air into his mouth and then repeating the process I learned during the lifesaving course I took at the Dalplex. Pushing, pinching, blowing, and all the while Lucas's eyes are like those of the fish displayed on ice in the Empire Room. Vacant. Unseeing.

And then something returns to them. Lucas cries out, water bubbling from his lips, and he coughs and chokes and coughs. But he's breathing, and I'm gathering him into my arms, telling him that he's going to be all right, that everything's going to be all right. And for the first time in nearly a year, I believe what I'm saying, believe this can really be true.

Lucas sobs into my chest, his body shaking against mine, and I hold him closer. I stroke his hair, whisper his name over and over, make shushing sounds, and in a few moments I feel him begin to relax, his sobs subsiding.

"I'm so sorry, Jace," says Connor, dropping onto the sand beside us. When we'd gotten Lucas out of the water, Connor started to run for help, but I called him back, made him stay here with me. I couldn't be alone. Not this time.

"He's okay now," I tell him.

"I'm sorry," he says again, looking away from me. He takes a deep, shuddering breath.

Neither of us says anything for a long moment. I turn and look far down the beach, where swimmers and surfers are oblivious to the drama we've experienced, the tragedy we've sidestepped on this Caribbean sand. I'm suddenly struck by how much we miss, how much happens around us without our knowledge. And by how much unfolds inside us without our ever knowing it's there.

Connor draws another deep breath. "He was just reeling in the line like before," he says. "But this time something took the hook. Ran the line out." He stops for a moment and looks away again, shaking his head before continuing. "I started shouting, telling Lucas to wind her in. But he just stood watching the line zing out, so I grabbed the rod from him."

I want to ask him questions, but I don't. I just let him tell it. "It was a grouper, I think. Thirty-five, maybe forty centimetres long. The rod bent almost double. I thought it was gonna break, but then the fish began to tire, and I reeled it most of the way in before I gave the rod back to Lucas. But when he pulled the fish up onto the sand, he started to scream."

"Scream?"

"It was awful. He just . . ." He pauses, clearing his throat. "He just screamed."

I allow myself one more question. "How did he end up in the water?"

Connor looks out at the waves and I imagine him picturing those moments over again, imagine him considering what else he might have done, how else those moments might have unfolded. "He just scooped the fish up in his arms and ran with it. Rod and all. Straight into the water." He swallows here and the sound is thick and full, like mustard being squeezed through a tube. "He was so fast, I couldn't . . ." He stops, swallows again. "He was so fast."

I reach out to put my hand on his shoulder, but then I don't, letting it fall instead to the sand. "He *is* fast, Connor. I know," I tell him, remembering our first day here when Lucas left me holding only his trunks.

Connor clears his throat before continuing. "Once the fish was in the water again, it started to swim, but the hook was still in its mouth. It kept swimming in circles. I thought Lucas would stop then, expected him to just toss the rod, but he kept going, kept moving through the waves with the rod in his hand. I went after him, but it's a lot deeper here . . ." He pauses again before finishing it. "Before I could catch up to him, he went under. Christ."

I feel Lucas's heart beating against my chest, and I wonder what went through his mind at that moment. What was there about the fish? I wish I could ask him, wish he could tell me.

And then, miraculously, he does. "Fan," he says simply.

The word catches me, like a stitch when I'm running.

Connor turns puzzled eyes toward me. "What does he mean? What's 'fan'?"

But I can't reply. I can only hug my brother. Who could never say our older brother's name.

26

"I'm glad you decided to eat with us this evening, Jace," says Mara, as the four of us leave the Empire Room. "We haven't seen much of you lately. It's nice spending time together as a family again."

"Are you going to the show tonight?" I ask quickly, although I'm already worn out from talking all through dinner. I've been entertaining Mom and Mara with non-stop invented histories of the people sitting around us so they wouldn't have time to ask about my day—which couldn't possibly suck harder than it already has—or, for that matter, about Connor, who went to Cozumel after all. I made him go. He kept apologizing for what happened with Lucas, kept telling me how sorry he was, that it was all his fault, and I just couldn't listen to it any more. I know a lot about the subject of blame. I could, in fact, fill Bradford's notebook with what I know. But it turns out I don't know everything. Listening to Connor repeatedly blame himself for what happened on the beach, I learned something more. That being sorry isn't a solution. That admitting guilt is sometimes all any of us can do.

"Wouldn't miss it," says Mara. "They're doing songs from famous Broadway musicals like *Evita*, *Cats* and *Phantom*, along with some newer ones. I talked to a woman who saw it last week, and she said it's amazing, especially the costumes. Are you and Lucas coming, Sophia?"

I seize my opportunity. "Mara, would you mind taking Lucas? I want to talk to Mom about something. We'll come in a bit."

Immediately, I see written on Mara's face the warning she gave me this morning—*your mother doesn't need to know*—and I feel like climbing one of the Empress palms and announcing from the top that Jace Antonakos is *not* gay, has never *been* gay, and has no plans to *turn* gay. But I don't. I just clench my teeth and smile. "It's okay. We won't be long."

She looks at me for a moment, opens her mouth to say something, but then she nods. Taking my brother's hand, she tells us, "We'll save you seats," and the two turn onto the path leading toward the outdoor theatre. I watch Lucas as he leaves with her, imagine under his clothing the marks carved into his chest and arms by the fishing line. I wonder if they'll leave scars, the story of what almost happened forever written on his flesh.

My mother was upset when she saw those marks, pissed at me for letting Lucas get tangled in fishing line on the beach, which is what she assumed happened. She took him back to their suite to put some peroxide on the cuts, but not before ripping me a new one for being so careless with him. She didn't see the marks on my own hands, hidden inside clenched fists. Lucas, of course, couldn't tell her what happened, and I said nothing. Not telling isn't the same as lying. At least, that's what I've been telling myself for nearly a year.

But I know differently now.

When Lucas and Mara are out of sight, my mother turns to me. "If this is about your brother—" she begins, but I interrupt her.

"Let's go sit someplace, okay?"

She nods, and I lead her toward the swimming pool, where all the loungers have been repositioned perfectly for the morning. They're equally spaced and arranged in unbroken lines following the contoured perimeter of the pool, and it seems strange to see them unoccupied like this. For that matter, it's strange to see the pool unoccupied, too, but evenings are when Empress workers clean and treat it for the following day. They've already finished, and soft underwater lights now make it glow like phosphorescence in the darkness. It's like seeing day trapped inside night.

My mother sits sideways on a lounger and I sit on the one next to it, facing her. Even in the darkness, I see something in her eyes that surprises me, makes me wonder if I can do this. Fear.

But I think about what I said to Connor: *You can't spend the rest of your life worrying about people finding out. You need to deal with this. It's not going away.* It's only now that I understand who I was really saying this to.

And there's something else I understand, someone else to think about: Lucas. Who, I realize now, knows loss in ways none of us can imagine.

I take a deep breath. "There's something I need to tell you. Something you don't know."

"About what happened on the beach?" Somehow she sees it already. Even without knowing, she knows.

I look across the pool at the island in the centre with its silhouetted marble fountain surrounded by exotic flowers. The spray of water that jets upward is invisible in the darkness, and the sound of its return seems disembodied, like rain from a cloudless sky.

I nod. "Yes, about what happened on the beach." I can think of no other way to say this. "Lucas almost drowned."

Her intake of breath is so sudden, so sharp, it's as if I've struck her. *"What?"*

I take my time, try to make her understand the sequence of events, the sheer unpredictability of them, and I'm surprised that she lets me continue without interrupting. I tell her about the casting and the reeling in of the line and how much Lucas enjoyed both. I tell her about leaving him with Connor while I talked to Kate. I tell her about the fish and the screaming and Lucas's rush toward the water. I tell her about the fishing line and the coral, about his open and unseeing eyes. I tell her everything. I want there to be nothing she does not know.

She stares at me, her dark eyes like open wounds in her face, and when I finish, she doesn't speak. It's as though she's listening to the story all over again in her head, making the movie of those moments, and I watch as her lower lip quivers.

Finally, "How could you *do* this, Jace?" her voice ragged, a whispered rush of words.

For a strange moment, I wonder what she's asking me here, whether it's how I could have put Lucas's life at risk, or how I could now put these images in her mind. But there isn't time to ask. "There's more," I say to her.

"More?" Her voice is little more than a croak, and for a moment I wonder if she's strong enough. If *I'm* strong enough.

But it doesn't matter any more. Nothing does. Except the telling.

═══

The night before Stefan killed himself, he dropped by the house for supper. Unannounced as usual. And, as usual, it was like a member of the royal family had just arrived, my mother tearing around the kitchen to whip up something special, my father pulling on coveralls so he could give Stefan's old Civic the once-over, checking tire pressure, topping up fluid levels, making sure everything was in proper working order. It wasn't like Stefan asked for any of this. It's just what he was accustomed to.

Mom was quieter than usual that night—I thought she was probably coming down with something—but Stefan was uncharacteristically cheerful, sharing funny stories about people in his classes and telling off-colour jokes that embarrassed our parents but had both of them laughing before long. He was extra-attentive to Lucas, too, following him down to his basement regatta room and watching as he launched his newest miniature boats. I stood at the top of the stairs listening for a while as Stefan commented on each vessel, and I was surprised when, from time to time, Lucas seemed to acknowledge what he said.

Later, when I was in my room working on my Chem lab, the door opened and Stefan walked in, carrying the large hockey bag my parents had gotten him when he'd first joined triple A. He surprised all of us when he didn't try out for the Saint Mary's hockey team, because everyone was sure he'd make the cut, but he said he wanted to focus on his courses so he wouldn't lose his scholarship, said he just wanted to play recreational hockey now, which he usually did a couple of times a week.

He dropped the bag heavily on the floor by my desk.

"I don't want your shit stinking up my room," I told him. When Stefan was living at home and didn't have a game coming right up, it wasn't unusual for him to forget his gear and leave it sitting unwashed in that bag for days. My mother once went through a whole bottle of Febreze trying to get the odour out of the canvas. But she never seemed to mind. After all, this was Stefan.

"It's clean," he told me.

I doubted that, but it didn't matter anyway. "You can't just dump it here till you need it. I don't have room for it."

"I'm not dumping it. It's yours, if you want it."

I looked up from my Chem lab, mole-mass interconversions and Stefan's offer making my head spin. "You're not serious," I told him.

"Yeah. I am." Stefan knelt down and unzipped the bag. He took out the skates my parents had scrimped to pay over a thousand dollars for, and he held them in his hands for a few moments before laying them carefully on the worn hardwood floor. Their blades reflected the light of my desk lamp like knives. Inside the open bag I could see his helmet, jersey, gloves and all the other paraphernalia that's part of the world of rinks. "Someone might as well use this stuff. I won't be needing it any more."

"Why not? You giving up recreational, too?"

He didn't answer, just reached into the bag, running his hands lightly over its contents. After a moment, he looked up at me. "Look, you want this stuff or not?"

"You know I don't play hockey."

"Afraid to try a *real* sport?" When I didn't respond, he said, "Fine, forget it," and began picking up his gear.

There was something in Stefan's tone and the way he bent down to collect his stuff, the *finality* of both, that made me uncomfortable. Made me tell the lie that formed easily on my lips. "Sure, I want it."

He looked up, his eyes studying mine for a moment. As if looking for something.

"I told you I want it," I repeated, annoyed at him now.

He stood up. "We tell each other a lot 'a things," he murmured, moving toward the door.

"You're sure about this?" I asked him.

"As I'll ever be."

Those were the last words he ever said to me. The following night he sat on a lawn chair in our garage, put the barrel of a rifle in his mouth and pulled the trigger.

===

My mother looks at me now, but I can't meet her eyes, don't have the courage to see what she's saying with them. I don't stop talking, though, don't stop the telling.

"I knew something was wrong," I continue, but my voice shatters, syllables colliding with each other, fracturing, fragmenting. I draw in a lungful of flower-scented Caribbean air mixed now with the smell of chlorine and other pool chemicals, all of them designed to sanitize the water before us, the water I'm looking at to avoid seeing my mother's eyes. I long for something that can sanitize *me*, that can wash away the blood on my hands. Stefan's blood. "I knew," I tell her again. "I should have said something. Done something. But I didn't."

There. I've said it. After all this time.

I thought I'd feel better somehow. Thought I'd feel immediately lighter, like a weight fell away. Instead, it feels like I'm the one falling, tailspinning out of control. I grip the plastic edges of the lounger, the cuts on my fingers opening, stinging, but even this does not diminish the feeling of freefall, of plunging headlong into darkness. I breathe in deeply, and then deeply again, but I can't ignore the wedge of sensation that moves through me now, the sounds that slip out of me there by that pool.

I feel a hand on my shoulder, but I don't look up. Still can't bring myself to face her.

"You didn't know," my mother tells me. "You couldn't."

I need more than anything to hear her tell me this lie, but it doesn't change anything. Doesn't change what I knew about Stefan but didn't tell. And what I know about myself. How frightened I've been for so long. I begin to sob openly now, and some part of me knows I should worry that people will hear, will see me crying on this lounge chair by the Mayan Empress pool, but I don't. Nothing exists for me now but this moment, this release.

My mother puts her hand under my chin, draws my face up so my eyes finally meet hers. "You can't blame yourself, Jace," she says. "You didn't know."

And then, before I can tell her she's wrong, she adds, "But I did."

27

This time, the knock on my door is more insistent, but I ignore it, as I have the last two. I know it's Connor out there. I was sitting on my balcony looking at the stars when I saw him staggering up the walkway toward Ocean 1, so I quickly slipped inside. I really don't have the energy to let him in, don't have the energy to listen to him tell me again how unhappy he is. I don't want to listen to anyone. I'm still trying to make sense of what my mother told me by the pool an hour ago.

The knocking becomes pounding. "Jace! Open up! I *know* you're in there." And then, "I saw you on your goddamn balcony, for Christ's sake!"

I sigh. He's an *observant* drunk, I'll give him that. I know now that he won't stop hammering, so I make my way to the door and unlock it. When I swing it open, he nearly collapses inside.

"What took you sho long?" he slurs, weaving unsteadily toward the common area. He nearly stumbles as he makes his way down the steps and over to the leather sofa, sprawling along its full length.

"Connor," I begin, "this isn't a good time—"

"You got any beer left?" he asks, seeing the empty bottle on the coffee table and the one in my hand that I was working on when he arrived.

"You don't need any," I tell him.

"Who the hell are *you* to tell me what I need?" he snarls.

I'm surprised by his outburst, but he has a point. After the past hour, it's obvious I have no idea what *anyone* needs. Or needed. "You're right." I make my way to the cabinet and fling open the refrigerator door. "Drink yourself shit-faced. You're almost there anyway."

He blinks. "You're still pissed at me over what happened with Lucas, right?"

That's when I lose it. "Do you ever stop to think that maybe everything isn't always about *you?*"

He pulls himself up to a sitting position. "What crawled up *your* ass?"

"You! *You* crawled up my ass!" And then both of us realize at the same moment the implication of that remark.

I feel my face flame as Connor drawls, "I think I woulda remembered *that.*"

I sit down on the other end of the sofa and let myself sink back into the plush leather. "I'm tired, Connor. It's been a hell of a day." I take a final swallow of my beer and set the bottle beside the other empty.

He doesn't say anything for a bit, and I'm glad for the silence. It's what I've been hoping to hear in my head for the last hour. Thoughts have been racing around in there, caroming off each other like NASCAR competitors, and I'm worn out. It's not easy admitting that the hell I've made out of my life is my own invention. I can't blame Stefan any more. As much as I'd like to.

"You wanna do somethin'?" Connor asks finally. "Maybe go to the disco or take a walk or somethin'?"

I look at him. "You aren't afraid your buddies will see us together?"

"They're not comin' back tonight. They're stayin' in Cozumel with a bunch they met at a casino over there." He releases a long belch.

"Connor, I'm not gay."

He shrugs. "Yeah, I got the memo."

"So why would it matter if they *did* see us?"

He looks at his hands in his lap, begins picking at the nail on his left thumb, doesn't speak right away. Then, "It's just easier, okay? No questions."

"And no need to lie, right?"

He shrugs again.

"Connor, doesn't any of this piss you off?"

He looks up. "Whaddya mean?"

I think of the time I've wasted this year. The opportunities I've let slip away. I think of Cynthia and how much I loved her. *Still* love her, despite the fact that she's moved on with Corey. It's not something I can just switch off, as much as I've wanted to, as much as I thought I could. I think of the condoms in my sock drawer and suddenly feel like shredding every goddamn one of them.

"Don't you wish you could show people what's really inside you?"

He looks away. "We already talked 'bout this."

"No, we didn't," I say. "I don't just mean being gay." I've been thinking about Cynthia in my room after Stefan's funeral, about her telling me there's nothing wrong with showing how you feel. And about the things my mother told me by the pool. "I mean about everything," I tell him.

"That's easy for you to say," Connor observes.

I suddenly want to punch him. So I do, ramming my fist into his upper arm.

"Ow!" he shouts. "What the—?"

"It *isn't* easy for me to say," I tell him. "*None* of this is. The *easy* thing is saying nothing. Doing nothing. I've spent the last year of my life thinking about things I *should* have done. I'm through with that."

Rubbing his arm, he asks, "What d'ya mean things you *shoulda* done?"

For a moment, I consider telling him, but it wouldn't matter. I can see that now. Instead, I ask, "What are you doing here, Connor?"

"Came for a beer."

"You could've gotten a beer at the bar. *Ten* beer."

A look that I can't read passes over his face, and he hoists himself to his feet. "Fine, I'll get a goddamn beer at the goddamn bar." He turns.

"I don't think that's why you came here," I tell him, standing up.

He staggers around the coffee table heading for the stairs.

I follow him. "I think you came here for something else."

He makes his way up the stairs, nearly stumbling over the top one.

"I think you came *hoping* for something else," I say to his back.

"You *wish*," he mutters, reaching unsteadily for the door and gripping the knob.

"That's not what I meant."

"I don't give a goddamn *what* you meant." But he still stands there with his hand on the doorknob.

"You need someone to talk to, Connor. That's why you're here. You need someone to know what you are. *Who* you are."

He shakes his head, his words still directed toward the door. "So suddenly *you're* the expert on what everyone needs?"

"I know you're a coward," I say as I come to stand behind him.

Connor turns to me, his face dark with throttled rage. "Watch your mouth."

"And I think you'll go on being a coward, crawling inside bottles to make yourself feel more like a man."

"You don't know shit."

"Yeah, maybe, but I know what it's like to be miserable and alone and—"

"Shut the fuck up!"

"Why? Truth hurt?"

I fully expect him to roar, to lunge at me, to plough me squarely in the face. But he does the one thing I don't expect. He turns, opens the door and leaves.

I stand staring at the open door for a full minute before finally closing it. I walk back down the stairs into the living room, see the two empty beer bottles and put them in the recycling container behind one of the cabinet's doors. Then I move to the desk by the window and stand staring at the phone for what seems like a very long time. I hear myself telling Connor he's a coward and wonder how I could have thought for so long that I was any different.

I pick up the receiver and press "0" for the hotel operator.

| 28 |

It's hard to believe the week's over already. Keeping this notebook has really helped me to

I reread that crap for the tenth time, feel no more inspired to finish the thought now than when I wrote it three hours ago in Cancun Airport, and I cross it out. I'm screwed. I managed to record the required number of observations in Sanderson's Global Geography notebook—most of them written last night, although I dated them as separate entries spread out over the week—but I've done dick-all for Bradford. I was supposed to write at least 2,100 words this week, but the only thing I've got is the poem about Stefan, and I haven't decided whether I'll leave that in or tear it out. It's too personal for a teacher's eyes, but if I tear it out I'll probably lose it, and I'm not ready to let it go. I don't want to draw lines through it, either. It'd be like saying it was a mistake. But it isn't. It's probably the most honest thing I've ever written.

I think again of what Bradford said about cross-outs, how she won't read something we don't want her to, and then I remember her telling us we can put Post-its over anything that's private and she'll just glance at it for length. Right. Like I believe that.

Everyone knows teachers have no lives of their own. These note-
books are candy for people like Bradford.

It took a couple of days, but I was finally able to dry mine out
after that downpour on the beach. The cover and pages swelled
so the notebook is almost twice as thick as before, which now
makes the job of filling it seem twice as tough. I've spent the
entire flight racking my brain for things to write, and those
godawful prompts have been zero help, especially since the rain
washed a lot of them off the page. I scan down what remains on
Bradford's handout, many of the words missing or faded or run
together, and I find a few prompts I can still read.

The emptiness of
I wonder if
Everywhere below

Christ. Bradford must have been in maximum moron mode
when she came up with those beauties.

The emptiness of these goddamn pages is going to cost me
major points in English.

I wonder if I could just copy some stuff from Air Canada's in-
flight magazine without her finding out about it.

Everywhere below us people are shovelling driveways and
scraping snow off their . . .

Hmm. I think for a moment, feel the stirring of an idea.

Everywhere below us people are shovelling driveways and
scraping snow off their cars. Shortly after we took off from
Cancun, the pilot came over the PA and told us he hoped we
enjoyed the sun in Mexico because we won't be seeing it for a
while at home. A winter storm that began in New England has
moved into Atlantic Canada, and a thick mass of cloud below the
plane now stretches clear to the horizon. A flight attendant told my

aunt that snow has been falling in Halifax since late last night and we should expect delays driving home from the airport because the roads are treacherous.

Okay, so maybe a weather report isn't exactly what Bradford had in mind, but, hey, it's at least a hundred words. Only two thousand more to go.

Tanned passengers have exchanged T-shirts, shorts and sandals for sweaters, long pants and shoes.

Jesus. Sounds like Air Canada fashion commentary, but thoughts are finally coming and I don't want to jinx this.

I even saw a couple at Cancun Airport putting on boots before we boarded. That seemed like overkill at the time, but now I wish I'd done the same thing.
There are some things I wish I hadn't done, too,

I stop and think about what I almost wrote, then consider the Post-it possibility and wonder if maybe I should just keep going. It's all about word-count, right? I can worry later about Bradford reading this stuff. I shrug, pick up where I left off.

things like avoiding Kate ever since our chat at the Beachside Café two days ago. It only made the hour we waited together in the departure lounge this morning a hundred times more awkward. Our limousine arrived at the airport after the bus delivered the other hotel guests who are on our flight, and she was one of the first people I saw there as Mom, Mara, Lucas and I made our way toward four empty seats. The moment she saw me, she began pawing at the bottom of her carry-on in that intense kind of rummaging that's designed to ward off unwanted interaction with others. If I'd been a vampire, she'd have held up cloves of garlic or a crucifix.

I think about Kate sitting somewhere behind me now, and I wonder if her boyfriend will be waiting at the airport to meet her. Which would certainly explain her reluctance to have any contact with me. But I really don't care. I'm just glad that First Class deplanes before Economy.

Across the aisle from me, Mara is drinking ginger ale, and the morning light through her window reveals tiny lines around the corners of her eyes. I'm not sure if they were there all along or if they're new, compliments of the Caribbean sun, but I'm pretty sure Mara won't be booking cosmetic surgery any time soon. The two of us had a long talk yesterday. We spent our last afternoon on the beach taking a walk beyond the point, and she told me she'd made some decisions about her marriage. She'd already phoned a lawyer and told him to begin divorce proceedings, and she'd contacted a realtor friend to look for a condominium she could move into right away. She has yet to tell Stavros any of this, but she said she needed to do that in person.

When I asked what had brought all this about, she said she owed it to me, that if I was brave enough to live <u>my</u> life, she could try to be brave enough to live her own. Then I realized she was talking about my <u>gay</u> life, and I spent the next hour clearing up that huge misunderstanding once and for all. When I sorted out everything that had happened, she felt pretty foolish but, fortunately, not foolish enough to rethink her decision to give Stavros the boot. I even offered to be with her when she told him—wanted, in fact, to see that son of a bitch squirm when he learned what her lawyer had assured her: that she'd walk away with half of everything he owned—but she said it was something she had to do by herself. I don't know why I'm continually surprised that so much of what's important in our lives we need to do alone. I used to think when I turned eighteen that I'd understand everything. No such luck.

I look across the other aisle at my brother, asleep by the window, and my mother awake beside him, an arm's length and a world away. I can't help but wish there was something I didn't understand, something I wish she hadn't shared with me by the pool two nights ago. There are moments when I find myself choosing not to accept it, wondering if she made it all up for my benefit. I've played and replayed it in my head so many times it's like watching a film loop over and over. Even now I can hear her, can see the way her face looked as she described the last time she spoke with Stefan alone, see her lips form the words that I found impossible to believe.

======

"I won't listen to any more of this," she said, looking up from the table where she'd been working with Lucas. She was glad she'd allowed him to go down to the basement to play. She was never quite sure how much Lucas understood from conversation, but she was relieved she didn't have to worry about that now, relieved he hadn't heard what Stefan had told her. "You should be ashamed for saying such a thing to me."

"Mom—" Stefan began again, but she cut him off.

"No." She put her hand up as if to deflect his words. "Your father and Jace will be home soon and I don't want them walking in on this nonsense."

Stefan stood over her, his face working oddly as if trying to hold back a flood of words. Then he sat down in the chair opposite her. He reached across the table to take her hands in his, but she pulled away. He looked at her for a long moment, and then he shook his head sadly. "Do you think I'm saying this just to upset you? That I *enjoy* telling you I'm not the person everyone wants me to be, *expects* me to be?"

"I don't know why you're saying *any* of it. It isn't true."

He looked down at the tabletop, smooth and gleaming from years of polishing. "How can you be so sure?"

"You're my son. I carried you inside me for nine months. You think I don't know my own flesh and blood? I know."

He glanced up sharply. "And what about what *I'm* feeling? What about what *I* know?"

She shrugged. "You're confused. Overtired. All the studying you're doing to keep your scholarship—"

"It's not like mono or a vitamin deficiency. You can't treat it with antibiotics or diet. It won't just go away."

"It *will* go away. You need to forget about it. Erase it from your mind."

"Don't you think I've *tried* that?" Stefan got up and moved to the sink, looked out the window at the backyard. "Don't you think I'd give anything *not* to be this way?"

"You're just not trying hard enough."

He laughed harshly, the sound like pennies in a rolling jar. "Yeah. I'll be the little train that could. I'll just try harder."

She pushed her chair back from the table and went to stand beside him. "There must be people you can see, people who treat this kind of thing."

He turned to her, the expression on his face almost savage. "You just don't *get* it, do you? This isn't something that can be fixed."

"Not if you don't want it to be," she said. "If you really *wanted* it fixed, it could be fixed."

He looked out the window again, and this time she saw he was looking at the garage. "And it doesn't matter that I'm not happy?" he asked her finally. "That I haven't been happy for a long time?" He drew a breath before continuing, "That not a day goes by when I don't wish I was dead?"

She reached up, grabbed his shoulder, jerked him around to face her. "Don't you *ever* say such a thing again! Do you hear me?"

He nodded. "Sure. Like I won't say I'm gay. Ever again."

They stood staring at each other for a long moment, neither

giving ground, until Stefan shrugged, sighed. "You're right," he said. He drew another deep breath before continuing, "I guess I just need to try harder."

Her relief was visible as she relaxed against him. "That's what I'm saying, Stefan." And then, as if it explained everything, "These are confusing times."

"I have to go," he said, turning toward the door.

As he was opening it, she asked softly, "You won't mention this to your father, will you?"

He paused for a moment, looking out at the garage again. Without turning, he said, "Mention what?" And then he was gone.

———

I look at my mother still pretending to read her magazine, the same one she brought on the plane a week ago, and I can tell she's not really in seat 2B on Flight 847. She's sitting in our kitchen with Stefan again, listening. Actually listening to him this time. And responding with all the things she now wishes she'd told him that night, anything except "You should be ashamed." I know this because I've spent nearly a year looking at the hockey gear in my closet and wishing I'd said something more than just "Sure, I want it." Stefan was right when he said we tell each other lots of things. Just seldom anything that matters. Language should bring people closer, not build walls around us like the one at Tulum. I think of our tour guide, Roberto, explaining how the Yucatan got its name, and I know my brother would have liked that story, how one word can say so much about what's wrong in our lives.

That evening by the pool as she told me about Stefan, I wanted to reach out to my mother, wanted to tell her what she needed me to say: that she wasn't to blame for what happened, that she'd done the best she could for him. But I couldn't. All I could think about was how much it must have cost Stefan to tell her his secret, how much it costs any of us to show others who we really are. Sitting on the resin lounger watching the lights reflect on the pool's surface, I thought of Alex Praeger and how he must have felt coming home from school each day to hear from his own family the same things that were snickered in the hallway or sneered in the cafeteria. Or worse—something like what Connor's dad said about perverts and child molesters.

And then I thought of Stefan's last evening at home with all of us, thought of how content he suddenly seemed, and I understood then that he'd already made his decision, that there was nothing I could have said that would have stopped him from putting that gun to his mouth. And as much as I hated what he'd done to me, what he'd done to all of us, I was grateful that, for one night at least, he'd been happy. I thought of Rod and how he never begins a book without reading the last page first, justifying it by saying, "If I don't like the ending, why would I waste time on the rest of it?" It's as though, once Stefan finally knew how it would all end, he could take some comfort in what came before.

I look up from my notebook, surprised at the words pouring onto these swollen pages. I'm not sure where they're coming from, or if I'll even leave any of them for Bradford to see. I think about her Post-it rule again, wonder if I really can trust her not to read what I've written. But I also wonder where these thoughts are taking me, wonder what else might flow from a simple two-word prompt like *Everywhere below.* I flex the cramped fingers of my right hand for a moment, then press the pen to the page once more.

The passengers in Economy have had a much quieter flight back to Nova Scotia than the one we took to Mexico. I haven't heard a thing from any of the Torrents. Most of them were pretty subdued at Cancun Airport, sprawled across vinyl seats like accident victims, probably nursing the after-effects of final-night partying. The only one who showed any real energy was Connor, who spent most of his time prior to boarding chatting up a woman working at the American Airlines desk.

I haven't seen Connor to talk to since he came to my suite that last time. I felt lousy about how he left, how I'd reamed him out for being a coward. It's just that the news about Stefan was so much to take in, so freakishly coincidental. Or, as Bradford would no doubt have described it, tragically ironic. I mean, what are the chances of meeting a closeted gay hockey player thousands of kilometres from where my brother, a hockey player, killed himself because he couldn't handle being gay? It wouldn't take Ms. Surette more than a minute of Math class to prove the statistical improbability of that event. It's about as unlikely as winning the CDD anti-lottery.

Yesterday, though, I woke up remembering something that one of Pop's regulars, Mrs. Mouskouri, says all the time: "Things happen for a reason," followed by a slow, sad shake of her grey head. As if that explains everything. Transfer truck wipes out a whole family on the 101, guy who worked hard all his life gets diagnosed with cancer the day he retires, smart-as-a-whip preschooler forgets what it means to be a brother and a son. Things happen for a reason? Give me a break. Only losers like Mrs. Mouskouri—whose husband choked to death years ago on a false tooth, for Christ's sake—cling to fatalistic crap that always makes it somebody else's fault when their lives turn into shit storms. Every time I hear her sombrely offer those five words like she's reading a bumper sticker on the back of God's big silver Buick, I feel like upending an entree over her head or ramming a dinner roll down her throat.

But for some reason, when I woke up yesterday morning those words were on my mind and wouldn't go away, like a song you hate but catch yourself humming for the tenth time. I lay there for a while thinking about Connor and what he'd said that morning on my balcony. And what my mother had said by the pool. Mostly, though, I thought about things that don't get said. And about regret.

Finally, I crawled out of bed, got dressed and headed to Garden 2, where Connor and his buddies were staying. I had no idea what I'd say to him, or whether he'd even let on he knew me if his friends were there. But I went anyway, thinking that maybe some things do happen for a reason, after all.

As I was looking for his room, though, something bright caught my eye in a cart that a maid had left parked in the hallway. It was poking out of the bottom of an industrial-sized garbage bag hanging beneath sponges and cleaning supplies: an amber finger caught in sunlight that streamed through an open doorway. It took me a moment to recognize it as a piece of the lightning glass we'd found on the beach, and another moment to realize what Connor had done: smashed it and thrown it in the trash. I was still staring at it when the maid returned and asked me, in halting English, if there was anything I needed, anything she could do. I told her there was probably nothing anybody could do. And I left.

Connor passed me in the lobby last night and didn't even nod, all his attention directed toward a hot brunette attached to his arm, and this morning in the airport he seemed to go out of his way to avoid me. It made me think of that Leah Delaney song about silences and all the things that people never say to each other. After the last eleven months, I can't imagine anything harder than choosing to live with those silences.

I hear the plane's flaps ratchet down and feel the nose dip, and I know it won't be long before we land and we're going through customs. At least I don't have to worry about some official in Halifax finding my stash of condoms—I left them behind at the Mayan Empress, and I expect someone will put them to good use. Someone who knows a lot more about intimacy than I do.

I've already filled out the customs form declaring what I'm bringing back from Mexico, but it's not what I'm bringing back that's important. It's what I've left behind. And it isn't latex wrapped in coloured foil.

I only had three purchases to write on the form the flight attendant gave me. One was a T-shirt I got for Rod from a street vendor just outside the Empress gates. Rod had given me money to buy him "something uniquely Mexican," and I was pretty sure this T-shirt fit the bill. It had "Riviera Maya" written across the top in large letters and, in smaller letters crammed at the bottom, "If you can read this you're much too close, but while you're down there, why not give me a blowjob?" It's not like he'll be able to wear it anyplace, but I know he'll get a kick out of it.

My second purchase was a gift for Pop, a CD by the group Kate and I heard. I was walking by the bar last night where they were playing again, and I went in and listened to them one last time. They were just as amazing as before and, afterwards, I went up and asked if they had any music I could buy. Turns out they've recorded three CDs, but lots of other guests had been asking the same thing because they had only a single copy of one of their CDs left. I guess maybe I bought it as much for me as for my father.

Pop called me last night. He had something to tell me, but he wouldn't say what it was until I'd promised him there was nobody else in the room. I wondered why all the secrecy. In the past year, we've only really talked about what's going on at the restaurant, so I figured it was trouble with the waitresses again. Monica and Estelle are good servers, but they often get into it with each other over one thing or another—scheduling the hours they work or dividing up tips or deciding who gets to wait on good-looking male customers, stuff like that—and my father has no patience with them, usually threatens weekly to fire them both. They like me, though, and respond well to my teasing and joking around, my way of smoothing things over when things get ragged. I figured I had some major smoothing over to do when I got back.

But that wasn't it.

Pop told me he tore down the garage while we were away.

He wasn't planning to. Driving into the yard the first night we were gone, he noticed that a piece of siding over the garage door was rotted and sagging, and he sat in the car for a long time staring at it, caught in the twin pools of his headlights. He doesn't remember getting out, doesn't remember walking into the backyard, or even coming to stand in front of the garage door. What he does remember is the way he looked at the siding, the way he had to tilt his head so he could examine the rotted wood without seeing through the window. When he finally reached up to tug on it, to test it, the piece of siding came away easily, as though whatever had held it there was now long gone.

He intended to replace it, he told me. He even thought for a minute about where he'd have to go to get a piece that would match, how he'd probably do it the following Monday, leave the restaurant after the lunch rush was over and drive out to that sawmill just off the highway near Sackville.

But even as he thought about replacing it, he knew he wouldn't. The wood felt good in his hands. Felt <u>right</u> in his hands.

He paused in the telling, then, and I began to think the telephone connection had failed, but then he said, "I know this'll sound crazy, Jace, but at that moment I felt . . ." He paused again before continuing, "I felt Stefan standing beside me."

I expected to feel rise within me the resentment I've always felt when my parents speak of Stefan. Now all I felt was loss.

My father told me about going into the garage for the first time since the suicide, how he began dragging everything outdoors and piling it in the snow. How he found his sledgehammer and started first with the windows. Stan Foster, who lives next door, almost called the police until he saw what was happening. Then he offered to lend a hand, but Pop told him this was something he had to do by himself. It took him six nights to finish it, six nights to bring it all down and load the debris into a dumpster he'd rented from Scotia Demolition.

"Do you think it was the right thing, Jace? Tearing it down?"

My father was asking what I thought. Was asking <u>me</u> what was right. I couldn't speak, could only hang on to the phone and that moment.

"Jace?"

"Yeah, Pop," I finally managed to say. "It was the right thing to do."

"Your mother—" he began.

"I'll handle it," I told him.

"I know you will," he said. There was another pause, and then, "I've missed you, son."

"I've missed you, too, Pop."

There was a sound on the other end of the line, a strangled kind of cough. Then, "I don't just mean—"

"I know, Pop." And I did.

The third purchase I recorded on the customs form was my first: the nesting Jesus that I bought in Playa del Carmen. I'm not keeping it, though. I'm taking it over to Cynthia as soon as I get home, even if I have to wade through snowdrifts to get there. She knows I'm coming—I called her two nights ago from Ocean 1 and asked if I could drop by today. There was a long silence on her end, and I knew she was imagining me re-enacting the meltdown I had when she told me about her and Corey. But I said I wouldn't be staying long, that there was just something I wanted to give her. And to tell her.

She asked me if I could just tell her then what it was, but "Thank you" isn't something you can say over the phone. And besides, I want to see her open that wooden Jesus, watch her face as she frees all those figures inside.

ACKNOWLEDGEMENTS

Every time I begin a book, I'm certain I'll never finish it. My completing any project has a lot to do with the people in my life, and I'd like to thank my wife, who has more faith in me than I have in myself; and my daughters, whose love and enthusiasm make me want to do better, to *be* better. I also want to thank my editor, Lynne Missen, whose unerring sense of story keeps me honest; and my agent, Leona Trainer, for continuing to take chances on a part-time writer.

Also, I'd like to thank the many teachers in my life. Having taught for several years, I know the frustration that accompanies large classes, expanded curricula, and increasing inequities, but I also know what a privilege it is to play a part in a person's learning. I have known many fine teachers and I regret that I can't possibly list them all here, but there are some whose impact on me as a human being, as an educator, and as a writer continues to resonate in my life: my parents, who taught me that the right thing and the hardest thing are often the same; Margaret Young, who showed me that teaching is more art than science; Lynn Bloom, who knew I was a writer long before I did and who gave me the encouragement I needed to believe it myself; and, finally, the hundreds of students who have shared my classroom and taught me more than they ever learned from me.